"Tell me you don't still feel it."

"Feel what?" Jenna asked, ignoring the way his gaze kept drifting to her lips.

Jake hauled her against him. "This."

The next thing Jenna knew, Jake had wrapped his arms around her back and lowered his lips to hers. His kiss was hot, sure and so sensual it took her breath away. Despite herself, she had missed this, missed him and the special...and yes, powerful way he made her feel.

Jenna knew if they didn't stop soon they would end up in one of the beds upstairs. And while that was all she had wanted when they had been together before, she also knew this was no way, and no place, to lose her virginity....

Dear Reader,

It's another wonderful month at Harlequin American Romance, the line dedicated to bringing you stories of heart, home and happiness! Just look what we have in store for you....

Author extraordinaire Cathy Gillen Thacker continues her fabulous series THE LOCKHARTS OF TEXAS with *The Bride Said, "Finally!"* Cathy will have more Lockhart books out in February and April 2001, as well as a special McCabe family saga in March 2001.

You've been wanting more books in the TOTS FOR TEXANS series, and author Judy Christenberry has delivered! *The $10,000,000 Texas Wedding* is the not-to-be-missed continuation of these beloved stories set in Cactus, Texas. You just know there's plenty of romance afoot when a bachelor will lose his huge inheritance should he fail to marry the woman he once let get away.

Rounding out the month are two fabulous stories by two authors making their Harlequin American Romance debut. Neesa Hart brings us the humorous *Who Gets To Marry Max?* and Victoria Chancellor will wow you with *The Bachelor Project*.

Wishing you happy reading!

Melissa Jeglinski
Associate Senior Editor

The Bride Said, "Finally!"

CATHY GILLEN THACKER

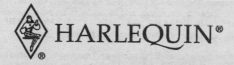

HARLEQUIN®

TORONTO • NEW YORK • LONDON
AMSTERDAM • PARIS • SYDNEY • HAMBURG
STOCKHOLM • ATHENS • TOKYO • MILAN • MADRID
PRAGUE • WARSAW • BUDAPEST • AUCKLAND

ISBN 0-373-16841-1

THE BRIDE SAID, "FINALLY!"

Copyright © 2000 by Cathy Gillen Thacker.

This edition published by arrangement with Harlequin Books S.A.

® and TM are trademarks of the publisher. Trademarks indicated with ® are registered in the United States Patent and Trademark Office, the Canadian Trade Marks Office and in other countries.

Visit us at www.eHarlequin.com

Printed in U.S.A.

ABOUT THE AUTHOR

Cathy Gillen Thacker is a full-time wife/mother/author who began typing stories for her own amusement during "nap time" when her children were toddlers. Twenty years and more than fifty published novels later, Cathy is almost as well-known for her witty romantic comedies and warm family stories as she is for her ability to get grass stains and red clay out of almost anything, her triple-layer brownies and her knack for knowing what her three grown and nearly grown children are up to almost before they do! Her books have made numerous appearances on bestseller lists and are now published in seventeen languages and thirty-five countries around the world.

Books by Cathy Gillen Thacker

HARLEQUIN AMERICAN ROMANCE

Dear Reader,

The fictional town of Laramie, Texas, exemplifies everything I know and love about the state. The people are warm and friendly and helpful as can be, their desires bold, their dreams big. It's a place where opportunity is limitless and people are encouraged to live and enjoy life to the fullest.

So much so that I knew when I started writing the books about John and Lilah McCabe and their four sons that I'd also write another series set in Laramie. But this one would be about a family of four sisters who, like the McCabes, find the love that has eluded them in Laramie.

Look for the first two books about the Lockharts in August and September 2000. The third and fourth books will be published in February and March 2001.

In the midst of all this, I am also writing a bigger, more in-depth story about Sam McCabe, John and Lilah McCabe's nephew. A widower with five lively boys, he returns to Laramie when his life soars out of control. TEXAS VOWS: A McCABE FAMILY SAGA, will be published in March 2001.

I hope you enjoy them all as much as I enjoyed writing them.

Happy reading!
Cathy Gillen Thacker

Chapter One

"I need a favor. And I need it from you," the low, distinctively male voice drawled.

As the velvety sound surrounded her, tingles of awareness slid down Jenna Lockhart's spine. She knew that rich, familiar murmur. Unless she was hallucinating... The blood rushed hot through her veins. She turned slowly toward the door, telling herself all the while she had to be imagining it. That the romantic notion was prompted by the equally shocking elopement of her sister, Dani, and Beau Chamberlain several weeks before. Just because Dani had found the man of her dreams and married him, just because wedding fever was sweeping the town of Laramie, Texas, did not mean that the man of Jenna's dreams would waltz back into her life on a moment's notice. Did it?

Drawing a deep breath, Jenna lifted her eyes, curious to see who had entered her exclusive boutique just seconds before she closed for the day. And promptly felt her knees turn to jelly. Well over six years had passed since she had seen the man who had broken her heart all to pieces, but Jake Remington hadn't changed a bit. Except, perhaps, to become even more handsome and self-assured. He was a good six inches taller than her five-foot-nine-inch frame, with a penchant for casual clothes, and an even more casual manner that belied his enormous wealth and good fortune.

"What are you doing here?" Jenna demanded.

Looking completely at ease with himself in the ultrafeminine surroundings, he circled around the one-of-a-kind wedding and evening dresses on display. Once at her side, he tipped back his black Stetson, revealing layers of thick jet-black hair. As he scanned her from head to toe, reluctant pleasure tugged at the corners of his lips. "I wanted to congratulate you on your success." Jake lifted his glance back to her eyes. "Your clothing designs have been in the news all month. Dani created quite a stir when she wore one of your dresses to the premiere of Beau Chamberlain's new movie. Reportedly, every starlet in Hollywood now wants one of your originals."

That was true. Due to her growing success, Jenna was booked solid with appointments. She was taking the time between now and then to prepare for the onslaught. And perhaps look at hiring someone besides Raelynn to help her in the shop. But not wanting to disclose all that to Jake, Jenna merely shrugged and returned his steady glance, albeit with a lot less admiration. "You've done very well for yourself. *I* hear J&R Industries is a multimillion-dollar conglomerate."

Jake pushed back the edges of his black sport coat, and placed his hands on his waist. His sexy grin widened. "You've kept up."

Jenna turned away, trying hard not to notice how taut and trim his midriff was beneath his olive-green shirt and snug black jeans. "Hard not to, if you read the business pages of all the major Texas newspapers—and I do."

Following her around the shop, Jake said, "I would have called for an appointment, but I didn't think you'd see me."

Struggling not to recall how good it had felt to be held against that warm, strong chest, Jenna refused to look at him as she shut down her computer for the night. "You were right." She remembered without wanting to how much he had hurt her, abandoning her the way he had. "I wouldn't have."

Jake looked at her steadily, serious now. "What happened between us was a long time ago."

Funny, Jenna thought. It seemed like just yesterday to her. Though in reality it had been six years, eight months, ten days and...nineteen hours. But who was counting?

She smiled thinly. "What's your point?"

Jake's expression was suddenly as vulnerable as it was grave. "I want us to be friends again."

Jenna didn't want to think of Jake as vulnerable, because if she did it meant he had a heart, and that was *definitely* not true. Jenna locked her cash register. "Not possible."

He leaned across the sales counter. "How will you know unless you try?" he asked.

Every muscle in her body went stiff with tension. "I'm not interested in trying, Jake," she told him flatly, ignoring the unsettling way her senses stirred at his close proximity.

Jake regarded her with so much smug male assurance it took her breath away. "Same old stubbornness and fiery temperament."

"Same old arrogance and conceit," she shot back, refusing to be distracted by the enticing, woodsy scent of his skin.

Instead of being insulted, Jake merely grinned, and looked all the more entranced. "Jenna, I have a proposition for you."

As Jenna recalled, what he'd said was that he needed a *favor* from her. In her opinion, those were two very different things. "I'll just bet you do," she replied. Grabbing a clear plastic garment bag, she slipped it over a wedding dress on the overhead rack.

"I need you to make a complete wardrobe."

Jenna knelt and gently folded the edges of the beaded satin gown into the bag. "I don't design men's clothing." And even if she did, she wouldn't design anything for him!

Jake also knelt to help, holding the bottom of the bag straight. "It's for the lady in my life."

Resisting the urge to deck him, Jenna zipped the garment bag closed. "Now I'm *really* not interested."

Jake stood, and hand beneath her elbow, gallantly helped Jenna to her feet. "I'll do anything you want."

Still tingling from his brief, but sure touch, Jenna carried the gown back to the storeroom. Wishing her heart would stop pounding and resume its normal beat, she carefully hung the gown on the rack. "I'm still not interested, Jake." To her dismay, Jake showed no signs of leaving despite her less-than-gracious hints.

He moved back to let her pass and continued speaking as if she had already agreed to accommodate him. "The thing is, it's a rush job."

Her exasperation mounting by leaps and bounds, Jenna strode back out into the carpeted showroom. She went to the desk behind the sales counter and reached for her Rolodex. "I'll give you some names and send you on your way."

"I don't want anyone else. I want you."

"Too bad," Jenna replied, forcing herself to remember how much he had hurt her instead of how very well he kissed, "because you're never going to have me." *Ever again.*

Jake quirked a brow. Desire, pure and simple, was in his eyes. "Don't make promises you may not be able to keep."

Her temper flaring, Jenna poked a finger at his chest. "And don't you presume to know what is in my heart or on my mind."

Outside, a red sport utility vehicle with tinted windows pulled up to the curb and parked just ahead of Jake's charcoal gray truck and Jenna's sporty white convertible.

Obviously perturbed by the interruption, Jake glanced at his watch and frowned. "She's early."

Like that matters! Jenna thought, incensed.

Unable to believe his audacity, never mind his lack of consideration for her feelings, Jenna turned to Jake furiously. "You are so out of here," she said just as the driver alighted from the truck. To Jenna's amazement, it wasn't some glamorous young babe Jake was dating, but a plump, pleasant-looking woman in her mid to late fifties, wearing jeans, boots and blue denim work shirt. She had a straw cowgirl hat pulled over wild salt-and-pepper curls and a red bandana tied around her neck. She walked to the rear door on the passenger side. Realizing this woman was only the chauffeur, Jenna began to frown again.

Jake moved between Jenna and the window, adeptly blocking her view. He tugged her behind a three-mannequin display of evening wear in the boutique window. Meanwhile, though the chauffeur had opened the passenger door and was holding it wide, no one was getting out.

"Look, I'm begging you," Jake said urgently. He clamped both his hands on Jenna's shoulders and held her there in front of him when she would have bolted. "Alex's been through a really rough time. When she saw your designs on TV she fell in love with them. I promised her I'd get you to design her some dresses, just for her. Exactly what she wants. Down to the very last detail."

Finding his request more unbelievable than ever, Jenna snapped at him, "So break the promise. That's certainly not anything you've hesitated to do before."

Reminded of the heartless way he had betrayed her in the past, he showed a moment's regret. Then, recovering, he went on matter-of-factly. "It's not that simple, Jenna."

Jenna scoffed again. " It is to me. Besides, I have confidence in you," she continued sweetly, favoring him with a long, withering look. "You'll think of something, Jake. You always have."

The driver turned to Jake and lifted her hands in exasperation. Jake nodded his understanding signaling the driver to wait.

"I'll double your usual fee," Jake said urgently, fastening his attention on Jenna once again.

Jenna shook her head, thinking, *This man really needs to have his head examined.* "No!"

"Triple."

Jenna rolled her eyes. "You must *really* be desperate."

Jake muttered, lifting one hand from her shoulder and, rubbing the back of his neck. "You have no idea how much."

Jenna wasn't sure whether to tell Jake what she really thought of him, or just pity him. "Find some other ex-girlfriend to torture," she said in a low, bored tone.

Jake dropped his other hand, stepped back. Where he had gripped her shoulders, Jenna continued to tingle warmly. Too warmly.

"There is no one else," he said, dispirited.

Looking into his mesmerizing silver-gray eyes, still feeling the awareness that shimmered through her at his touch, Jenna could almost—almost—believe that. Which only proved that once a fool, always a fool, she reprimanded herself. "No one else who knows how to operate a sewing machine, you mean," she replied archly.

Without warning, the limo driver snapped to attention once again. Sensing something was about to happen, Jake and Jenna both looked in the direction of the car. Seconds later, Jake's "lady" vaulted out, clutching what looked to be a squirming bullfrog in both hands. She was muddy, unkempt, with a baseball hat planted backwards on her head, covering a mop of long and tangled strawberry blond hair that obviously hadn't seen a brush all day. Olive-green overalls and a dingy T-shirt, several sizes too big, hung from her slender figure. She wore pink-rimmed sunglasses, high-topped basketball sneakers. A backpack in the form of a monkey was slung over one shoulder. Relief and amusement—and irritation at Jake for not having explained further—flowed through Jenna in equal quantities, making her want to deck him all over again.

"This is the *lady* in your life?" Jenna asked, guessing the little girl's age to be about five or six.

"The one and only," Jake smiled as the little scamp marched toward him. Jake turned to Jenna, sexy mischief in his eyes. "What did you think I meant?"

Too late, Jenna realized it had been a test, to see if she still had feelings for him, and she had failed. Hardening her heart against any further involvement with him, she said, "I don't design children's clothing, either."

Outside, the chauffeur waved cheerfully at Jenna, gestured to Jake she'd be back in a minute, then took off down the street after she ushered the child toward the shop.

"I was hoping you'd make an exception for Alexandra, here," Jake continued as the child sidled up to him for a one-armed hug.

"That's okay, Daddy." Alexandra leaned against Jake's side, her head resting against his waist. "I didn't want any dresses anyway. And stop calling me Alexandra. You know I only wanta be called Alex." Carefully transferring the frog to one hand, she grabbed onto the sleeve of Jake's casual black blazer with the other and tugged fiercely. "Let's go, Daddy."

His eyes still on Jenna, Jake shook his head. "Not yet, honey. I've got business to do."

The pout that formed on Alexandra's pretty face was immediate—and potent. "You've been doing business all day," she grumbled as the frog leapt from her hand and hopped across the floor of the shop. "I want to go to the ranch house now," she repeated stubbornly. Racing after her frog, she called over her shoulder, "It's brand-new. Daddy built it just for us, so I'd have somewhere I could play outside, and have horsies and dogs and cats and stuff. Only I don't have none yet."

Jenna looked at Jake, too surprised by his revelations to be concerned with the amphibian escapee. "I didn't think your family was summering here anymore." They had stopped at the time of Jake and Jenna's failed elopement.

"My folks don't, although they keep the ranch for an investment and loan out the house to friends from time to time."

"Then why would you build a place here, if you no longer have family vacationing in the area?"

Jake shrugged. "I loved coming to Laramie when I was a kid." He shot a glance at Alex, who had throw off her monkey backpack and pink sunglasses and was hopping around after her frog, well out of earshot. "I figured Alex would love it, too."

Jenna smiled, unable to resist a dig after the way his family's snobbish attitudes had hurt her. "Are you sure that's wise? Laramie is a great place. Friendly. Warm. Caring. Intimate. But on the social register—well, we really can't compare with your native Dallas now, can we?" She looked at him steadily, daring him to claim otherwise.

Jake stared back, regarding her with the same steady intensity. "I never thought you'd be a snob."

"Me?"

"Okay, reverse snob," Jake amended.

Before they could continue their discussion, Alex's chauffeur stepped into the shop. Jake turned to the older woman, affection etched on his face. It was, Jenna noted curiously, a feeling that was returned. "Jenna," Jake said warmly, "this is Clara, our housekeeper, the lady who keeps us all sane. Clara, I'd like you to meet Jenna Lockhart, the lady I've been telling you and Alex about."

"I heard you two knew each other as kids," Clara said.

Jenna nodded. "We used to see each other every summer. But that ended a long time ago. We haven't seen each other since."

Jake gave Jenna a look that said: "And it's a loss to us both."

Jenna gave Jake a look that said: "Speak for yourself."

Alex popped up from behind the sales counter. She waved the bullfrog in the air. "Hey, everybody, I got him!"

"Well, nice meeting you all, but as you can see I'm closing my shop for the day."

"Goody! Did you hear that, Mr. Froggie? We get to go to the ranch!" With a wave at Jenna, Alex darted back out the door.

"Nice meetin' you!" Clara said, waving as she headed out the door after Alex.

Jake frowned at his daughter, who was already climbing

back in the truck. "This probably isn't a good time for us to talk," he conceded with a frown.

Jenna breathed a sigh of relief. "I'm glad you finally realize that."

"We need to go to dinner together," Jake said firmly.

Jenna's eyes widened. Determined not to put herself in an emotionally vulnerable position with him again, she scoffed derisively. "In your dreams!"

Jake's eyes darkened with legendary confidence. "I'll be by to get you around eight o'clock," he promised as she stalked away from him.

Jenna concentrated on putting the Closed sign on the front door. Then opened it and held it wide for him. "Don't hold your breath," she muttered sweetly as she waved him toward the exit.

But clearly, Jake was counting on getting his way. As always. "Wear something casual," Jake advised as he sauntered toward the door. "I want you to be comfortable." He gave her a smile that reached his eyes. "We have a lot to talk about."

"THE NERVE of that man!" Meg Lockhart fumed short minutes later at the emergency meeting of all four Lockhart sisters. Having come straight from work, she was still in her nurse's uniform.

"I'll say!" Kelsey agreed with a snort of disgust as they all gathered around the dining table in Jenna's apartment above her Main Street boutique. Kelsey put down the stack of catalogs of ranch gear she'd brought in with her, pushed back her cowgirl hat and pulled up a chair.

"To come around after all these years, acting as if nothing much at all had happened!" The happily married Dani shook her head in a reproach too deep for words. A movie critic by profession, she liked drama and excitement as much as anyone, but this was too much—even for her!

Dani leaned toward Jenna urgently. "I mean, I know how

much you loved him once, Jenna. But for him to think—after all this time, no less!—that you would still be carrying a torch for him… How foolish is that?''

Pretty foolish, Jenna thought, aware it was uncomfortably close to the truth. As much as she hated to admit it, no man had ever come close, before or since, to engendering the passionate emotions in her that Jake Remington, captain of J&R Industries, did.

All four sisters sipped iced tea with lemon, their heads bent together thoughtfully.

''Actually, I think the smartest thing would be for you to go on that date,'' Meg decided after a moment as she took the pins out of her long auburn hair and shook it out.

Everyone turned to Meg—the oldest and most responsible of them all—in shock. Meg regarded them determinedly but saved her advice, which came straight from the heart, for Jenna. ''You need to prove to him once and for all that you are so over him it isn't funny,'' Meg told Jenna sternly. ''Let him wine and dine you and even pull out all the stops if that's what he wants to do. Just play along with nary a word of protest and let him go for it. And then—'' Meg paused and raised a cautioning hand ''—when he's expended his full bag of rich-boy tricks, let him know straight out there's no going back to the way things were when you were teenagers. Let him know it's over, once and for all.''

More discussion followed. By the time her sisters left to take care of their own dinnertime commitments, consensus had been reached. Meg's plan was the one Jenna was going to follow. So Jenna dressed in the prettiest, sexiest sundress she owned, for the express purpose of making Jake Remington eat his heart out and realize what he gave up when he dropped her like a stone after their failed elopement.

PROMPTLY AT NINE o'clock, Jake bounded from his truck and took the exterior steps leading up to Jenna's apartment above the shop two at a time. He rang the bell, wondering all the while if she was even going to be in. Part of him wouldn't blame her if she did stand *him* up this time.

A second later the door swung open. He took her in and immediately had the exact same thought he'd had earlier in the day. Damned if she wasn't the most beautiful woman he had ever seen. And damned if she wasn't the only woman who could make his heart turn cartwheels in his chest. Especially in that body-hugging off-the-shoulder white sundress that made the most of her high perfect breasts, slender waist and trim but oh-so-curvaceous hips. High-heeled white sandals and a hem considerably shorter than the one she'd had on earlier made the most of her sexy showgirl legs.

And her wish to drive him mad with desire had not ended there.

She'd taken down her thick red-gold hair and let it fall around her shoulders in tousled sexy layers that teased her shoulders and framed her delicate, oval face. She'd scented her soft ivory skin with perfume, the same kind she had worn when they were young and in love. Her clear blue eyes were bright with challenge and an *I-dare-you-to-try-anything-cowboy* sass. Jake had always been the kind of guy who loved a challenge. And nothing more than the challenge Jenna Lockhart presented. He just regretted it had taken him so long to get back to her. But since he had, and since she was still so clearly ticked off, maybe it was best he slow down a tad, take it nice and easy. And to that end, he waggled his eyebrows at her and teased, "You going out with me or someone else?"

Jenna propped her hands on her slender hips. She still looked like she'd like nothing more than to take a swing at him. "What do you think?" She plucked her purse and keys off the entryway table and, her head held high, strode past him.

Jake held the door for her, followed her out and waited while she locked up. "I think if anyone else shows up, intending to squire you around, he's going to have to do battle with me first."

Jenna pinned him with a debilitating glare. "I figured we should just get this over with," she said dryly.

Jake grinned at her fiesty tone, liking the warm flush of color that had come into her high, elegant cheeks. "Such enthusiasm," he drawled.

"What did you expect?" Jenna watched her step as she headed down the stairs. "Me to jump up and do a cheer the moment you waltz back into my life?"

Jake grinned at the thought of Jenna in the short pleated skirt and sleeveless sailor top that had comprised the Laramie High School cheerleading uniform when Jenna was in school. "You used to be pretty great at that," he said, recalling how good she had looked in burnt orange and white. "In fact, I loved seeing you cheer at the few games I was able to get to." Jake opened the door, and gave Jenna an unasked-for hand up into his truck.

Her delicate brow arched as he climbed behind the wheel and started the engine. "What do your parents think of you asking me to create a wardrobe for their granddaughter?"

Jake frowned as he shifted into Drive, turned onto Main Street and headed out of town. He had known they would have to talk about all the things that had separated them before; he hadn't expected to do so this soon. "I don't have to ask my parents for permission anymore, Jenna," he replied quietly, slanting her a glance.

Jenna's clear blue eyes radiated both hurt and unhappiness. "Meaning they don't know," she guessed, just as quietly.

Jake's shoulders tensed and he had the urge to rip off the tie he had put on just for her. "Meaning I don't care if they do or don't know. Meaning I am a man with my own life now. Just like you're a woman with your own life." He speared her with a look, wanting to be clear about that much.

Jenna cut him off, her voice unexpectedly devoid of joy. "Speaking of your life, where's Alex?"

Jake relaxed as they passed the last of the traffic lights and headed out into the Texas countryside toward their destination.

He smiled as he thought about his daughter, and Jenna's interest in her. "Alex's back at the ranch." Jake turned down the air conditioner. "She's supposed to be in bed. But I imagine she's talked Clara into letting her stay up late and they're playing potato-chip poker and chomping on cigars about now."

Jenna quirked a brow. Jake grinned. "Alex's, of course, will be made of bubble gum."

"What about your wife?"

Jake could tell by the way Jenna looked at him, the fact she was even here with him, that she—along with everyone in Laramie and half the people in the state of Texas—had heard about his divorce from Melinda Carrington the year after Alex was born. Melinda had wanted—and won—a large chunk of Jake's trust fund from his parents. He had considered it a small price to pay for his freedom and custody of his beloved only daughter. "Melinda is in Europe, getting over the end of yet another romance, this one was with an Italian count. She's upset because she really wants to get married again, to someone who can give her the kind of ultraglamorous life I never did. Apparently, the allure of single life has worn thin." Jake understood that. He was tired of being alone, too. Tired of regretting the way his romance with Jenna had ended. The way both of them had been hurt.

"I've seen her pictures on the society pages of the Dallas papers. She's very beautiful."

"On the outside," Jake confirmed.

"And well-bred," Jenna continued in a way that let him know she was determined to lay all their cards on the table. "Your parents must have approved of her."

And still did, unfortunately despite everything. But he didn't want to get into that now, and certainly not with Jenna on what was supposed to be *their* night. Jake slowed the truck as he approached the turnoff, some fifteen miles outside of Laramie. The native limestone country inn was set back from the highway in a grove of live oaks. It was softly lit from within.

The grounds were landscaped and very private. Glad to see the owners had followed his instructions to a T and cleared everyone else out, including the staff, before they arrived, Jake parked in front and cut the motor. "I hope you don't mind. I selected the place."

"Obviously not in Laramie," Jenna added, her accusatory look reminding him of all the times they had seen each other on the sly when they were teens. Too late, Jake realized how it seemed to Jenna. She was wrong if she thought he was ashamed to be seen with her. Quite the contrary. "I wanted something more private, so we could talk without interruption," Jake explained. "So I rented the inn for the evening."

"You mean the dining room?" Jenna ascertained.

Jake shook his head, "The entire inn."

Shock widened Jenna's eyes, then turned them an icy blue. "You're kidding."

"Nope."

Once again, to Jake's dismay, Jenna obviously suspected his intentions were not at all chivalrous or forthright. "You really are pulling out all the stops," she said, clearly displeased.

Jake got out of the truck, his hopes of a lovely intimate dinner with the only woman he had ever loved fading fast. He knew he'd made mistakes in the past where Jenna was concerned. Whether she was ready to admit it or not, she had done the same by him. Nevertheless, he was getting tired of defending himself, and having her look at him as if all he were trying to do here was take her to bed. He circled around to open her door. "I have money. I'm not afraid to put it to good use. Getting you on my side—and Alex's—is very good use."

Reluctantly, Jenna allowed Jake to escort her up the front steps and across the porch. "Speaking of Alex, you really should be home with her this evening."

"Funny." Jake held the door and guided her through the wide front hall to the beautiful dining room to their left. The long table for sixteen had been pushed against the wall. It was covered with a linen tablecloth and a variety of silver chafing dishes. A smaller table had been placed in front of the huge stone hearth, and was beautifully set for two. In deference to the summer heat outside, and the air-conditioning inside, there was no fire. Instead, a dozen lit candles were artistically arranged in the grate. Vases of freesia and baby's breath—Jenna's favorite—abounded. Soft music from their youth filled the room.

"And yet," Jenna continued, looking at Jake as if he were anything but a good guy to have around, "you're here with me."

Jake uncovered their salads and poured the wine. "In order to get you to help out Alex and me."

Jenna accepted the wine with a nod. "Texas is full of designers." She kept her eyes on his as Jake sat down opposite her.

"But only one of you," Jake countered, trying to imagine what it would be like to have Jenna back in his life again, not as the grief-stricken teen she had been when they parted, but the strong, self-assured woman she had become.

"Why me?" Jenna whispered, suddenly looking as torturously unhappy as he had felt all these years without her. *"Why now?"*

Jake wasn't about to apologize for doing what should have been done years ago. "Because I haven't been able to stop thinking of you." *Because all this time I thought I had hurt you enough and I was doing you a favor by staying away. And then I saw you on TV and realized I would never love anyone the way I loved you.*

For a moment, Jake thought Jenna felt the same way, but the feeling faded, and the sweetly nostalgic look in her clear blue eyes faded and turned to ice once again. "That's a shame," Jenna said crisply. "There's nothing worse than wasting energy or time. Which is exactly what this is." She started to rise.

Jake caught her wrist and pulled her back down into her seat. He wanted nothing more at that moment than to haul her into his lap and kiss her soundly. But—for Alex's sake, for the sake of them—he kept his mind strictly on the business at hand. The business that would have Jenna and him spending time together and getting to know each other again. "You haven't heard my proposition," he pointed out calmly, releasing her only when he was sure she wouldn't try to flee.

Not looking at him, Jenna speared a piece of lettuce with her fork, lifted it to her lips. "I don't want to hear your proposition."

"Sure now?" Jake taunted as he too dug into his crisp, delicious salad. "It could do wonders for your design business."

Jenna paused. So it was true, Jake noted, with equal parts satisfaction and disapproval. Her design business *did* mean everything to her.

"I'm listening," she said eventually.

Jake reached into the inside pocket of his blazer and pulled out a neatly drawn-up business agreement. "I'm offering to provide the financial backing via J&R Industries to make and distribute a clothing line bearing your name."

Jenna put down her fork and studied the paperwork for an extraordinarily long time. "And the catch is…?" Jenna said eventually.

Jake polished off his salad and took a sip of wine. "Alexandra needs a wardrobe."

Jenna narrowed her eyes at him and observed with a faint note of disapproval in her voice, "Why, when she seems to have one she is perfectly happy with?"

Jake shook his head, cutting Jenna off. "She needs to look like a little lady," he said firmly. "The sooner, the better."

Jenna arched a delicate brow and went back to eating her salad. "Says who and why?"

Famished, Jake broke open a roll and lavishly spread it with butter. Reluctantly, he imparted, "Melinda is concerned about

Alex's tomboyish phase. She thinks it proves I'm not capable of rearing Alex on my own.''

Jenna paused, her fork halfway to her lips. ''But you have custody, don't you?''

Jake took another sip of wine. ''Sole custody since she was two, yes.''

Jenna's brow furrowed. Finished with her salad, she also reached for the bread. ''Isn't that unusual?''

Jake shook his head. ''Not when the mother doesn't want custody. And Melinda didn't. All she wanted in the settlement was money. Which, as you and everyone else in the Lone Star State knows, she got.''

''I'm sorry,'' Jenna said. ''For Alex. I know how tough it is to lose a mom when there's no helping it. To have that happen when it doesn't have to be that way, well, it's got to be tough.''

Jake sighed and got up to retrieve the main course, blackened redfish, scalloped potatoes with jack cheese and French beans. ''When Alex was younger, she didn't seem to mind the fact that her mother lived in Europe and rarely jetted over to see her.'' Jake filled the plates and brought them over, one at a time. He sat down opposite Jenna and dug in. ''The truth is, even when we were still married, when Alex was a baby, Melinda never paid much attention to her. So when Melinda moved out—well, Alex couldn't miss what she'd never had. I wasn't about to leave her home alone. And though my parents would have taken her, that wasn't an option, either. I didn't want Alex adopting some of their snobbish attitudes. So she traveled with me on business. Everywhere I went, Alex went—with Clara usually coming along and doubling as driver and nanny, depending on what I needed at that moment.''

Jenna regarded Jake with the inherent kindness that was so much a part of her personality. ''And Alex was happy with the arrangement?''

''Very.'' Jake exhaled. ''But when she went to school this past fall and all the other kids in her kindergarten class had moms fussing over them and picking out their clothes, it hit her hard. And suddenly, she just started refusing to wear dresses—not that she'd ever really liked them. But at least when I needed her to brush her hair and wear a dress so I could take her to some fancy restaurant, I could get her to do so."

"But no more?" Jenna guessed, as the CD player switched from a Trisha Yearwood album to one of Garth Brooks's.

"No more. I guess Alex figured if she couldn't be like everyone else and have a mom and a dad living at home with her, she'd just be different. And that was when Alex went full-bore into this tomboy stage. I thought it was a phase and just didn't push it. But now Melinda has heard about Alex's increasingly disheveled appearance from mutual friends. She's embarrassed, upset. Thinks it reflects poorly on her. Next thing I know she's threatening to sue for custody and planning to leave Italy—where she's been living the past couple of years—for good."

Jenna looked at him quizzically. "You don't want Melinda to come back to the States?"

Jake sighed, knowing it sounded lousy of him, but also knowing if he was going to drag Jenna into the middle of this mess, he owed her the plain, unvarnished truth. "If I thought it would do Alex some good," Jake hedged. "If I thought Melinda would be any kind of loving mother, or positive influence in Alex's life, I'd be lobbying for it in a red-hot minute."

Jenna's eyes softened compassionately. "But you don't think that'd be the case."

Jake sighed. "Bottom line, Melinda doesn't have a maternal bone in her entire body. She cares about money and appearances and finding another husband whose only goal in life is to make her happy, and that's it."

"So in coming to me you're trying to head Melinda off at the pass."

Jake nodded, more sure than ever now—from Jenna's sympathetic reaction to his dilemma—that he had been right to come to her. "Unfortunately, clothes aren't all she needs." Jake looked at Jenna seriously. "Alex needs a crash course in being a lady before her mom gets back."

Jenna made a face, no longer quite as eager to help out or get involved. She went back to polishing off her redfish. "Can't you get your mother to help with that?"

Jake shook his head, knowing that as much as he loved his mother, and he did, that she was long on lecturing and interfering and short on patience. "My mother is not the one for the job," he said firmly. "You are."

Jenna looked at him as though he had lost his mind. Finished with her entrée, she got up to see what else was on the side table. Jake stood up, too.

"Think of it this way," he said as Jenna helped herself to very small slivers of chocolate cake, praline cheesecake and warm peach-and-blueberry cobbler. "You'd be doing something for me I desperately need." Jake settled on just the chocolate cake. "I'd be doing something for you that you desperately need. We'd be helping each other."

They returned to the table in silence. Jenna shook her head in silent censure, even as she enjoyed her dessert. "After the way you treated me—" she said, as if unable to believe his gall.

Tired of taking all the heat for what had happened between them, Jake angled a thumb at his chest. "Hey! I'm not the one who got cold feet and refused to elope at the last minute!" In fact, he still felt if Jenna had just gone off with him then, they would be married today.

Jenna rolled her eyes as she got herself a cup of coffee. "We were caught, suitcases in hand, by your parents!"

Jake discounted that with a shrug. "We still could have gotten away," he said levelly, pouring his own cup of coffee. "What would they have done? Chased after us?" He mocked her with a lift of his brow. "I don't think so. That's way too undignified for my folks."

As for the rest of the complications, they had thought about everything. Jenna was underage, but she was also just a couple of weeks away from her birthday. As long as she went willingly with Jake, and they didn't cross any state lines, and waited until Jenna was legally of age to actually consummate the marriage, then they wouldn't be breaking any laws. Of course, if they married without the permission of her guardian their marriage would have been technically invalid. But they had that covered, too, deciding if they just waited until after Jenna's birthday to return to Laramie that no one would kick up a fuss about what was more or less a "done deal" for nearly three weeks. They recognized that his family's lawyers could easily take care of any legalities, even if it meant another quickie ceremony.

Jenna sighed. "Okay, so maybe there wouldn't have been a car chase or some big scene at the justice of the peace, even if your parents had managed to figure out exactly where we were going as well as physically head us off before we got there." She waved a lecturing finger beneath his nose. "But your folks still would have tried to convince you to have our marriage annulled when we returned and my big sister probably would have done the same thing."

"So what?" Jake argued right back. "If we had already been married, a baby potentially on the way, my parents and Meg both would have backed off, if only to avoid an even bigger scandal than just us running off and getting married." He knew Meg. She cared about Jenna and wanted her to be happy. And he knew his folks. No way would they want any grandchild of theirs born out of wedlock, or Jake taking advantage of a young innocent girl. In fact, it was their training on that fact that had kept Jake from ever making love to Jenna in their younger days. Even at the very end, when she'd been willing, he had insisted on waiting until they were actually married. And, truth to tell, as much as he still wanted to make love to her, he still didn't lament that fact. He was glad he had treated Jenna with respect, glad they had waited until they were old enough and or the time was right. The truth was, as much as they had wanted to be married then, they hadn't been ready for it.

"Your parents didn't approve of me, Jake. Not from day one. They didn't even want us being friends." She looked at him steadily, all the hurt she had felt, then and now, in her clear blue eyes. "Over the long haul, a marriage between us never would have worked and you know it."

Jake reached across the table and covered Jenna's hand with his own. "All I know is that we let our relationship go," he confessed huskily, "and I've spent every day since regretting it." He didn't want to spend the rest of his life the same way, and if he were right in his assessment of her feelings, Jenna didn't, either.

Jenna jerked her hand from his. She pushed away from the table angrily and vaulted to her feet. "If that were true, you would have come after me then. You would have called, tried to see me. Something. Anything—"

Remembering how miserable they both had been, Jake pushed to his feet, too. "I wanted to," he said roughly, going after her.

"Then why didn't you?" Jenna squared off with him, tears glistening in her eyes.

Jake clasped her shoulders. "Because I couldn't," he told her with a weariness that came straight from his soul. "Not without destroying your life. And that of your sisters."

Chapter Two

Jenna stared at Jake in raging disbelief. *What did he think he had done in abandoning her, if not ruin her life?*

"My parents said if I pursued you in any way, they'd use our reckless elopement as proof that Meg was not a proper guardian for you and your younger sisters. They said that in even asking you to marry me, as young as you were, given what had just happened to your folks, that I was taking advantage of you in the worst way. You and I might view the situation romantically, but it was quite possible Meg and the police would view the situation as my parents did—as simply running away. They reminded me that if the authorities stepped in to help locate you that you could have been deemed a juvenile delinquent just for attempting to marry without your guardian's permission. And that I could be put in jail for contributing to the delinquency of a minor, whether Meg agreed with the court's decision or not. They said if I wasn't strong enough or mature enough to walk away while you and your sisters put your lives back together that they would do 'the right thing' for me. They promised to do everything in their power to see the courts removed Meg as your guardian, split you and your sisters up and put the youngest two—Dani and Kelsey—in foster care."

Jake shoved a hand through the tousled layers of his inky-black hair. "You would, of course, have been legally free after your eighteenth birthday to do what you wanted. But for Dani, who was sixteen-and-a-half at the time, and Kelsey, who was fifteen, it would have been devastating.'' Jake paused, his eyes filled with a mixture of regret for all the time they'd lost and compassion for what they'd been through. "I couldn't do that to you. There was no doubt in my mind my parents would follow through on their threat. They really thought they were doing the best thing for you and your sisters. And knowing how devastated you all were by the sudden loss of your parents, I began to think maybe my folks were right, that I was wrong to take your youth from you like that, that you deserved the same chance to go to college and be a normal teenager that I'd already had." Jake shrugged, pain sharpening the handsome lines of his face. "So I walked away from you, and didn't look back."

Doing her best to absorb all he had told her, Jenna felt for a chair and sat down. Jake slid a chair over and sat down in front of her, so they were sitting knee to knee. "You should have told me what was going on," Jenna said, trembling.

Jake leaned forward and took both her hands in his. "How would that have helped you?" he asked softly. "To be told you needed to choose between being with me and the continued welfare of your sisters? Do you think that would have made you feel better to be put in a situation like that, after all you'd already been through?"

Jenna sighed. Of course it wouldn't have. If he'd told her, made her choose, it would have torn her apart, and caused even more stress and heartache for her and her sisters.

Jake shook his head, recalling. He searched her eyes as he continued filling her in. "I wanted to fight my parents—you don't know how much—but at the same time I had to be realistic about the odds of success. I was only twenty-two. I had not yet inherited the trust fund from my grandparents. I didn't have the means or influence at that point in my life to help keep you and your sisters together on my own. Plus, you know the age thing, the fact I was four years older, finished with college, and you were still in high school had always been an issue. It's not much of an age difference now, of course, but back then…well there's a big difference between being in high school and being in college." Jake sighed and ran a hand through his hair, "As mature as you were, there were times when I did feel I was pushing you to grow up too fast, so the two of us could be together the way we felt we were meant to be. So I felt guilty for ever asking you to elope with me. I felt like I'd been really unfair to you."

Jenna saw the regret shimmering in his eyes and knew this was true. "I knew you were incredibly vulnerable, that you weren't in any state of mind to even be thinking about taking such a monumental step. But at the same time I didn't know what else to do. I didn't know how to help you then, how to make it better, except by loving you."

"Which you did," Jenna said softly, recalling how good and warm and safe he'd made her feel in the first dark days after her parents had died. Jake had been there, holding her when she cried, attending the funeral with her, helping her take it one day, one moment at a time. Even now, she didn't know how she would have made it through those first dark days if he hadn't been there.

Jake swallowed hard. His hands tightened over hers. "But when we were caught, suitcases in hand, and when I saw your doubt, when you called it quits before we'd even gotten all the way out of Laramie, and said you had changed your mind, you didn't want to elope with me, I knew you probably did need to be with your sisters more than me. That you needed the chance to grow up, free of any serious entanglements or pressures from anyone else—the chance I'd already had."

Jenna recalled the euphoria she'd felt as she packed a bag, sneaked out of her house and met up with Jake in the Laramie High School parking lot, well after midnight. Then the humiliation and dismay when she realized his parents had followed him to the secret rendezvous. She only had to look at Patricia and Danforth Remington's faces as they stepped from their Mercedes to know they were dead-set against her marriage to their only son. "Of course I had second thoughts," Jenna defended herself hotly. It had been natural to back out of the elopement at that point. Withdrawing her hands from Jake's grasp, she pushed back her chair, got up and began to pace. "I'd just lost my parents. I wasn't going to willfully separate you from yours, which was what a hasty marriage to you would have done. So yes, of course I called it off."

Jenna swallowed around the growing knot of emotion in her throat. "When you said you'd call me as soon as you could, I believed you, Jake." She hated to think how many hours she had sat by the phone, just waiting for it to ring. How many nights she had gone to sleep with it in bed beside her. "I didn't expect you to walk away from me forever," Jenna murmured as she went to the window and turned her back on Jake. She'd thought—hoped—they'd continue to see each other and wait a few years. Hoped with time his parents would come to know her and realize how much she and Jake loved each other and change their minds, even endorse the marriage. She shook her head as she stared out at the dark Texas night. "I thought you'd come back for me as soon as you got things straightened out with your parents," she confessed in a low, choked voice. "I thought we'd figure things out together." Arms folded in front of her, she whirled around to face Jake. "Instead, I never heard from you again—not one word, not ever, until today!"

Jake grimaced and stood. "I thought I was doing what was best for you and your sisters in walking away. I thought I was being selfless and gallant. If it helps to know—I've regretted it ever since."

Jenna glared at him, her heart thudding in her chest. "Not enough, apparently, to stop you from getting married to Melinda that same summer," she shot back.

Jake stepped closer. "It was a mistake, a rebound thing. Although," he amended with a frown, "I didn't know it at the time."

Jenna, who'd eventually had her own rebound fling, equally

disastrous, understood that. But just because she understood it
didn't mean she was willing to trust him again. Now or ever.
"It still doesn't answer my question, Jake." Hands on her
hips, she regarded him contentiously. "Why did you come to
me for help with Alex? Why now?" Why hadn't he left well
enough alone? Yes, she was hurt, but it was a hurt she had
recovered from. This new hurt was something else indeed.

Jake blew out a weary breath. He looked deep into her eyes
and said firmly, "Because I want us to be friends again."

"Friends." Jenna studied him carefully, knowing with the
two of them it had never been platonic. "Or more than
friends?" she asked bluntly.

Half of Jake's mouth slanted up in a slow, sexy smile. "You
choose."

Jenna lifted her brow and, her eyes holding his all the while,
challenged dryly, "You sure don't ask for much, do you?"
Even if, in his dark blue sport coat, casual khaki slacks, light
blue shirt and tie, he was as sexy as ever in that distinctly
blue-blooded Texan way.

Jake closed the distance between them and clasped her
hands between the two of his. "Tell me you don't want the
same thing and I'll go away," he whispered, his warm cal-
lused palms caressing the backs of her hands. "But if you
do—if you have it in your heart to repair our relationship and
at the same time help me with my little girl—" Again, that
slow sexy smile that always turned her knees to water. "I'll
owe you, for a long, long time."

WASN'T THIS what she had wanted? For him to come crawling
back to her on his hands and knees? Okay, six plus years had
passed, but he was still back. Eligible—handsome as ever.
And he was offering to make all her business dreams come
true, to boot. So what was wrong with this picture? Why,
despite everything, did his incredibly presumptuous proposition look and sound so good to her? Why was she suddenly
so willing to forgive him for taking her heart and stomping it

to pieces? It wasn't like she was still in love with him—or would ever love him again.

Jenna looked him square in the eye, determined to let him know where they stood before things progressed any further. ''I'm not going to sleep with you.''

Jake merely grinned at her, as if to say: *I wouldn't make bets on that if I were you.* Shrugging, he held her gaze and retorted dryly, ''I didn't expect you would. It may surprise you to know that making love with me is not usually part of my business deals.''

''Let me guess. But in our case, you'd be willing to make an exception.''

His deliciously mischievous grin broadened all the more. Jake rubbed his jaw thoughtfully, allowing finally in a deep, sexy murmur that sent shivers coasting up and down her spine, ''We never did have that wedding night.''

Jenna flushed despite herself as she reminded him, ''We never had the wedding, Jake.''

''Then, sure.'' Jake spoke as if now were a different matter entirely.

''We won't now, either,'' Jenna continued flatly. Figuring this had gone on long enough—much more of it and she'd be fantasizing about his return to her life in a romantic sense, too—Jenna pushed past him. Wishing all the while, as she glared at him, that he didn't have the power to rile her so. She didn't need this kind of all-encompassing emotion in her life. She didn't need him. And if she had her way, and she planned to, she never would again, either.

Looking as relaxed as she was upset, Jake paused to drop an envelope on the table, then swaggered after her as she turned to head for the door. She was nearly there when he clamped a hand on her bare shoulder. Ignoring her resistance, he gently guided her around to face him. Looking down into her face with an intensity that took her breath away, he taunted softly, ''You're telling me you don't still feel it?''

Jenna swallowed hard and forced her knees to stop trembling. Darn it all, why had she worn such a sexy dress, anyway? She could have worn something casual that wasn't the least bit provocative. She could have worn something not designed to make him eat his heart out for all he'd given up. "Feel what?" she asked instead, ignoring the way his gaze kept drifting to her lips and the exposed swell of her breasts.

Jake hauled her against him. "This."

The next thing Jenna knew Jake had wrapped his arms around her back and lowered his lips to hers. His kiss was hot and so sensual it took her breath away. Furious, Jenna made a muffled sound of protest. But then she was surrendering to the emotions swirling through her at breakneck speed, threading her hands through his hair and kissing him back with every fiber of her being. Loving the taste and feel and scent of him, so dark and male and sexy. Loving the way he had always kissed her, as if he didn't care how many roadblocks she threw in their way, as if he meant to possess her, heart and soul. Damn, but she had missed this, missed him and the special…and yes, powerful way he made her feel. Jake deepened the kiss even more and stroked his tongue intimately with hers, as if she were the only woman in the whole world for him.

JAKE HADN'T MEANT to kiss her while they were at the inn, maybe not at all that night. He'd wanted to take things nice and slow this time. Show her how much he still cared about her, and always would, before asking anything remotely intimate or physical in return. But when she looked at him like that, as if she were just daring him to love her, he never had been able to resist, even if his hot-blooded pursuit of her was likely to incense her. He wanted to feel the softness of her body cuddled against his. He wanted to taste the honeyed sweetness of her lips, feel the sensual twining of her tongue as it wrapped around his, inhale her sexy perfume, and thread his fingers through the thick red-gold waves of her hair. He wanted her to tell him—by the passionate nature of their embrace—how she felt about him. Even if she wouldn't admit it out loud.

JENNA KNEW if they didn't stop soon they would end up in one of the beds upstairs. That was exactly what she had wanted when they had been together before—the ultimate culmination of their love in the most physically intimate union a man and woman could enter into. But she also knew this was no way, and no place, to lose her virginity.

Furious that Jake had managed to evade all her carefully erected defenses—again—Jenna splayed both her hands across his chest, tore her lips from his, and pushed him away.

Stumbling backwards, Jenna glared at him. "You haven't changed one bit," she sputtered angrily. Darned if he hadn't turned her whole world upside down, and with just one measly, heart-stopping kiss!

Jake grinned and rubbed his jaw. He looked like one thoroughly satisfied male, pleased as punch that it had taken her a good five minutes to summon up the will to make him stop. "The kiss was that good, huh?" he teased.

Even better, Jenna thought wistfully, not above admitting—to herself, anyway—that she had the same physical desires and needs, not to mention emotional yearnings, as every other woman in Texas. But she couldn't let her desire for Jake sway her. So what if the two of them together had passion unlike anything she had ever felt before or since? So what if he alone had the power to make her tingle from head to toe and want him with every fiber of her being just by being in the same room with her? Physical desire still did not equate happiness. Jenna looked him up and down disparagingly. Seeing the depth of his desire, she returned her gaze to his face. "You still think everything and anything is there for the taking. You only have to want it badly enough for it to happen."

The happiness in Jake's eyes faded. It was replaced by irritation. "Everything and anything is there for our taking," he shot right back. "And don't give me that woe-is-me look, either, honey. 'Cause you have done your fair share of setting your sights on something—like being the premiere new clothing designer—and making it happen.'' Jake regarded her steadily, then finished with velvet determination, ''So there is no reason on earth you can't do the same thing in regards to your personal life. You just have to want it.''

Guilt assailed her anew. ''Well, I don't want it!'' Jenna jerked away from him, angry that he was making her want more than what she had, what she couldn't—and never would—have: a satisfying love life with him.

He sized her up, skeptical of her self-serving fib. ''Could have fooled me.''

JAKE DROVE her back to Laramie in silence. Jenna slammed out of his truck and stormed up to her apartment above the shop. To her dismay, he didn't even attempt to follow, just made sure she was inside safely and then drove off. Not loudly, with a screech of tires, as he might have after one of their quarrels in his impetuous youth, but calmly and quietly.

Tears streaming down her face, Jenna locked the door behind her, muttering invective about his character all the while. Then, really letting her temper fly, she slammed her purse against the wall, and for good measure, kicked off her shoes, too.

Without warning, Kelsey's head rose over the back of the sofa, nearly scaring her to death. Jenna gasped and slammed a hand against her chest. She had forgotten Kelsey was bunking here with her until she and her partner, Brady Anderson, could move out to the old Lockhart ranch. That wouldn't be possible until the contractor they'd hired had finished sanding and varnishing all the floors and cabinets and installing new electrical wiring and plumbing. Meanwhile, the two had plenty to do, staking out pastures and putting up fences that would divide their property into separate cattle and horse operations, one half of the ranch being his, the other half hers. It was quite an undertaking for two people, who—up until a month or so ago—had been strangers, and all the Lockharts, save Kelsey of course, were feeling a little nervous about it. They just hoped their baby sister knew what she was doing. Which was more than Jenna could say for herself, given the thoroughly unrestrained way she had just kissed Jake Remington, behaving as if the two of them had never been apart!

Kelsey studied Jenna's face. "The date was that good, huh?"

Jenna scowled at Kelsey. "The man is absolutely impossible! Not to mention arrogant, assuming and antagonizing."

Kelsey nodded with exaggerated indignation. "And those are just the As."

Jenna gave Kelsey a warning look. She was in no mood for jokes. "I mean it." Feeling like she was burning up all over, Jenna lifted her skirt, peeled off her pantyhose, then padded barefoot to the refrigerator. "I'd hoped otherwise, but that Jake Remington hasn't changed one bit."

Kelsey followed Jenna to the kitchen and accepted a cold beer. "Neither have you, apparently."

Jenna paused, her hand curled around the bottle cap in midtwist. "What's that supposed to mean?" She set the long-necked brown bottle on the counter and finished opening it with a sharp twist.

"Come on, Jenna." Kelsey grinned as she opened her beer and took a long thirsty drink more suitable for a rough-and-tumble cowboy than the fine Texas lady she'd been reared to be. "This is your baby sister you're talking to here." She waggled her eyebrows at Jenna. "The one who used to sneak into your room at night and hear all about your clandestine dates with Jake. All those summers you two sneaked around to see each other, so his parents wouldn't find out he was smitten with a poor local girl instead of one of the rich debs from Dallas they wanted him to marry."

Jenna went to the pantry and brought out a bag of blue corn tortilla chips and an unopened jar of salsa. "He did marry one of them. He married Melinda Carrington."

Kelsey shrugged and leaned against the counter, her Texas Rangers baseball-style pajamas molding her slender frame. She watched as Jenna poured chips and salsa into serving dishes and carried them back into the living room. "Yeah, and from what I heard Jake divorced her, too."

"Your point, being...?" Jenna asked, as the two settled back onto the sofa.

"That," Kelsey spelled out gently, "it's pretty clear you never stopped loving him. And he probably hasn't stopped loving you, either. Or else he wouldn't be here."

"The only reason he is here is because he thinks he can make money off my clothing designs. Lots of it. And, as a matter of fact, I do, too," Jenna confided as she rubbed her tense shoulders with her hands. "I've known that for a long time. All I've needed was the money—and the backing—to expand."

Kelsey loaded a chip with salsa. "I hate to burst your bubble, sis, but Jake could make money off dozens of other businesses in Texas, if that's all he's after."

Unfortunately, Jenna knew that was true, too. She sighed and took another sip of beer. "He also wants me to help turn his little girl, Alexandra, into a lady and get her outfitted in some pretty dresses."

"There are hundreds upon hundreds of children's clothing shops in this state. Why come to you for that, when you don't even design children's clothing?"

"Because Alex is hard to please," Jenna answered, remembering without wanting to how cute and lively Jake's little girl had been, even if she had been out of control.

Kelsey shrugged and reached for another chip. "People who specialize in selling to the super-rich are well versed in 'difficult,' Jenna. Probably even more so when it comes to their spoiled-rotten kids."

Irritated at having her theories shot down one by one, Jenna frowned at her baby sister, and continued trying to convince them both that Jake's actions were not due to any long lost love for her, as he claimed. "There is no where else in Laramie to go for lah-de-dah clothing. He just built a ranch here. He and his daughter are living here now."

Kelsey made a dissenting face. "He could still drive to Dallas."

"His ex-wife will be here in two days."

Kelsey rolled her eyes. "It's a two-hour drive there, even less to San Antonio from here. So don't give me that. He could easily go there to buy dresses for Alexandra if he wanted to."

Jenna sighed.

"Face it, sis." Kelsey leaned forward earnestly. "Jake Remington is here for one reason and one reason only. He wants you back in his life. Probably as his wife. Which is why he's trying so hard to get you and his daughter together. Before he can make a real move on you, he's got to make sure the two of you can get along."

Kelsey had never stayed any guy's girlfriend for long—she was way too fickle for that—but she was very good at analyzing what was going on between a man and a woman. Too good sometimes, Jenna thought, as her baby sister's words hit close to home. "That door is closed," she retorted stubbornly, refusing to let herself hope, even for one second, that her sister might be right about Jake's intentions.

"I see." Kelsey grinned and peered at her in a parody of Dr. Ruth. "And iss that vhat you told him vhen he kissed you?"

Jenna's jaw dropped open. Her hand flew to her mouth. "How did you—?"

"Please." Kelsey rolled her eyes, her exasperation with her older sister mounting. "With the two of you alone on some romantic excursion! With Jake in hot pursuit? Don't forget, I used to hear about those kisses." Kelsey clasped her hands to her chest and pretended to be overcome with an intense longing of her very own. "Just hearing about them was enough to make me swoon."

Deciding it was high time she got in her nightclothes, too,

Jenna vaulted to her feet and headed for her bedroom, Kelsey right behind her. Jenna was still flushing self-consciously as she took off her earrings and dropped them onto her vanity. "I was young then. Impressionable." She lifted her hands to her neck and began struggling with the clasp of her necklace.

Kelsey gave her a knowing look as she stepped behind her to lend a hand. "And now you're old enough to do all the things you used to only dream about," she teased, releasing the clasp.

It was Jenna's turn to roll her eyes. She dropped her necklace beside her earrings and turned. There was really no way to tell how experienced Kelsey was—she acted like she had done everything there was to be done and then some—but Jenna had a feeling that was all an act, meant to intimidate the guys and keep them at bay. Jenna shook her head. "You're incorrigible."

Kelsey acknowledged this with a mischievous grin. Then her smile faded as abruptly as it had appeared. She looked at Jenna steadily, her eyes brimming with concern, then said softly, "And you're dreaming if you think a man like Jake is just going to go away."

Jenna steeled herself against the hurt she was sure would come if she didn't shield her heart. Jake had devastated her before. It had taken her years to recover. She didn't care what he said, she was not going to let him do it again. She folded her arms in front of her stubbornly as she slipped out of her dress. "I don't care what he wants! He's not going to get it this time." Jenna stomped over to her closet and hung up her dress. "I'll do business with him. I'll outfit his daughter, but that's it."

JENNA WAS HALF HOPING Jake would send his daughter over to her shop with someone else to order a few dresses, but of course that didn't happen. The next morning, his charcoal-gray truck pulled up in front of her shop and parked at the curb, followed by the red sport utility vehicle with Clara at the wheel. Jake and Alexandra stepped out of the truck, Clara stepped out of the S.U.V. Clara waved and headed off down the sidewalk on some other errand. A few seconds later, Jake held the door for his daughter and Alexandra Remington stomped in with all the petulance an almost-six-year-old could muster. While Jake put his briefcase down next to the sales counter and took off his black Stetson, Alex planted her hands on her hips and glared at Jenna as if she were the enemy. "I figure I might as well tell ya straight out," she said, in a cute imitation of her take-charge daddy. Her scowl deepened, as did the fire in her blue-gray eyes. "I don't want ta be here." Her lower lip shot out stubbornly. "I'd rather be home looking for a new frog—Daddy made me let Mr. Frog go last night, so if I want to play with one I'm gonna hafta find another one, and maybe a snake, too, this time."

Jenna's eyes widened with distaste at the mention of reptiles, as Jake frowned and looked down at his daughter. "Alex. No snakes," he said firmly. "I mean it. Snakes can be poisonous. And so can some frogs, for that matter."

Alex sighed loudly. Tilting her head to one side, she sized up her daddy and decided, against all odds, to try again. She put her hands out to her sides and balanced herself on one foot. "You could always buy me one that's not poisonous," she suggested hopefully.

"No." Jake's mouth was set, his attention only on his daughter.

"Why not?" Alex challenged, her chin shooting out pugnaciously once again.

"Because I don't like snakes," Jake explained.

Neither did Jenna. In fact, she shuddered just thinking about them.

"You might if you had one," Alex countered optimistically.

Jake's expression remained firm and unyielding. "Well, we'll never know, because we're never getting one. And I explained to you why we had to let Mr. Frog go—he is a wild frog and wild frogs belong in nature. Mr. Frog would have died if we had kept him in captivity too long."

"What other kind of pets do you have?" Jenna asked, guiding Alex over to her long, cozy sofa.

Alex sighed and looked all the more dejected and disappointed. "I don't got any."

Jenna shot Jake a look. Given Alex's obvious love of animals, this was a surprise. "We just moved from a high-rise in Dallas," Jake explained. "The building did not allow pets. I've been hoping to rectify that, now that we've moved to the ranch. I just haven't had time."

"Ah." Jenna got out her sketch pad and seated herself on the sofa next to Alex. That sounded better. *To her, not necessarily to Alex.* Jenna began to sketch a simple, princess-style dress with a pinafore. Ignoring Jake entirely, she smiled down at Alex. "What kind of pet would you like to have, if you had your choice?"

Alex pushed the brim of her cowgirl hat out of her eyes and rested her chin on her hand. She crossed her blue-jeans-covered legs. "Maybe a zebra or a bear cub."

"I think kittens and puppies make better pets," Jenna said.

"How come?" Alex asked.

Jenna smiled. "Because they're soft and fluffy and fun to cuddle and they're meant to be indoors."

"Maybe I'll get a kitten then," Alex said after a thoughtful pause. "Or a puppy. Maybe both." Her eyes lit up enthusiastically as she drew a yo-yo from one pocket and a cap gun from the other.

"That might be possible, if you cooperate and start wearing dresses again, when I ask you to wear a dress," Jake said.

Alex slid off the sofa and fired her cap gun at the ceiling. Loud pops and acrid smoke permeated the air. "Maybe you should get me a kitty and a puppy first and then I'll see if I feel like wearing a dress," Alex countered.

Jake confiscated the cap gun and shook his head. "Behave first."

Alex shook her head. The stare down between parent and child continued. "I don't hafta wear dresses at school," Alex said finally, when she realized her daddy wasn't any more likely to give in than she was.

"No, you don't," Jake said calmly. "But you could wear a dress if you wanted to wear one. And what's more you'd look very pretty if you did." He gave her a gentle, coaxing smile.

Alex made a face and with a loud sigh flounced back over to sit beside Jenna. "I don't want to look pretty." She leaned over to see how Jenna's sketch was progressing.

"How do you want to look?" Jenna asked as her pencil flew across the page.

"So right now."

"You can look 'so right now' in a dress," Jake said enthusiastically.

Alex glared at Jake.

"Can't you, Jenna?" Jake said, looking to Jenna for moral support.

Jenna shrugged and refused to take sides. "Depends on the dress," she said. Pausing, she looked at Alex, who had gone back to playing with her yo-yo. "What's your favorite color crayon?" Jenna asked.

That, Alex had to think about. "Red," she said.

"What else?" Jenna prodded, making a few notes to herself on the side of her page.

"Blue."

"Dark blue or light blue?"

"Both."

"What about green?"

"It's okay," Alex replied seriously, "but I like blue and red better."

"Okay. What grade are you going to be in next year?"

"First. I went to kindergarten last year."

"Did you learn about letters and numbers?"

Alex nodded vigorously. "I can sing the alphabet song."

She paused to demonstrate. "And I can count to twenty!" She demonstrated again.

"All right! Way to go!" Jenna enthused, and won a shy smile from Alex that made her smile in turn. "Did you draw pictures?"

"Mmm-hmm."

Jenna finished the sketch and then filled it in with Alex's favorite colors. "What was your favorite thing to draw?" she asked.

Alex furrowed her brow. "Kitties and puppies. And one time I drawed a kite and a big tree with lotsa leaves."

Jenna nodded. Clearly, she and Alex were on the same page now. "I want to show you something in the storeroom." Indicating Alex and Jake should follow, Jenna rose and went to the back of the store, where there were bolts of fabric. She pulled down three different shades of blue. "Which of these do you like best?" she asked Alex. "The dark blue, the medium blue or the light blue?"

Alex touched each of the three bolts of fabric. "I like the one that looks like blue jeans."

"Ah yes, indigo. Okay. Now…what about these reds? Scarlet, fire-engine or rose?"

"Fire-engine."

"Good choice." Jenna went back out to the showroom. She sat down, picked up her sketch pad and colored pencils and added the hues Alex had just selected. "Well, what do you think?"

Alex looked down at the short blue-denim jumper and fire-engine-red blouse. The jumper was adorned with kittens and puppies and letters of the alphabet, and paired with red cowgirl boots and a saucy blue cowgirl hat. "Now, granted, this is a dress, but it's not your average dress," Jenna said. "'Cause the jumper—the blue part here—is going to be made out of blue denim and looks more like overalls, except of course it's not. And I've got you wearing boots instead of black patent-leather shoes. Do you think you could wear something like this?''

For a second, Jenna thought Alex was going to shout a resounding *yes* or a Texas-sized *Yee-ha!* But her delight faded as soon as it appeared, replaced by a pout as big as the Lone Star State. "No. No dresses. Not even ones with kitties and puppies on 'em. Daddy, I want to go now.''

Jake knelt down in front of his daughter. He shot Jenna a brief grateful glance then turned back to Alexandra. "Alex, we talked about this. You have to have a few dresses now, like it or not."

"No." Alex dug in even more stubbornly. She folded her arms in front of her. "I don't. I want to go home now. And I know you got to go to work. Can you please have Clara take me back to the ranch?"

"Honey—" Jake looked both exasperated and desperate. The clock was ticking. Before they knew it, Melinda would be here, and Alex wasn't anywhere near even picking out a dress, never mind putting one on.

Jake shot an anxious look at Jenna.

"I think we've done enough for now," Jenna said, knowing there were just some things that couldn't be rushed, like it or not. "Clearly, Alex has other things she'd rather be doing. And I for one think she ought to have that opportunity." Jenna looked at Alex. "Are you busy this afternoon?"

"Why?" Alex glared at Jenna suspiciously, clearly not about to be tricked into wearing any dress.

Jenna shrugged in a way that let Alex know she at least wasn't going to force her to do anything she didn't want to. Aware Jake was watching her every move, she knelt down so she and Alex were at eye level with each other. "I thought I might come over to play, say around one o'clock, if it's okay."

Alex blinked in a combination of surprise and delight. "You want to play with me?"

Jenna nodded. This was one little girl in need of some

tender loving care if she'd ever seen one. "If your daddy say it's okay."

Alex looked up at Jake.

Clearly at a loss as to what Jenna was up to now, Jake shrugged. "It's okay with me if it's okay with you, pumpkin."

"Okay, I'll see you then. Bye, Daddy." Alex kissed Jake goodbye, then skipped out the door to the curb, where Clara was leaning against her vehicle and talking to Wade and Shane McCabe.

Jake waited until they'd driven off, before he turned back to Jenna. "You were supposed to back me up on this dress issue."

Jenna gathered up her sketch pad and pencils and carried them back to the storeroom, Jake right on her heels. "Oh, relax, would you?" she said, wishing he weren't so close, and that he didn't smell so good, like soap and man and woodsy, masculine cologne.

Jake's silver-gray eyes darkened sexily. "You do remember what kind of time schedule we're on here, don't you?"

Jenna rolled her eyes and tried not to notice how very close he had shaved that morning. "Rather hard to forget with you breathing down my neck like that."

Hands braced on his waist, pushing the edges of his sport coat back, Jake said, "You were supposed to convince her to at least order one dress."

Ignoring the way he was towering over her, Jenna held her ground. "I did. Didn't you see her face? Alex loved the alphabet dress I designed just for her. Granted, it's a little casual," Jenna shrugged, "but we have to start somewhere."

Jake's frown deepened all the more. "So she loved it for a second, before she dug in her heels," he countered, exasperated. "She is still not going to wear it."

"Yes," Jenna retorted patiently, "she will. But only when she wants to."

"Which is where you were supposed to come in," Jake added.

Jenna made a face at him, designed to show him how ridiculously panicky he was being. "Which is where I am *still* going to come in if you will just take a chill pill and let me do my thing." She turned on her heel and headed back out into the showroom.

Jake followed. "You have a plan?" he asked, the hope in his low voice as annoying to Jenna as his scolding had been.

"Of course I have a plan. I always have a plan," Jenna snapped back irritably, wondering when Jake would give her some credit. She paused, aware her emotions were starting to get out of control again—something that happened frequently when Jake was around. She drew in a bolstering breath. "I'll work on it this afternoon, when I go over to play with her," Jenna finished calmly as she walked over to the sales counter and checked her schedule—she had been rescheduling appointments with customers right and left to make room for Jake.

"Oh." The wind temporarily knocked out of his sails, Jake paused and raked a hand through his hair. He blew out an uneasy breath, looked at her seriously. "Good. 'Cause you know what is riding on this."

"Absolutely." Jenna smiled tightly, reminding herself to keep this strictly unemotional and aboveboard. She wanted this discussion with Jake finished within the next ten minutes, which would leave her plenty of time to prepare for her next appointment. "The expansion of my business."

Briefly, disappointment flickered in Jake's eyes. "And Alex's custody," Jake added, as he sauntered around to join her behind the sales counter.

"And Alex's custody," Jenna agreed, then paused as her next thought hit. She tilted her face up to Jake's, so she could see into his eyes. "Does Alex know what's going on between you and her mother—that Melinda is threatening to sue you for custody because Alex is such a tomboy?" Jenna asked curiously.

"No." Jake rested his shoulders against the wall. "And I

don't want her to know. Bad enough we're divorced and Melinda has shown practically zero interest in her since day one.''

"Did you expect this to happen?"

"No, but I probably should have. My attorney warned me at the time of the divorce that custody arrangements are often challenged after several years have passed. Sometimes for money. Sometimes because one parent doesn't approve of the way the other parent is rearing the child. She was particularly worried in my case because Melinda so easily gave up all rights to Alexandra. She thought Melinda might eventually realize she'd made a mistake and want to become more a part of Alex's life.''

"Surely Melinda couldn't win," Jenna said, concerned.

"When it comes to fighting over a child, no one ever wins. The whole point is to avoid the battle," Jake said. "And in this case, also to placate Melinda so she won't be compelled to overreact to make up for lost time and opportunity. Right now, as far as I can figure, Alex is an accessory to Melinda's life that doesn't quite fit. Alex's tomboy ways are embarrassing Melinda. Melinda doesn't like being embarrassed. If I weren't here, she'd probably send Alex off to boarding school to keep her out of sight of all our mutual friends in Texas. Since she can't do that, more drastic action is called for. One way or another, Melinda is going to make sure that Alex doesn't detract from her mother's public image.''

"Or in other words," Jenna guessed, "as long as Alex is a perfectly behaved little lady, the fact that Melinda's not around never comes up. But let Alex be 'clearly needing a mother in her life' and Melinda's absence is all people talk about."

"Right. Which brings us back to square one," Jake sighed wearily, looking for a moment as if the weight of the world were on his shoulders. "How to get Alexandra in a dress, so all this unwelcome attention will go away."

"Simple." Jenna smiled victoriously. "You just have to make her want to wear a dress."

Jake gave Jenna a droll look. "That's what I've been trying to do," he explained.

"Yes, I know. But a master is on the scene now. So leave it to me, and stop worrying about it. And start worrying about how you're going to pull the expansion of my business together by the time I get your daughter into a dress."

Jake opened his briefcase. "Actually, I've already been working on this. I think we should come up with a complete line of designs—formal, casual and business wear—to be mass-marketed and then try and sign up a whole host of department stores to carry it. From there, we'll contract with factories to make the clothes and—"

Jenna cut him off with a look. "No."

Jake blinked as if he hadn't heard right. "No?"

"I want a single, small but distinct, line of clothing bearing my name," Jenna said firmly. "Marketed at one store. Made in one factory, right here in Laramie."

Jake regarded her in consternation. "Jenna, I know you are used to being a one-woman operation, more or less, but you don't have to limit yourself that way."

Jenna folded her arms in front of her and regarded Jake sternly. "I want to keep things small so I can insure the quality."

Jake put his papers back in his briefcase. "Obviously, you've thought about this."

"A lot. I always knew I would expand and do it in a carefully controlled way. Do we have a deal?"

Jake nodded, his eyes never leaving her face. "I'll start looking for a factory site this morning."

"I already have one." Jenna smiled. "The old carpet warehouse about twenty minutes outside of town. It's standing empty and it's for sale." It would be the perfect place for them to set up shop.

Jake paused. He leaned against the sales counter and clamped his arms over the rock-solidness of his chest. "I'll look into it, see what the asking price is."

"Maybe we could go see it this afternoon, after I spend some time with Alex."

Jake looked through his calendar. "Four o'clock?"

Jenna nodded and handed him his hat. "I'll see you then."

"LOOK, DADDY, we're having a tea party!" Alex said, several hours later.

Giddily she spun around showing off her wool beret, long chifon scarf and white elbow-length gloves. "And I even got high heels and pearls!" All of which she had added to her usual T-shirt and jeans. Beginning to see where Jenna was going with all this, Jake grinned and joined the group where they were gathered around the table in the second-floor playroom at the ranch, sipping from child-sized cups, and eating tiny little tea sandwiches and petits fours. "And what a nice tea party it is," Jake answered, admiring the cozy camaraderie that had cropped up between the women in his life. Jenna in particular looked very happy and content. He wondered what it would be like to have the full wattage of Jenna's smile aimed at him once again.

"And tomorrow we're going to have another one and really play dress-up, too," Alex enthused.

Jenna met Jake's eye and grinned as she adjusted the silk stole around her shoulders and the genuine bridal-shop tiara perched on her head. "I didn't have time to dig through the treasure trove in my storeroom," she explained, "but tomorrow I'll bring some sample garments and the clothes my sisters and I used to wear as kids."

Aware the J&R ranch house hadn't been filled with this much love and laughter since he, Clara and Alex had moved in, Jake took off his hat, and pulled up a chair. "You still have them?"

Jenna nodded. "Mom never could bring herself to get rid of them. She thought her grandkids might use them someday, and as it turned out, Meg's son Jeremy has, as well as his friends."

Jake was glad Jenna and her sisters had done what they could to preserve the Lockhart family heirlooms, with their sentimental value. No doubt they'd mean a lot to them all someday. "How old is Jeremy?" Jake asked, as a bonnet-and-shawl-clad Clara handed him a plate.

Jenna's lips curved fondly. "Same age as Alex, almost six."

Alex tugged on Jenna's sleeve. "Can Jeremy come to our tea party, too?"

"If his mom says okay," Jenna allowed kindly, before shooting a look at Jake. "But you're going to have to ask your dad."

Alex looked at Jake for permission.

"Sure, honey." Jake smiled, happy Jenna had become buddies with Alex and Clara so quickly. "Go ahead and invite him."

Alex studied Jake as Clara handed him the plate of peanut-butter-and-jelly and cucumber-and-cream-cheese sandwiches. "Daddy needs a funny hat, too."

Jenna gave him a flowered-brim garden hat. Alex giggled riotously. "Not that one, silly. Let him have...this one." She ran to her toy chest and returned with a child-sized magician's hat.

Jake put the small black top hat on his head. "Much better."

Alex beamed. "Would you like some apple juice?" Being careful to be very prim and proper, instead of rowdy and out-of-control, Alex reached for the tea set.

"Don't mind if I do, thank you," Jake told Alex. While Alex poured Jake some apple juice, Jake traded glances with Jenna, silently telegraphing his appreciation.

"The petits fours are delicious," Clara said.

"They're from Isabel Buchanon's bakery, over on Main Street," Jenna explained. "If you haven't been there yet, you ought to give it a try. She's got the best baked goods in town, no question.'

Clara smiled. "We'll have to run by there."

The pager clipped to Clara's belt began to beep. Clara looked down at the number flashing across the screen. "That's my daughter, Lisa." Jake reached into the pocket of his blazer and handed over his cell phone. Clara made the call, said hello, and listened. "Honey, you can't be in labor yet. You're not due for another two weeks—oh, dear. Yes, that's a definite sign. Have you called your obstetrician? Is Randall on the way? Of course I'll meet you at the hospital, honey. I wouldn't dream of missing this."

"Problem?" Jake said.

Briskly, Clara untied her bonnet and removed the shawl from her shoulders. She looked calm and in control. "Lisa's water broke and she's started having contractions."

"Do you want me to drive you to the hospital?" Jake said.

Clara shook her head. "This being a first baby and all, there's no telling how long it will take."

Jake stood and helped Clara with her chair. He wrapped his arm around the older woman's shoulders and gave her a hug. "Give Lisa and Randall our love. Let me know if there's anything they need."

Clara hugged Jake back. "I will. Bye, precious." Clara knelt down to give Alexandra a hug and a kiss.

"Can I see your new grandbaby after it's borned?" Alex asked.

Clara smiled. "You sure can." She said goodbye to Jenna then was off.

Silence fell over the playroom. Suddenly, no one was much in the mood for a tea party. But that was okay with Jake. He looked over at Alex. "I've got a surprise for you."

Alex perked up immediately. "You do?"

"It's on the back porch." Jake smiled at his daughter, but did nothing to give away the nature of the surprise. "Want to see?"

Alex vaulted out of her chair and wobbled over to him on her high heels. "Can I wear my dress-up clothes?"

Jake frowned. Now that Alex was actually wearing something feminine, even if only for dress-up purposes, he hated to have her take it off. But given what he had on the porch, there was no helping it. "I think you better take them off for this," he said.

"Okay." Alex sighed, clearly disappointed, but not about to give up her surprise for the sake of arguing. She ripped off hat, gloves, scarf and high heels, but hesitated at the long double strand of pearls—which looked a little ludicrous with her jeans, T-shirt, and buckskin vest. She looked over at Jenna hopefully. "Can I keep these?"

"Sure," Jenna said, smiling, as she too took off her tiara and stole and excess jewelry.

"Thank you," Alex promised sincerely, giving Jenna an admiring look. "I'll take good care of them. I won't lose them or anything."

Jenna reached over to squeeze Alex's shoulders. "I know you won't, sweetheart."

Jake waited for Alex to put on her boots. "Ready?"

Alex nodded. She took his hand, glanced over at Jenna. "You come, too, Jenna."

Jake nodded, seconding the invitation with a frank, sexy look.

Obviously curious, Jenna followed as Jake took his daughter's hand in one of his, Jenna's in the other, and led the way downstairs, past the dining room, through the kitchen and onto the large and homey screened-in back porch.

To Jake's amusement, at first Jenna—like Alex—saw nothing amiss. Both scanned the rough-hewn furniture with red plaid cushions, the abundance of green, leafy plants and blooming geraniums, the Navajo rugs strewn across the cool cement floor and the ceiling fan whirring overhead. Then they heard it. The quick, frantic scampering of little feet. A yelp. A howl. A hiss. Alex and Jenna barely had time to draw surprised breaths before they caught sight of a fast-moving bundle of butterscotch fur and a pair of lively dark brown eyes. And an even faster bundle of gray fur. Both dashing past in a blur.

"Daddy, you did it!" Alex exclaimed, clapping her hands together with all the delight Jake had expected.

Jenna turned to Jake. "Did you ever!" she agreed dryly.

Chapter Three

"You look…surprised," Jake said, a little irked Jenna didn't look more impressed by what he had done. To his relief, his daughter, however, had no such reservations. Alexandra was already down on the floor, tumbling around with the cutest golden retriever puppy Jake had ever seen while her fluffy gray-and-white-striped kitten watched from a distance.

Jenna paused and bit her lip. "I am."

Jake edged closer, until their arms were almost touching. "Because…?"

Jenna shifted slightly, her shoulder brushing the curve of his biceps. "You got her a kitten *and* a puppy."

Jake shrugged, unable to see what the big deal was, and for whatever reason Jenna did seem to think this was a big deal. "I didn't want her out hunting down snakes and I thought this would keep her busy."

Jenna knit her brows together. "It'll do that, all right," she drawled, the hint of bemusement in her clear blue eyes.

Jake refused to feel inferior just because he had never been allowed to have any pets as a kid. Whereas Jenna, who'd grown up on a ranch, had nurtured an abundance of them.

"Just out of curiosity, Jake…" Jenna clasped a soft, slender hand around his upper arm and tugged him out of earshot. She backed him up against the exterior limestone wall that separated the porch from the interior of the house. "Have you ever house-trained a puppy?"

"No," Jake said uneasily, unable to help thinking how pretty Jenna looked in her two piece turquoise cotton dress, with its loose, cropped blouse and long flowing skirt. "But how hard can it be?"

In response, Jenna just shook her head. And sighed—loudly. Her high, perfect breasts rising and falling against the demure button front of her blouse. "Did you at least get their shots?"

Jake's eyes traced the glimpse of creamy skin visible in the open collar of her blouse. He liked the way the armholes were cut on it, dipping in slightly to reveal Jenna's slender shoulders and pretty upper arms. "Uh, actually we have an appointment to do that at five, at the Laramie Animal Clinic. I thought we could run by the warehouse, take a quick look, then go straight to the vet's office and the pet-supply store from there."

"We," Jenna repeated, lifting a skeptical brow and planting both hands on her hips.

Jake gestured off-handedly. "Well, I would have asked Clara to help with the pets." And hoped like heck Jenna, a real animal lover if there ever was one, would volunteer to help out some, too. "But since Clara had to go off to Laramie Community Hospital to see her new grandbaby born…" Jake shrugged, to show there was no way he could have foreseen Lisa going into labor a good two weeks early.

Jenna blinked in surprise. "Clara's married daughter lives here in Laramie, too?"

Jake realized they hadn't covered that earlier. He nodded. "It's one of the reasons we moved here. So Clara could be close to her daughter and son-in-law. She's been with us since Alex was an infant and has rearranged her life on more than one occasion on our account. I thought it was time we did the same for her."

Jenna studied him with a mixture of blatant approval and suspicion. "What were the other reasons?" she asked warily.

That was easy, Jake thought, relaxing all the more. He

smiled down at Jenna, said softly, "My happiest memories of growing up were all here. I thought it'd be a good place to bring up Alex, too."

Before Jenna could respond, Alex ran up to him. "Daddy, my new kitty is hiding behind the sofa and she won't come out."

"She's probably just shy," Jake said as the puppy began to bark. He glanced at his watch. "I think we better get these animals rounded up in their carriers."

"Why?" Alex asked, clapping her hands over her ears to shut out the high-pitched noise. Smiling, Jenna knelt and scooped up the puppy, cradling him close to her chest. To everyone's relief, the frantic barking stopped immediately.

Briefly, Jake explained what they had to do next, which was take both kitten and puppy to the vet for their vaccinations and exams, and then go by the grocery store to pick up pet food and other essentials.

"In that case, maybe we should reschedule looking at the warehouse and do that tomorrow morning," Jenna said as she continued to pet Alex's new puppy with gentle, loving strokes. She buried her face in the puppy's fur, looking as ecstatic as Alex to have access to such a cute and cuddly animal. Jenna pressed a kiss to the puppy's head and was promptly rewarded with a slurpy lick on the chin. "Given everything else we have to do this afternoon and evening," she continued.

Jake studied Jenna, realizing all over again how much he had missed having her in his life. "You wouldn't mind?" He didn't want Jenna to think she was playing second-fiddle to anything that was going on here, because she wasn't.

"Not at all." Jenna looked down at Alex, who was now cradling her kitten in much the same way Jenna was holding the puppy. "Meanwhile, these two critters need some names, Alex. Any ideas?"

Alex grinned. "I want to call my puppy Buster."

"Good choice," Jake beamed his approval. As did Jenna.

Alex kissed her kitten and cuddled her close. "And I want to call her Miss Kitty."

"I HAD NO IDEA one puppy and one kitten could be so exhausting," Jake told Jenna three hours later as they brought the carriers into the house and set them down on the floor. Alex followed, carrying a plastic sack filled to the brim with kitten and puppy toys.

While Alex stayed with her new pets, Jenna and Jake headed back to his Jeep for the rest of the stuff they had purchased. Jenna slanted him a glance, noting that he did look exhausted and out of his element. "You've only owned them for a couple of hours," Jenna said cheerfully as she lifted out the sack of kitty litter and the litter box. It was sort of fun to see the oh-so-confident Jake unsure of himself. "Just wait until tonight."

Jake got a panicked look in his eyes as he hefted the bags of puppy chow and kitten food into his arms. "What happens tonight?"

Alex came running to get them as they headed back inside. "Daddy," she said, "we had a disaster."

Unfortunately, Jenna and Jake soon discovered, Alex wasn't kidding.

"You can't leave Alex and me alone with this puppy," Jake said, after he and Jenna had finished cleaning up the puddle on the kitchen floor.

Hoping to avert a similar disaster, Jenna set up the litter box for the kitten in the laundry room. While Jake watched, she made sure there was nothing either animal could get into, and that all electric cords and so on were out of reach of even the most curious agile kitten or puppy. "Because?" Jenna asked as she washed her hands in the laundry-room sink.

Jake dropped the dirty paper towels into the trash, put away the floor cleaner, then went to wash his hands. "We'll never survive."

That, Jenna thought, with equal parts amusement and pity, was no doubt true.

Jake had taken on much more than he knew.

But there was no going back now. He had given Alex the two pets simultaneously. They would just have to muddle through. Jenna smiled at Jake, and because he seemed badly in need of some encouragement, touched his cheek. "Your heart was in the right place."

Jake chuckled wearily. "Even if my head wasn't."

Before Jenna could reply, Alexandra barreled in. She went straight to Jake and plucked on his sleeve. "Daddy, I'm hungry."

Which in turn, Jenna noted, caused Jake to look all the more desperate.

Jenna relented, figuring it would be cruel to make him ask. "Okay, I'll stay through dinner."

Alex cheered and Jake's sexy grin widened. "How about the whole evening?" he asked as Alex, satisfied food would soon be on the way, raced back out again to check on Buster and Miss Kitty.

"Well?" Jake said, when Jenna didn't answer right away.

Jenna shook her head and started for the door. "Typical Jake," she drawled. "Always wanting it all—now."

Jake caught her arm before she could exit the room and turned her to face him. "You're telling me you're not the same?"

That was just it, Jenna realized uncomfortably, as she looked up into his handsome, suntanned face, taking in the rugged line of his jaw, the stubborn set of his chin, his blade-straight nose and those sensually chiseled lips that really knew how to kiss. She *was* the same as him in that regard. But there was no sense in admitting it to him when she knew he would just use her weaknesses to his own advantage.

Jenna extricated herself graciously from his grip. "I'll show Alex how to feed Buster and Miss Kitty."

Jake's eyes twinkled knowingly. Looking delighted to have

her there with them, for whatever reason, he murmured happily, "And I'll see what I can do about rustling us up some grub ASAP."

While Jenna and Alex tended to the pets, Jake made the thirty-minute round-trip drive back into town. Jenna had her excuses all ready—she was going to use the opportunity to bow out—but when he returned with a mouthwatering bucket of crispy fried chicken, containers of mashed potatoes, gravy, creamy coleslaw and half a dozen fluffy, golden-brown biscuits, she found herself weakening. She was hungry, after all. He had enough food to feed an army. It would be a shame to see it go to waste. And even more cruel to disappoint Alexandra, who by now was as desperate as Jake to have her stay and eat with them. So she did.

And the three of them had a very good time, talking and laughing about Buster and Miss Kitty's antics as they ate. Not surprisingly, by the time they had finished the delicious meal, Alex was visibly drooping. It was all Jake could do to get her upstairs, into her pajamas and into bed.

"She was asleep almost before her head hit the pillow," Jake reported minutes later as he joined Jenna in the kitchen.

Jake frowned, seeing she had just about finished cleaning up after dinner. "I was going to do that."

Jenna refused to let him win her confidence this easily. He might think he was a changed man. But she still knew the way he had deserted her once because of family and social pressure and she knew he could probably do it again. All too readily, if and when his own interests were at stake or he felt the situation called for it.

Jenna gave him a deadpan look meant to provoke. "You know how?" Jenna scoffed in a disbelieving tone as she put a twist tie around the garbage sack and set it by the back door.

The hot-tempered denial she expected never came. Jake merely picked up a dishrag and began mopping the tabletop. While his palm moved across the table with long powerful strokes, he said. "I've learned a lot since we last saw each other."

Jenna's eyebrows rose in cool disbelief as he went back to the sink and submerged the cloth into the soapy water. She watched him wring it out again and tackle the counters. "So it seems," she said, refusing to be impressed. After all, any moron could competently clean a tabletop. Or run into town for her all-time favorite take-out meal. All it meant was that he was trying to get into her good graces so she would make a designer-quality wardrobe for Alex, quick as could be, and help get Melinda off his back.

The phone rang. Clearly resenting the interruption as much as she welcomed it—she didn't want to be alone with Jake, and certainly not like this, in such an intimate setting!—Jake strode across the kitchen and plucked the receiver off the wall after the first ring. He barked a hello, then frowned intently, his mood softening visibly as he listened to whoever was on the other end of the line. "Stay as long as you need to," he said. "No. Don't worry about a thing here. Jenna and I've got everything under control. Just give Lisa and Randall my best."

Jenna quirked her brow as he hung up. "How is Clara's daughter doing?" she asked curiously.

Jake frowned. "She's still in labor. It looks like it's going to be a long night, for all of them."

And for Jake, too, Jenna thought, given the new pets in the household.

Jake looked around. "Where are Buster and Miss Kitty?"

"Sleeping in their crates on the back porch. They're as exhausted as Alex."

"Speaking of Alex…" Jake took Jenna's hand and led her into the living room, further delaying her departure. "It looked like you had a really good time together today."

Realizing she did want to sit a moment, after the way they had been running around all afternoon, Jenna let Jake settle her on the sofa and drop down beside her. Jenna kicked off her sandals and curled her legs up beneath her. "We did."

Jake watched as Jenna smoothed her long cotton skirt over her legs and feet. "You do realize, however," he pointed out, "that a whole day has gone by and you still haven't gotten her into a dress."

Jenna grinned as she thought about their tea party, and how much fun she'd had. "But I did get her into hat, scarf, pearls, gloves and heels," she bragged. Given Alex's attitude toward all things feminine, that had been no small accomplishment.

Unfortunately, it did little to appease Jake, who frowned worriedly and raked a hand through his hair. "Somehow I don't think that's going to satisfy Melinda. And we can't just go out and buy a dress at the store. Melinda'll throw a fit if she sees *her* daughter in off-the-rack anything."

Melinda sounded like a real piece of work. If she was really as snotty as Jake described her, he had reason to want to steer clear of her. And shield Alex from any snobbish maternal explosions, too. Jenna just hoped she did not have to meet or deal with Jake's ex. "Never fear, cowboy. I also got this." Tranquilly, Jenna reached into the pocket of her skirt and handed him a folded piece of paper.

Jake stared at the letters and numbers scribbled on the page. "What is it?" he demanded, completely clueless.

Jenna grinned. Shaking her head, she explained, "Alex's measurements. I'll start her denim jumper when I get home tonight."

Jake took Jenna's hand and absently rubbed his fingers over the back of it. "She agreed to wear it?"

"Not yet." Jenna sighed, refusing to think about how relaxing it was to sit here with Jake like this, or how good, how right, how gentle and loving his casual touch felt. "But she will."

Jake's stroking hand stilled abruptly and he looked over at her. "How do you know?" he demanded.

Jenna's lips curved ruefully. "Because I know little girls, Jake. I was one once, too, you know."

JAKE REMEMBERED. Oh, how he remembered. The first time he had laid eyes on Jenna, she'd been coming down Bowie Lane with her three sisters. He'd been all of fourteen. Sent to the ranch for the entire summer—to get away from some boys Patricia and Danforth had considered a bad influence and learn to manage a ranch—while his parents were off in Europe. Lonely as could be without anyone his age to hang out with, he'd talked Esther and Buck, the couple caring for him, into letting him go into town and hang out at the Armadillo Miniature Golf Course while they hit the hardware store and grocery-shopped. Seeing the four laughing, talking Lockhart girls headed for the same activity had made his impromptu plan seem all the better.

"What are you thinking?" Jenna asked.

"About the first time I saw you," Jake told Jenna honestly. Though nearly fifteen years had passed, he could still recall it as clearly as if it had happened yesterday. Jenna had been dressed in a pair of blue-jean shorts and a snowy-white T-shirt, a bandana tied jauntily around her neck. Although all the Lockhart sisters were pretty as could be, and Meg closer in age to him, it was Jenna, with her thick mane of red-gold hair and sparkling clear blue eyes who'd caught his attention. Jenna alone, who had seemed to sense how lonely and out-of-place he felt, how much he needed and wanted to feel as at home in Laramie as they did. It had taken Jenna all of two minutes to invite him to join them in their putt-putt game— and in many more fun-filled group activities at the Lockhart ranch before the summer was out.

Until that point, he had never seen a family as happy and content and lively as the Lockharts. He had envied Jenna her family's closeness, their infectious sense of fun and spontaneity, and wished he could have shared the same with his own folks. Which was maybe why he was back here now. To see if he couldn't get for Alex what the Lockharts and the Mc-Cabes, and all the other close-knit families in Laramie seemed to take for granted. The overwhelming sense of love and belonging. The knowledge that things were the way they were supposed to be. The people here had dreams and goals. The difference was the dreams didn't consume them, or force families into second place. Here, kids counted as much as—maybe more than—any business deals or acquisitions. It hadn't been that way in the high-class neighborhood of Dallas where he had grown up.

Jenna's eyes softened in recollection as Jake studied her.

"You remember that afternoon, too," Jake guessed finally, liking the curve of her lips.

"Of course." Jenna looked suddenly self-conscious. "It wasn't every day a great-looking teenage boy came to Laramie in a long black limousine."

Jake winced, recalling the stares his folks' limo had always gotten. It wasn't the kind of attention Jake had welcomed, then or now. Although he knew why his parents had insisted upon it. It had been to set him apart, keep the locals at arm's length.

"My parents never did know when to scale it back," Jake remarked dryly, remembering how much fun it had been to socialize here, hanging out at the Armadillo and the Dairy Queen, and going riding at the McCabe Ranch. Even the twice-weekly summer dances at the Laramie Community Center had been a lot of fun.

"Which is why you have Clara driving Alex around in a truck instead of a limo," Jenna guessed.

"I want her to have as normal a life as possible," Jake said. One of these days his daughter would realize she stood to inherit a good deal of wealth. The kind that could rob you of your ambition and humanity, if you weren't careful. Jake didn't want Alex thinking she was better than anyone else because of it, because it simply wasn't true. If anything, wealth the size of theirs was a handicap. Jake turned to Jenna and confided seriously, "I want Alex to have a happy childhood, full of family and friends and pets and normal everyday things. I don't want her growing up in a high-rise, or living behind the walls of a gated community, either. That's why I built the ranch and brought her back to Laramie. So she can have the kind of happy-go-lucky childhood every kid deserves.'' The kind he hadn't had, much as his parents had loved him—and still did.

Jenna nodded her approval. "That's good," she replied, her eyes serious. "It's important Alex be allowed to enjoy her childhood as much as possible and not be forced to grow up too fast."

"Like you did?" Jake asked compassionately. The death of Jenna's parents had nearly destroyed all four sisters. Had they not had each other, he wasn't sure how they would have gotten through it.

Pain flickered in Jenna's blue eyes, making him want to hold her in his arms and never let her go. Only the knowledge of how such a move would likely be received kept him from doing it. Jenna didn't want his pity, or anyone else's. Never had, never would.

"I don't deny my parents' death changed everything for me—for all of us—but we survived," Jenna said stiffly, turning away. "Just like you will survive this battle with Alex over wearing a dress."

"Is that what you think it is—a contest of wills?" Jake asked as he watched Jenna uncurl from the sofa and bend to slip her sandals back on. Her bare feet were pretty and feminine, her toenails polished a soft and sexy pale pink.

"Isn't it obvious?" Jenna stood and, slipping her hands into the pockets of her long, swirling turquoise skirt, began to pace.

Feeling restless, Jake stood too and stretched. "It would be except she's never been a particularly difficult child. Until now. Over this." Jake sauntered to Jenna's side, achingly aware how pretty she looked in the fading evening light. He studied Jenna's upturned face. "Do you have any thoughts on why she might have taken this stand—having been a little girl once yourself?"

Jenna shrugged her slender shoulders, the action lifting her breasts against the soft cotton of her blouse. "Maybe she realizes how vitally important it is for you to suddenly get her into a dress, and she's worried about it," Jenna supposed quietly. "Maybe you should just level with her, tell her how much this will mean to Melinda."

"No," Jake said stonily, not about to have Alex molding her personality in an endless effort to please people. "I told you before I don't want her under that kind of pressure."

Jenna looked at him as if he just didn't get it. "So instead you're just behaving mysteriously."

Jake grinned. He liked sparring with Jenna. Maybe because she was the one woman who refused to let him get away with anything. "That's a man's perogative. All women know we men don't make any sense, and vice versa, right?"

Jenna rolled her eyes at his teasing tone.

"Besides," Jake continued earnestly, moving close enough to inhale Jenna's perfume, "maybe Alex will get so into this tea-party stuff she'll end up just wanting to wear a dress. And not just denim, but something really frilly." At least that's what he was hoping.

Jenna grinned. "That's what I'm bargaining on, cowboy. Meantime," she shaped her thumb and index finger in a sassy L and angled both at his chest, "you've got to figure out what you're going to do with the pets for the night." As if on cue, in the distance, Buster began to whimper, signaling his need to go out back.

Jake and Jenna rushed to the back porch, lest Buster increase his carrying-on and wake Alex. Jake slanted a glance at Jenna as he followed her. "I can't just leave them on the back porch in their crates?"

Jenna shook her head as she knelt down to let Buster out of his crate and led him to the back door, into the yard. As soon as he hit the grass, he began running and sniffing. But instead of getting right down to business, he snatched a twig off the ground and ran off with it clenched between his teeth. Grinning, Jenna watched as Buster trotted back and forth, tossing his little blond head and showing off his prize. "Miss Kitty can spend the night in the laundry room, with her water dish and litter pan. All you have to do is leave a night-light on for her and shut the door so she can't get out and roam the house. She'll be fine until breakfast. Depending on how you want to house-train Buster, it gets a little more complicated. He is going to need at least two, maybe three more 'backyard' breaks before morning. That is, if you want to train him to relieve himself only outside. If you want to try and paper-train him inside, you could confine him to a bathroom with newspaper on the floor. And then clean up in the morning."

Jake made a face as he considered that. "I'd rather not have to mess with newspapers at all."

Jenna accepted his decision enthusiastically. "Crate-training it is, then. All you have to do is confine Buster in his crate most of the time. Then every three or four hours, you take him out to the backyard, let him do his stuff, play with him for thirty minutes indoors, or as long as you want outdoors, then put him back in his crate. Buster will quickly get the idea that his crate is a safe good place to be—which will help you and Alex immensely when you travel with him—and that the outdoors is where he should be doing his business."

That sounded simple enough, Jake thought, as dusk descended around them like a soft warm blanket. "He won't soil his crate?"

Crossing her legs at the ankles, Jenna leaned against a nearby tree. "Not if he can help it. Dogs are den animals who keep their quarters clean by nature."

Jake tucked an errant strand of red-gold hair behind Jenna's ear, wishing that the idea of staying so close to Jenna, of perhaps even kissing her again, carrying her to his bed and making wild passionate love to her was a little less appealing. He was supposed to be getting her to trust him again. She would never trust him if all he ever did was put the moves on her. "How will I know when Buster needs to go out tonight?" Jake asked.

Jenna leaned back against the trunk of the shade tree, getting all the more comfortable. She didn't seem to mind it was beginning to get dark around them.

"He'll whine, the way he just did."

Jake gave her a level look, trying not to notice how thick and velvety her lashes were, or how well they framed her clear blue eyes. "What if he whines and I take him out to the backyard and he doesn't go?"

Jenna shrugged and cast a supervisory glance at Buster, who was now busy moving in circles and sniffing the grass. Jenna moved restlessly away from the base of the tree, straightening her spine, and inundating Jake with the clean floral scent of her hair and skin. "Then put him back in his crate for a while—half an hour, an hour—take him back out and give him another chance to go."

Jake swallowed and ignored the feelings of desire generated by her closeness. "It sounds complicated," he said. Maybe too complicated.

Jenna gave him a droll look and stepped away from the tree altogether. "I'm sure you can handle it."

Jake followed her out onto the unshaded part of the lawn. "You're really going to just leave me here with Alexandra, Buster and Miss Kitty?" Jake did his best to get her to take pity on him once again. To stay and help out. And spend time with and get to know him all over again.

To his disappointment, Jenna refused to apologize for jumping ship. "It was your idea to purchase the pets," she reminded him with a knowing smile.

"True," Jake acknowledged. "But then," he drawled, deciding maybe he was being too conservative here, maybe just one kiss wouldn't hurt. Giving in to the desire that had been plaguing him all day, he drew Jenna into his arms, ignoring her soft gasp of dismay, and lowered his lips to hers. "So was this," he continued, kissing her soundly, the softness of her body giving new heat to his. "And this." Jake lifted his lips, then took her mouth all over again, kissing her as if they'd never been apart. He kissed her because he had missed her.

Because they'd let so many things drive them apart. He kissed her to remind her what they had shared, and what they could share again, given half a chance. "And this." Delighting in her helpless response, Jake swept his hands down her spine, fitting her to him, softness to hardness, woman to man. Satisfaction rushed through him, along with the raw aching need, as he tormented her with lazy sweeps of his tongue, over and over again, until she moaned.

Jenna knew she should have left before Jake kissed her again. She'd meant to, really she had. But it had felt so good just to be with him, spending time and talking with him, she'd stayed. And now here she was, in his arms, her hands splayed across his chest, her lips fused to his. Here she was wanting and needing him the way she had never wanted anyone else. Here she was, wearing her heart on her sleeve, practically begging to be hurt.

Achingly aware of the warmth and solidity of the muscles beneath her fingertips, as well as the fact she had promised herself she was not going to let this happen to her—again!— Jenna forced herself to ignore the yearning that welled within her. She broke off the kiss and pushed him away.

Trembling from head to foot, doing her best to quell her breathlessness, she looked into his eyes and reminded him, "This is not on our agenda, Jake. We're supposed to be helping each other in business only."

Jake's grin widened all the more as he swept his thumb across the curve of her lower lip. "Sure about that?" he teased, his silver-gray eyes glimmering playfully as he slowly, surely, inevitably lowered his mouth toward hers. His eyes closing lazily, he whispered, "'Cause I could have sworn I felt you kissing me back." Wrapping his arms around her, he bent her backwards from the waist, leaning the weight of her on one braced leg. His tongue teased her lips apart, and then plunged into her mouth, stroking and arousing in a highly erotic way he'd never employed in their youth. He grinned as she made a muffled protest and then they were lost in the swirling, tempestuous meeting of their hearts and minds. When at last he released her, he said, "Yep, I'm sure I felt you kissing me back."

Damn it all, Jenna thought, as he slowly, deliberately set her back on her feet. Her arms still wreathed his neck and her body curved helplessly into the strong, warm shelter of his. Jake always had been impossible to resist. Especially when he kissed her like this. Like he meant it. "I'm serious, Jake," she whispered, giving in to impulse and standing up on tiptoe to press her lips to his for what she promised herself was the very last time. "You really have to stop this." *So I'll stop it, too.*

"I know you are," Jake said solemnly, beginning to kiss her again, even more thoroughly and completely this time. And that was when they heard it—the soft purr of a car motor in the drive. Even before they broke apart, they were illuminated in the twin beams of headlights. The whole scene was reminiscent of another time, another night, another clandestine kiss. Except then it had been his parents catching them in a torrid embrace on the very night they had planned to run off and get married.

Jenna had only to look up to realize Jake remembered that incident, too. Releasing her reluctantly, Jake swore heatedly beneath his breath. "What now?" he demanded unhappily.

As the uninvited guest stepped out of the vehicle, they saw and knew that the evening not only could, but would, get worse.

"WHAT ARE YOU DOING here?" Jake asked as Melinda emerged from of the sleek black limousine and snapped her fingers at the uniformed driver, who immediately hopped to and began emptying the trunk of a dizzying array of designer bags.

Jenna gaped at Melinda's baggage. She didn't travel with that much luggage when she did a trunk show of her designs!

Illuminated by the interior lights of the car, Melinda gave

Jake a condescending look. "I wired you I was coming," she stated in a low, surprisingly cordial tone.

Jenna could see Jake straining to keep his temper. "But not until the day after tomorrow."

Melinda took the credit-card slip the driver presented, added a tip, signed her name and handed it back. "I changed my travel arrangements and took the Concorde instead. I thought it might behoove me to get here sooner instead of later." Melinda paused to look Jenna over from head to toe. "I see I was right." She paused, looking more annoyed by than jealous of Jenna's presence. "Aren't you going to introduce me to your...guest?"

Jake tucked his arm beneath Jenna's elbow and guided her forward. "Jenna Lockhart, Melinda Carrington, my ex-wife. Melinda, Jenna."

Melinda shook hands with Jenna, then turned back to Jake. She regarded him steadily, once again looking more annoyed than jealous. "I thought that was over a long time ago."

So did we, Jenna thought. Although given the way things were going, she was beginning to wish her romance with Jake had stayed over. She had no desire for these kinds of unpleasant complications in her life.

Jake signalled for the limo driver to stay for a moment. "I've got a room arranged for you at a country inn near here."

Melinda shook her immaculately coiffed blond bob. "Please. You can't expect me to stay anywhere that dull. Although I must say," Melinda went on as she looked askance at Jake's brand-new two-story limestone ranch house, "this place is a lot more pedestrian than I expected." Melinda turned to Jake in amazement. "What's gotten into you? Selling the condominium in Dallas, moving out here to the boonies. I mean, I understand you wanting a summer place. Everyone in our circle has two, three, four homes, at a minimum. But the least you could have done, for Alex's sake, is build a suitable residence. Like your parents'—"

"Mansion," Jake supplied.

Melinda smoothed a hand down her slim marine-blue skirt. "Yes. Something along those lines."

Aware he was still holding on to her, almost like a shield, Jenna edged away from Jake. "Maybe I'd better go," she said.

Melinda tapped the toe of her expensive Italian pump. "Perhaps you should," she agreed, giving Jenna a sweet, cordial smile that did not reach her eyes.

"No," Jake interrupted, tightening his hold on Jenna's arm even more. He gave her a significant look she couldn't begin to decipher, then said firmly, "We have plans."

What was he talking about? Jenna wondered, confused. What plans could he have that seemed—unless she was mistaken—to include her, too?

Jake turned back to Melinda officiously. "You're welcome here, of course, as long as you like."

Melinda shook her head as if she were about at the limit of her patience. Clearly, she expected a lot more than Jake was currently willing or ready to give. "At last you've come to your senses."

"Just understand," Jake continued, regarding Melinda with a level look, "you're not going to be our only house guest. Jenna is staying here, too."

Chapter Four

Jenna had to hand it to him. The man had moxie.

On the other hand, so did she.

And she didn't like anyone telling her she didn't belong somewhere. She hadn't, since Jake's parents had told her she wasn't good enough for their son.

"You're joking, right?" Melinda Carrington said.

"Nope," Jake retorted in an edgy tone that just dared Melinda to disagree. "Jenna is a friend."

Melinda's thick-lashed eyelids narrowed disapprovingly. "One you almost eloped with years ago!"

Jake stepped closer, squaring off with the woman he had once called his wife. Maybe it was just ego combined with a broken heart, but Jenna had never been able to imagine him with anyone else. And certainly not this woman in her short peplum jacket and matching skirt and three-inch heels. A dazzling mix of diamonds and sapphires glinted at her throat, wrist and ears. Despite the fact Melinda Carrington had just been on at least two different jets, and a long limousine ride from Dallas Fort Worth, not to mention crossed half a dozen time zones, there wasn't a single strand of her platinum-blond hair out of place. Her makeup was equally perfect. And yet, there was a brittleness and a calculating bitterness beneath Melinda's beauty that was off-putting, to say the least. Whatever she was here for, Jenna was pretty certain, had nothing to do with Alexandra. And a lot to do with Jake.

Jake glared at Melinda. "Calling off my elopement with Jenna was a mistake. I knew it then. I certainly know it now."

Jenna warmed to the rock-solid certainty in Jake's voice. Even as she hated being caught between Jake and his ex.

Melinda merely lifted one perfectly shaped blond brow. "Say what you will," she retorted softly, "you are not going to chase me away, Jake."

Jake blew out a long, weary breath. "I didn't think I would." He looked Melinda up and down, then spread his hands wide on either side of him. "However, if you'd like to stay somewhere else, under the circumstances," he said graciously, while Buster ran in dizzy circles around his feet, "I certainly understand."

"Understand this." Melinda backed away from the puppy, her high heels catching in the thick carpet of grass and causing her to stumble slightly before she regained her balance and righted herself. She slapped her hands on her slender hips. "You and I have to talk about the way you've been bringing up Alexandra. So don't think you are getting off the hook this easily because you are just not! Now get me a drink and show me to my room." Melinda pressed her palm to her forehead. "I'm exhausted."

THE BACKYARD was flooded with yellow lamplight. Buster was still running around in circles trying to find the perfect place to relieve himself. Jenna was sitting on one of the swings in Alex's swing set, waiting for him to do so, when Jake returned a few minutes later. "Was Alexandra glad to see her mother?" she asked, somehow managing not to look him square in the eye. She knew it was unkind—even unrealistic— of her, and she hated the jealous way she felt, but she didn't want to see Jake with anyone else. Not Melinda. Not anyone.

Jake sighed and, positioning himself just to the left of Jenna, clamped both his hands on the support beam that ran across the top of the swing set. "She didn't see her."

Jenna put out a foot to stop her swaying. Both hands curled around the metal chain that supported the swing, she looked up at Jake. "You mean you didn't wake her?"

"No." Sorrow flashed in Jake's eyes. He briefly rested his head on his outstretched arm. "I mean Melinda didn't see her. She went straight to bed."

Jenna's eyes widened in incredulity. She pushed off with her foot and began swinging lightly back and forth again. "She didn't even peek in?"

Jake grimaced and then looked deep into Jenna's eyes. "Amazing, isn't it? The woman hasn't seen her own daughter in almost two years, she's extremely critical of the way I've been rearing Alex, and yet she didn't even ask for a glimpse of Alex while she slept. I offered, but she said no, she would wait until tomorrow."

Jenna saw the worry in Jake's face. Her heart went out to him, even as she tried to figure out a way to comfort him. "Given Melinda's behavior...you really can't think she wants custody of Alex," she said reasonably.

Jake straightened and ran his palm down the slick surface of the slide. "Not because she loves her, although I imagine in Melinda's own selfish way that she does love Alex as much as she is capable of loving anyone, but because there's something in it for her."

Jenna studied Jake's face. Clearly, he had given this a lot of thought. "Money?" Jenna guessed.

Jake scowled. Looking even more unhappy, he turned his back to the slide. "I've given her plenty. I offered her more. No, it's something else."

"What?" Jenna moved her hands higher up the chain.

Jake lifted a hand, let it fall. "That, I don't know. Aside from the fact she's self-involved and very image-conscious, Melinda can be a hard woman to figure out." His eyes narrowed as Buster, exhausted from all the excitement and his romp in the yard, plopped down on his tummy in the grass and took a breather. Jake smiled at the puppy fondly and, turning his glance back to Jenna, continued thoughtfully, "My gut tells me Melinda plans to use Alex for her own benefit and that this not-being-raised-a-lady is all just smoke and mirrors to cover her real plan."

There were other reasons Melinda could be here, too, Jenna thought. Reasons Jake didn't even want to consider. She looked at him levelly. "Or maybe Melinda just wants you back."

Jake shook his head in obvious consternation. "I wish it were that simple." He looked at Jenna steadily. "But our marriage was a disaster in every way, especially the bedroom. There's no way Melinda would want to go back to *that*."

Jenna found it hard to believe a man as skilled at kissing couldn't turn a woman on, but she also knew, from her own experiences in the dating game, that chemistry was either there or it wasn't. And yet... Jenna flushed. "But Melinda got pregnant right away." Within weeks of Jenna and Jake's botched elopement, as a matter of fact.

Jake nodded, grimly acknowledging this was true. "Because I was weak and she was determined," he said. "After that night, we didn't even see each other again until she told me the happy news."

Jenna wanted to believe he had never loved anyone else, the same way she had never loved anyone else. Aware she had started to tremble, she said, "And yet you married her."

Jake regarded Jenna without apology. "She was pregnant with my child. It was the decent thing to do. For Alex's sake, I'd do it all over again."

Jenna studied him, hearing what he didn't say as well as what he did. "Even though you didn't love her at all," she guessed, both troubled and relieved by what she was discovering.

But Jake refused to feel guilty about that, either. "We could have made it work, at least on some level, if Melinda had only met me halfway," he told Jenna honestly. "But she didn't and she wouldn't." He shrugged his broad shoulders indifferently. "I was as relieved as she was when our marriage ended."

Having met Melinda, Jenna didn't in all conscience see how he could have made that marriage work. The fact he was willing to try at all was laudable. She sighed. "Okay. That explains why the two of you don't get along and why Melinda seems so full of anger and resentment and impatience now. It doesn't explain why you want *me* to stay here with the three of you."

"I can't be alone with her, Jenna. Not again."

"You won't be alone with her." Jenna vaulted to her feet and stalked away from the swing set. "You'll be with Alex."

"Exactly the point." Hands shoved in the pockets of his jeans, Jake ambled up beside her. "I was counting on Clara to help me run interference, but she's not here and may not be for at least a day or so. And I was counting on Melinda bunking at the inn."

For that part of the current fiasco, Jenna had no sympathy. "You should have known *that* wouldn't work out."

Jake nodded, not above admitting he'd made a mistake. "I guess that was just wishful thinking on my part."

No joke, Jenna thought, even as she steeled her heart against him; she wasn't going to get involved in Jake's problems. "I don't see how my being here will make things any better." Restlessly, Jenna continued to stalk around the lamplit yard. Buster, similarly energized, got up to run along the landscaped hedges, sniffing and investigating tirelessly.

Jake kept pace with both Buster and Jenna. "Alex doesn't have any dresses yet. If you're here, working on them—well, at least I'll be able to demonstrate a good-faith effort to help our daughter conduct herself in a more ladylike manner."

Jenna had an inner bull-detector that worked like a charm. Folding her arms in front of her, she turned to square off with Jake. "You could do that just as well if I were sewing them in my shop," she pointed out matter-of-factly. Stepping even closer, she angled her chin up at him. "What's really going on here? What are you really afraid of?" There was something else going on behind Jake's silver-gray eyes; she was sure of it.

Jake exhaled roughly and shoved a hand through his inky-black hair. "Melinda can be critical to the point of cruelty, especially where Alex is concerned, since she sees Alex as an extension of herself." Jake's sensual lips thinned; his face hardened. "She's hurt her feelings before, but Alex was young, and I don't think she really understood what was going on. I'm not even sure she remembers. But if it happens again, Alex is old enough now that she will remember. I'm afraid it will crush her." He swallowed, shook his head. "Melinda is her mother, after all."

Jenna felt herself wanting to help, despite herself. "Have you talked to Melinda?" she asked softly.

Jake nodded grimly. "Many times, for all the good it did me. Melinda thinks her harshness will ultimately be helpful to Alex."

When all it would really do was crush Alex's spirit and damage her self-esteem, Jenna thought, beginning to share Jake's worry. "Which is where I come in," Jenna guessed.

Jake nodded. "I need someone willing to act as a decoy and take some flak from Melinda or, if the going gets rough, to vamoose with Alex. Clara would have done it had she been here. She's gotten very good at it—the two of them do not get along. But with just the three of us under one roof, it could be hell around here come morning."

Much as Jenna didn't want to be a part of Jake's problems, or the solution to them, she did feel for Alexandra. Jenna knew what it was like to be without a mother's love. When her parents had died, she had missed them terribly. To the point she was willing to do anything—even run away and elope with Jake in order to forget. But unlike Alex, Jenna'd had years of love and devotion from both her mother and her father. She had been almost eighteen when they died. Although there was no question that Jake loved Alex with all his heart and soul, and Clara did, too, Jenna guessed Alex had never really known a mother's love. Not from Melinda, anyway.

To have Melinda reappear in Alex's life, only to reject her... Well, that would be a pain that would be particularly hard to bear. Much as Jenna wanted to stay out of the situation and continue to guard her heart against Jake, she couldn't walk away.

"SO HOW WAS the factory site?" Kelsey asked half an hour later as Jenna let herself in to her apartment. Ignoring the ranch-supply catalogs and price lists Kelsey had spread out over the living room, Jenna went straight to her bedroom and began packing an overnight bag. "We didn't see it," she said, keeping her back to Kelsey as she began pulling clothes from the closet. She tucked them into her bag and then went to her bureau for undies.

"Why not?" Kelsey asked as she watched Jenna select a handful of silk chemises and matching underpants and fold them into her bag.

Briefly, Jenna explained about Jake's surprise for Alex and the much-earlier-than-expected arrival of Melinda.

Kelsey's eyebrows rose as Jenna took several long flowing nightgowns from her drawer. "That must have been some confrontation," Kelsey drawled.

Jenna shrugged, knowing there was no reason to deny it. Anyone who ran into Melinda would figure it out for themselves soon enough. "Melinda Carrington is a snooty handful, all right." She slipped into the bathroom and began gathering her toiletries. "Which is why Jake asked me to stay there with them, until his housekeeper, Clara, can take over once again. To help diffuse any tension between Alex and her rather difficult mother." Jenna dropped a vial of her favorite perfume into her bag.

Kelsey plucked it right out again. "I thought this thing you had going with Jake was going to be a fifty-fifty proposition.

Something that would benefit you both while reminding Jake what he had given up when he dumped you without a backward glance. But now it sounds like it's all about what Jake and his daughter need.''

Jenna added a pair of slippers—and the perfume vial—to her bag again. She shut it before Kelsey could snoop any more. ''Sometimes children's needs have to come first.'' Bag in hand, she headed downstairs into the shop on the first floor.

Kelsey followed her out the apartment door and down the stairs. She watched as Jenna picked up her portable sewing machine and carried it to the door. She returned for the heavy leather carryall bag that contained her portable sewing kit, favorite shears and marking tools, and placed it next to the door, too.

Still watching her disapprovingly, Kelsey folded her arms in front of her, ''That's what you and Meg both said about Dani and me when Mom and Dad died. 'Children's needs have to come first.'''

''They do,'' Jenna insisted.

But Kelsey, a free and fickle spirit if there ever was one, did not necessarily agree. She looked down her nose at Jenna, eyes somber. ''Sometimes I think we might have been happier if you and Meg had followed your hearts,'' she said. ''If you had said to heck with what Jake's folks thought and eloped with him anyway, and Meg had gone ahead and just admitted to one and all who fathered her baby and married him as well.''

Jenna couldn't deny that Meg's son Jeremy would have been better off knowing who his father was. If he had, Meg wouldn't be facing such a crisis with the increasingly curious and frustrated Jeremy now. She and Jake were a different story. Jenna plucked the bolts of fabric she would need from the racks and added them to the pile of things at the door. ''It wouldn't have worked even if I had married Jake.'' She sighed and shook her head, remembering. ''His parents' opposition was so virulent.''

Deciding she had everything she needed, not only to spend the night but to begin work on Alex's alphabet dress, Jenna unlocked the front door, and carried the fabric out to her car, which was parked at the curb. Kelsey followed with the portable sewing machine. "If that's the way you feel, why are you seeing him at all now? Why set yourself up for more heartbreak?"

Frowning, Jenna unlocked her trunk and set the bolts of fabric inside. "I'm not going to fall in love with him again."

"Of course not," Kelsey said dryly, as she fitted in the portable sewing machine next to the fabric. "There's no need since you never stopped loving him in the first place."

Jenna blew out an exasperated breath and kept her gaze averted. "I'm doing this strictly for business reasons, Kelse."

"Sure you are." Kelsey nodded knowingly as she returned for another armload.

Jenna bent to pick up her overnight bag. Kelsey got the leather carryall containing Jenna's sewing kit. Together, they marched toward her car. Jenna explained, "If I help Jake with Alexandra, he'll help me expand my business. I've wanted that for a long time." Everyone knew that. She just hadn't had the money or the connections to make it happen.

Once everything was neatly inside, Kelsey shut and slammed the lid. She turned and looked at Jenna, suddenly the baby in the family by age only as she warned softly, seriously, "Just make sure that's all you want."

BY THE TIME Jenna got back to the ranch, and parked her white convertible near the garage, the house was as quiet as could be. Jake was waiting for her on the front porch. "Everyone asleep?"

"Except Buster."

Jenna caught the worried look in his eyes and wondered how Jake's evening could get any worse. "What's wrong?" she asked anxiously.

"Let me carry your stuff up to your room and let you see where you'll be sleeping, then I'll show you," he said grimly.

Wordlessly, Jake escorted Jenna upstairs. Mindful that Alex and Melinda were both sleeping, they moved quietly through the hall, past the master bedroom where Jake bunked, the upstairs playroom and the other four bedroom suites, to the room at the far end of the hall. The spacious guest suite was decorated in a soft, soothing blue and had its own bath. "This gonna be okay?" Jake whispered.

More than okay, Jenna thought, noting this one room was almost half the size of her entire apartment. "Perfect, thanks," she whispered back, as Jake set her bags down where she directed. "Now show me what's wrong with Buster."

Jake crooked a finger and led the way down the back stairs, through the kitchen and mudroom and onto the screened-in back porch. It was lit up with soft yellow lights. Buster was in his crate, crying softly, and when he saw Jenna and Jake, his pitiful cries got even louder. "I don't know what's wrong with him," Jake said. "I fed him, gave him water, let him run around out back until he had done absolutely everything puppies need to do outside, and then brought him in. He was as happy as could be until I put him in the crate. Then he started crying. He didn't do that before."

"No," Jenna regarded Buster thoughtfully, her heart going out to the little puppy, who for whatever reason seemed to be suffering mightily, "he didn't."

Jake continued studying Buster anxiously, "I even put some of his new toys in with him, and a nylon bone—the kind the vet said would be good for him—in there for him to chew on. But nothing has helped. He's not going right to sleep like he did earlier today."

Jenna knelt in front of the crate and opened it. Buster shot out and, quivering all over, leapt into her waiting arms. As soon as he was nestled in her arms, he stopped crying. Jenna smiled down at him and stroked the soft, fluffy hair behind his ears. "I think he's just lonesome for his mama and his litter-mates. Usually, the first few nights they're separated they cry like this."

Jake hunkered down next to Jenna, looking both relieved that was all it was, and all the more worried, and petted Buster, too. "They do?"

"They want to go home, they want their mama." Jenna and Jake both got to their feet. Jenna settled into the rocking chair on the porch and still holding Buster close to her chest, began to stroke him softly from head to tail. "Did the breeder give you a cloth with the other puppies' smell on it to take home with you?"

Still looking mighty concerned, Jake shook his head. "Should he have?"

Jenna shrugged. "Sometimes they do. The cloths usually smell to high heaven, but they comfort the puppies, remind them of home, until they adjust to the new place."

Jake hunkered down beside Jenna and petted Buster again. "What are we going to do?" His eyes searched Jenna's face.

She smiled. "The same thing you do with a newborn baby. Love him a lot and rock him to sleep."

Jake, who was looking pretty exhausted, glanced at his watch, then back at Jenna. No question he was extremely grateful for all her help, but wary also of asking too much. "You don't mind?" he said cautiously.

Jenna smiled as she continued to pet Buster with long, soothing strokes. "To tell you the truth, I'm in heaven just holding this little guy," she admitted happily. "It's been so long since I had a dog. I've really missed having one."

Jake pulled up a ladder-back chair beside her, turned it around, and sat down backwards, folding his arms across the top of it. He rested his chin on his hands. "Why don't you have one? I remember you had four dogs and four cats when you were growing up."

"That's right. One for each of us."

Jake paused. His eyes gentled, as did his voice, "Is it because of what happened during the tornado?"

All of the cats and two of their dogs had been killed when the barn collapsed on their folks. In the most wrenching week of their entire lives, Jenna and her sisters had had to bury their folks and their pets. Jenna recalled crying until there were no tears left. And after that, just feeling numb. So very, very numb.

"Maybe." Jenna sighed as the puppy finally stopped trembling altogether and just snuggled closer. "I think there's only so much heartbreak and loss a person can take. And when our elopement fell apart and we broke up and everything else that could possibly go wrong for four orphans did, it just seemed more sensible not to tempt fate. Especially given the fact we had sold the ranch by then and were all trying to go to school. Plus, Meg had a baby on the way. We just figured the time for more pets would come later."

"Was that the only reason?" Jake prodded, his voice soft and low.

Jenna wondered if anyone would ever be able to read her the way Jake could. Heaven knew he saw things in her no one else ever had. Or would. Jenna forced a faint smile, met Jake's eyes and tried not to react to the compelling tenderness and compassion she saw there. "I think in a sense we were all trying to put the past behind us," she admitted honestly. "Forget the life we'd had, growing up on a ranch with all sort of animals around us, and do something different. Something more citified and sophisticated that wouldn't remind us of all we had once had and lost. But now that I'm holding this little guy, I'm beginning to think that was a mistake. I'd forgotten how much pets give you in return."

"He is pretty affectionate." Jake stroked Buster's head, too, and scratched behind his ears.

"And then some." With effort, Jenna turned her eyes from the compelling, gentle strokes of Jake's hand, and forced herself to forget how those same hands felt on her skin, in her hair. She smiled and forced her thoughts back to the subject at hand. "Wait until you and Alex have had Miss Kitty and

Buster awhile. You won't be able to imagine your lives without them.''

Jake continued petting Buster as he looked over and grinned at Jenna. "I like the difference in our lives already," he drawled. And Jenna had the distinct and unnerving impression he was not just talking about pets.

"DADDY, WAKE UP. Where's Buster?"

Jake groaned and looked at the clock. It was barely 6:00 a.m. Alex was wide awake.

"He's with Jenna."

"But she's not in her room. I saw her suitcases. Her bed is still made."

Which must mean, Jake thought, that Jenna had spent the whole night downstairs with Buster. Maybe even on the back porch. He had tried to get her to come to bed when he did, but she had insisted she stay out there and rock the homesick puppy a little longer before she tried to put Buster back in his crate.

Jake had suspected the puppy was just fine by then. It was Jenna who needed holding and comfort, and Jake who wanted to do the holding and comforting. But with Melinda and Alex just upstairs, he'd had no choice but to back off, accede to Jenna's wishes and head on to bed, leaving her to follow at will.

"Check the back porch, then," Jake advised. "But if they're sleeping, you've got to be quiet as a mouse and not wake them. They may not have gotten much sleep last night. And one more thing." He paused, wishing he did not have to deliver this particular bit of news, then pushed on cheerfully, "Your mom arrived last night."

Despite Jake's matter-of-fact tone, Alex went very still. "Where is she?"

Jake smiled reassuringly. "Sleeping. She had a long flight. So I think we better let your mommy rest as long as she needs to—she's very tired."

Alex sat down on the edge of Jake's bed. She tucked her legs beneath the hem of her long Winnie-the-Pooh nightgown, brought her knees up all the way to her chin, and wrapped her arms around her bent legs. She studied Jake with a wisdom older than her years. "How come she didn't wake me up last night when she got here?"

Because she had absolutely no interest in doing so, Jake thought.

But not wanting to hurt his daughter, he said, "Because she wanted you to get your sleep." He paused, knowing there was more to be said, for all their sakes, even if he didn't want to pressure his daughter by saying it, for fear she'd get the idea that what was outside counted more than what was inside a person. Reaching up, he tucked a piece of long tangled hair behind her ear. "I want you to look your prettiest today, on account of your mom being here. That means combing your hair and everything."

Jake expected Alex to scowl. To complain. To do all the things she normally did when confronted with the prospect of combing her hair. Instead she just looked at him, obviously thinking, reacting. But refusing to divulge what she was thinking and feeling about Melinda's sudden reemergence into her life.

Finally, Alex shrugged with typical nonchalance. She jumped up and bounded off the bed. "I'm going to go find Buster," she announced. And before Jake could protest, she'd dashed from the room.

"UH-OH. You wasn't s'posed to wake up on my account," Alex said as Jenna struggled to sit up in the rocking chair. Buster, having no such problems waking up after a night of sleeping on the back porch, leapt off Jenna's lap and into Alex's arms. Then, after a frenzy of kissing and tail-wagging, he wiggled free and jumped to the floor. "Better let him out back," Jenna said quickly, seeing the signs of an accident about to happen. "He's probably really got to go."

Alex raced over to open the back door. Buster zoomed out and squatted as soon as he hit the grass. "Good puppy!" Jenna called out enthusiastically as she stood and stretched.

Finished, Buster zoomed off to dash around the yard. Alex raced after him. Barefoot, her nightgown flapping around her legs, long curly strawberry-blond hair standing in wild tangles around her head, Alex was quite an untidy sight. But a deliriously happy one, Jenna noted.

Abruptly, Buster stopped, put his nose all the way to the ground, then circled twice, and squatted again. Alex, not understanding what was going on, just knowing she had finally caught up with her frisky puppy again, started to reach for Buster.

Jenna put up a staying hand and warned, "Watch out, honey, he's about to—"

"Oooh! Poop!" Alex said, pinching her nostrils closed.

"Now praise him, so he knows he's done a very good thing, going outside instead of in the house," Jenna said.

"Good puppy!" Alex said enthusiastically.

"Pet him, too!" Jenna said, coming outside to stand on the steps leading down into the grass.

Alex knelt beside Buster, who was now wagging his tail so hard he lost his balance and fell over. "Good puppy!" she said, petting him gently. "You are such a good puppy!"

Buster licked Alex's knee. Jenna smiled proudly. And then all heck broke loose as she heard a funny, sputtering sound, and saw the sprinkler heads popping up through the ground. Before she could do more than open her mouth, the lawn sprinklers were on. And Jenna had no idea how to shut them off.

"Alex, come here!" Jenna said. "You're going to get all wet!"

"I have to get my puppy first!" Alex raced after Buster.

Delighted at being chased, Buster ran all the harder. The water rained down, drenching them both, while Alex shouted and whooped with glee. Knowing there was only one way to end this—and that was catch Buster before he got any wetter—Jenna stepped down onto the lawn. She winced as the first cold spray of water hit her directly in the face. She knelt and held out her arms. "Buster, come here, puppy!"

Buster raced toward Jenna. Then raced away. Jenna jumped to her feet and ran after him. Alex ran after Jenna. Buster zigzagged between them both, in his glee charging right through the poop. Alex squealed. Jenna winced. Now they really had a mess on their hands. "Alex, stay right there!" Jenna said, hoping to at least keep the poop off Alex.

Too late. Buster had already changed directions once again, vaulted into Alex's arms, smearing poop all over her nightgown and onto her bare arms. Alex screamed, not liking that one bit. Buster leaped. The next thing Jenna knew, Buster was in her arms, smearing more poop all over both of them.

And at that moment Jake stepped out onto the screened-in back porch, with his ex-wife Melinda right behind him.

MOVING QUICKLY, Jake found the console located just inside the back porch door and shut off the sprinklers. Expression grim, he headed outside. Melinda, clad in a beautiful satin peignoir set and matching mules, was right behind him. She looked as horrified as Jenna felt. Alex, realizing this was her mother, whom she hadn't seen in nearly two years, stopped dead in her tracks. Her exuberance faded. She hung back. And with good reason. Melinda was not holding out her arms, or attempting in any way to warmly or joyously greet her daughter. Instead, she was scowling, shaking her head in obvious distaste.

"Un-believable," Melinda said, turning to Jake.

Afraid, for Alex's sake, what might come next if someone didn't do something, Jenna moved forward, a squirming, smelly Buster still in her arms. Someone had to diffuse Melinda's anger and take her fire. It might as well be her—it would hurt Alex less, and Jake would surely get his share sooner rather than later, too. "Meet Buster," Jenna said cheerfully.

"Keep that smelly animal away from me!" Melinda ordered shrilly. She backed up hastily toward the steps. She turned and glared at Jake. "I knew you were lax, but this!"

"Sure you don't want to pet him?" Jenna said, edging closer. "He's really very sweet!"

"No. Thanks." Melinda glared at Jake. "I'll see you inside." Ignoring Alex completely, she whirled and marched back inside the ranch house.

Alex, already apprehensive, looked completely deflated. She sank down to her knees in the wet grass. "She's mad," she whispered. "My mommy's mad."

"I think she's just tired from her long flight here," Jenna said.

"No. She's mad," Alex continued, looking all the more upset, "every time I see her she's mad." Tears welled in her eyes. Her lower lip began to tremble.

"Well, then, we're going to have to change that, aren't we?" Jenna said gently. She knelt beside Alex and wrapped her arm around her shoulder. Buster, not to be outdone in the comforting department, climbed onto Alex's lap and devotedly licked her chin. Unable to help herself, Alex giggled. She put her arms around her puppy. "He's as wet and smelly as I am!" she said, sighing.

"You know what else?" Jenna said. "I think we're going to have to give Buster a bath."

"We are?"

"Well, what else are we going to do?" Jenna grinned. "We can't let him go around smelling and looking like this."

"BUSTER STILL SMELLS kind of funny," Alex said twenty fun-filled minutes later, as they set an exhausted Buster in front of a bowl of puppy food.

Jenna dumped the tub of soapy water onto the grass. "That's because he's wet. Wet golden retrievers always smell like that. When Buster dries, he'll smell like the puppy sham-poo we washed him with.''

"Then he'll smell good."

"Yes, he will. And hopefully we'll be able to say the same thing about the two of us," Jenna said, as she wrinkled up her nose at her and Alex's damp, dirty clothes. "I think I need a bath, too. What about you?"

Alex looked down at herself. "I better get one, too. But I need help washing my hair."

Jenna smiled. "I can do that for you."

"Good. Daddy's not good at it. Clara says men don't know how to wash really long hair."

"Clara's probably got a point." Jenna waited for Buster to eat and drink his fill, then plucked him up and put him back in his crate, where he immediately settled down for a nap. "I doubt your daddy has ever had hair as long as yours."

Alex giggled, trying to imagine Jake with hair nearly down to his waist. "You're funny." With a happy sigh, Alex tucked her hand in Jenna's.

"Thank you." Jenna tweaked Alex's nose. "So are you."

Together, they headed inside, through the kitchen and up the backstairs. As they moved down the hall, Jenna literally held her breath, hoping they wouldn't run into either Melinda or Jake again until they got cleaned up.

Luckily for them, they saw neither. But they heard them, via the low hum of vaguely disgruntled voices emanating from downstairs.

Chapter Five

"You're leaving?" Jake and Melinda squared off in his study, behind closed doors. He stared at his ex-wife incredulously, beginning to regret his decision to do everything possible to foster a relationship between Alex and Melinda—sending Melinda regular updates about their daughter, and seeing Alex had photos and carefully filtered information about her mother, too.

He'd known there would be problems one day, caused by Melinda's emotional abandonment of her daughter. When she was old enough to understand what had gone on, Alex would probably resent the dickens out of Melinda.

But he had also known it was important for Alex and Melinda to have some foundation in place should Melinda ever realize her mistake and want to be more of a part of Alex's life.

He just hadn't expected this.

And he certainly hadn't foreseen Melinda's simultaneously pushy yet indifferent attitude toward Alex. Or expected she would be in such a hurry to get out of the house. But she clearly was.

Jake clenched his teeth. "You haven't even said two words to Alex."

Melinda shrugged her slender shoulders. "Is it my fault

she's out of control?" she countered. "You've turned our child into a little hoyden."

"With no help from you," Jake muttered, incensed.

"Exactly." Melinda straightened the hem of her peplum jacket. She removed her compact from her purse and checked her reflection. "Which is why I'm off to Dallas. I'm going to buy her a new wardrobe."

As much as Jake would have liked to veto this, he couldn't. Their custody agreement specifically allowed Melinda to visit Alex whenever it was convenient, which hadn't been more than four or five times since the divorce, and to bestow on Alex as many gifts as Melinda chose. Unfortunately, given their drastically different tastes and life-styles, having Melinda buy Alex a whole new wardrobe could only spell disaster.

Jake watched her pat her hair into place. "I'm having a wardrobe made here."

"By your little scamstress friend." Melinda closed her compact with a snap and sent him a wickedly derisive glance. "I know. I want her to have *real* clothes, Jake."

Jake's patience was fading fast. Melinda's snobbery was not something he wanted to pass on to Alex. "As opposed to what?" he shot back, unable to keep the sarcasm from his voice. "Imaginary ones?"

Melinda looked at him like he had lost his mind. She slipped her compact back in her purse. "You are not amusing."

He wasn't trying to be. With effort, Jake controlled his temper. He couldn't afford to get in an insult contest with Melinda when their daughter's well-being was at stake. "At least wait until Alex comes down," Jake urged gently.

Melinda released a long sigh. "I'll see her when I get back."

Jake studied the woman he had been married to for nearly two years. He wished he could feel something for her besides loathing and contempt, but given the way Melinda kept tromping all over Alex's feelings, he didn't think that was going to be possible. At least not any time soon. Trying like heck to figure a way to turn things around and make Melinda act like the mother Alex needed and deserved, Jake asked quietly, "When will that be?"

"I don't know." Melinda arched an elegant brow at Jake. "A few days is my guess. I've got to see my parents. And yours. Plus a number of our other friends."

All of whom, Jake realized sadly, took priority over their daughter.

Melinda glanced out the window. "There's my car and driver now."

"Maybe you could leave her a note." Jake was desperate not to see Alex hurt again. But how to prevent his selfish, self-centered ex-wife from doing that, he didn't know.

"Don't be silly." Melinda picked up her purse and flounced toward the door in a drift of expensive perfume, leaving Jake to follow at will. "She can't read."

"Actually, she can, at least the very basic words." Jake strode on ahead and opened the study door for Melinda. He escorted her through the foyer. "Clara and I started teaching her last year. She's a very quick study."

"Now—" Melinda looked at Jake unapologetically "—if only she could learn to be a little lady just as swiftly."

Jake stared at her. He didn't know what to say without making the situation worse. He only knew he wanted to read her the riot act for hurting Alex. And that was no way to feel about his ex-wife and the mother of his child. He might not be able to change Melinda's personality or value system. But for Alex's sake, he had to do a better job of making them get along peaceably. Even if Melinda couldn't care less about anyone else and wouldn't lift a finger to help.

"Goodbye, Jake." Melinda patted his cheek, then stepped outside. She signaled the driver to the front porch, where all her luggage was already stacked and waiting.

Wordlessly, Jake watched her tuck herself into the car. He was still standing there as Alex and Jenna came down the stairs and Melinda's limousine disappeared down the drive. "Where's Mommy?" Alex asked apprehensively.

Jake gave his daughter the most cheerful smile he could manage. "Mommy had to go to Dallas. She said she will try to be back in a few days."

"She didn't say goodbye to me." Alex's face fell. Her blue-gray eyes radiated hurt. And Jake's heart broke for Alex all over again.

Jake wrapped his arm around his daughter's shoulders, putting all the love he had into the hug. "Mommy asked me to say it for her." Or Melinda would have, he added silently, if she had a heart. Jake stroked Alex's shoulder with gentle comforting strokes as she wrapped both her arms around his middle and leaned against him. "Are you hungry, honey? We haven't had breakfast." Jake met Jenna's eyes, saw she was concerned, too. For Alex and for him.

"I know I'm starved," Jenna said cheerfully.

"Me, too," Jake agreed, glad for Jenna's help in distracting Alex from this latest slight, in a very long string of them.

The sound of a vehicle in the driveway had them turning to the windows once again. As curious as ever, Alex broke free of Jake and rushed over to the window just in time to see the red truck park in front of the house. "Clara's back!" Alexandra announced happily.

Seconds later, Clara strode in, beaming. "I'm a grandma!" she announced to one and all, hugging all of them ecstatically in turn. "The little rascal's name is Nathan James, and he weighs eight pounds and six ounces! And he's as healthy as can be. You ought to hear him! That child has a fiesty personality and set of lungs on him that would make any momma and daddy proud."

"I can see his grandma certainly is," Jake said with a wink. He hugged Clara again. "Congratulations." As they drew apart, he patted the older woman on the shoulder. "You must be exhausted."

Clara nodded as she shot Jake a glance. "That I am."

"How about hungry?" Jake continued fussing over her like an old mother hen. "I bet you could use something to eat, too."

Clara started to head for the kitchen. "I'll get it."

"Oh no you won't." Jake cut his housekeeper off at the pass. "You sit right there." With a gentle hand on her shoulder, he guided her to a comfortable-looking club chair. "Alex and I will wait on you this morning. Won't we, Alex?"

Alex nodded. She thrust herself back into Clara's arms. "I missed you," she murmured, hugging Clara fiercely.

Clara's eyes welled as she looked from Jake to Jenna and back again. She obviously suspected that something had gone on in her absence, to have Alex, Miss Independence herself, acting so clingy. "I missed you, too, honey," she said thickly.

Alex reared back to look at Clara. "Can I go see your new grandbaby?"

Clara smiled. "That's up to your daddy, but I don't see why not."

"We can go later this afternoon, after Nathan James and his mama have had a chance to rest," Jake said, grateful for the distraction. The trip to see the baby would help get Alex's mind off Melinda's slight. "Meanwhile," Jake said as he took Alex's hand and tugged her to her feet, "we've gotta rustle up some grub for Clara that's fit to eat. And some breakfast for us."

"I can help." Jenna, who'd sat down along with Clara, started to get up.

"No." Jake motioned Jenna to stay where she was. "You keep Clara company and we'll call you when it's ready. Alex and I will handle this." He looked at Clara. "You just take it easy now."

Clara nodded wearily and swept her hands through her curly salt-and-pepper hair. "Thanks. To tell the truth, I'm so tired I don't think I could fix anything edible right now anyway."

"Then you're lucky you have us, aren't you?" Jake teased. He and Alex departed, hand in hand.

Clara leaned forward and tugged off her cowgirl boots. "That man is something, isn't he? I don't know what I would have done without him the past seven years."

"How'd the two of you meet?" Jenna went to get an ottoman so Clara could put her feet up.

"It was just after my husband died of an aneurysm. Financially, I was okay. I didn't have to work. But with all four of my kids out of the nest and on their own, and no husband to take care of anymore, I was pretty lost. I wanted to work, but the only thing I was really qualified to do—the only thing I wanted to do—was keep a home and take care of children. The problem was, I didn't have any experience at all as a domestic.

"But Jake hired me anyway. From day one, he treated me like family and let me be me. He didn't make me wear a uniform or try to micromanage the way I kept house for him or what I cooked. Course—" Clara paused and rolled her eyes "—his wife at the time didn't feel that way."

"Melinda."

Clara nodded. "Sweet as pie when they were out in public or with his family, but mean as a rattler when she was at home with him. I felt so sorry for him. I mean, it was obvious why he married her...a baby on the way... He's always been such a decent man, even back then, when he was barely an adult himself."

Jenna knew she shouldn't put too much stock in what anyone else said about Jake, good or bad. What counted here was how he treated her, past and present. But it warmed her heart just the same to realize a woman as no-nonsense, as plainspoken and goodhearted as Clara, who had worked for him for so long, thought the world of him. Clara's respect and affection was not something that could have been bought; it was something Jake would have had to earn.

"I love that boy like he was one of my own kids," Clara continued as the tantalizing smells of bacon and coffee wafted out to the living room. "And I love Alex like she was one of my own grandkids. Of course, her problems now are mostly my fault." Clara shook her head ruefully as she fingered the red bandanna knotted around her neck. "I grew up on a ranch myself and I never did get very citified despite all those years I spent in the Dallas suburbs as a P.T.A. mom. Jake lets me wear jeans most every day of the week. I let Alex wear jeans and pants most every day of the week, too." Clara sighed. "So now she's turned into a tomboy, and it's a problem for Jake I sure as heck never intended he have."

Jenna patted Clara's hand. "Don't you worry. We'll get Alexandra into a dress yet."

"How?" Clara persisted, looking skeptical.

That, Jenna hadn't figured out yet.

"If my laxness causes trouble for Jake and Alex I'll never forgive myself," Clara whispered. "I know he comes on strong sometimes, but you could search every inch of the Lone Star State and not find anyone better."

Jenna felt that, too, sometimes. Other times she was afraid to get deeply involved with him again, for fear she'd end up getting dumped again. Heaven knew they had enough working against them: the past, his parents, Melinda. And now, a potential custody suit for Alex.

Jenna knew Jake.

If it came right down to it, if there was no other way, he would sacrifice his own happiness, and Jenna's, too, for that of his daughter. And when it came right down to it, Jenna reluctantly admitted to herself that she would not hesitate to do the same. Jenna wanted to be happy. She wanted—if anything and everything were possible—to be with Jake. But she'd be damned if she'd do it by stepping on the heart of a little girl who had already suffered quite enough.

Alex dashed back in. "Come on everybody! Breakfast is ready!"

Platters of fluffy scrambled eggs, crisp brown bacon, buttermilk biscuits and a medley of fresh fruit were piled on the center of the table, along with pitchers of milk and juice and a carafe of coffee.

"I set the table!" Alex said, as Jake poured coffee. "And took the biscuits out of the can and put them on the baking sheet for Daddy!"

"I see that," Jenna said, smiling. She gave Alex a congratulatory hug.

"You did a wonderful job." Clara hugged Alex, too.

"So did you hear all about Nathan James's birth?" Jake asked Jenna as he pulled butter and jam from the refrigerator and carried them to the table.

Jenna sat down and spread her napkin across her lap. "Uh, actually, we didn't get around to that."

Jake's brow rose in a way that let them know he didn't necessarily consider that a good sign. "What did you talk about?" He looked from Jenna to Clara and back again.

"You," Clara announced blithely, as Jenna ladled food on Alexandra's plate. "I was telling Jenna what a good man you are."

Jake's broad shoulders relaxed as he sank into a chair opposite Jenna. "Don't pay any attention to her," Jake teased with a playful wink. "She doesn't know what she's talking about."

"It's true!" Alex said enthusiastically, working hard to tuck a pat of butter down the split in the center of her biscuit with her spoon. "Daddy's one of the good guys. Clara says so all the time, and she's right."

Jake flushed and didn't meet Jenna's eyes. And Jenna even thought she knew why. This kind of easygoing camaraderie and unconditional familial devotion was new to Jake. Growing up, his relationship with his folks had been much more formal and instructional. His parents had made sure he had every material thing he ever needed, but they hadn't understood him. They had taught him how to behave, but they hadn't spent much time having heart-to-heart talks with him, or even asking him what he wanted. Jenna had a hunch, given Jake's reaction to Alex and Clara's unchecked adoration, that things were still the same with Patricia and Danforth Remington. They loved Jake very much. That had always been clear. But at the same time, they were more concerned that he behave in a blue-blooded manner, be financially successful in order to keep the family fortune intact, and marry his own kind—rather than try to find someone to love, have a family of his own, live a good, productive life and be happy. It was sad, Jenna thought, when family members couldn't seem to accept their differences and express their love for each other. On the other hand, as long as Jake's parents were still alive—unlike her own—there was still time to remedy that.

"So tell us all about Nathan James's birth," Jake said.

Beaming, Clara did. "Well, I have to tell you, witnessing a baby's birth is about the best thing in the whole world. I mean there is nothing—nothing—that can make a person happier than bringing a new life into this world."

"You go on to bed and rest. Don't even worry about us," Jake told Clara as soon as they had finished breakfast. "I've already called my secretary in Dallas and cleared my schedule until further notice. I'll see to Alex until Lisa and Randall are home again and all settled in with the new baby."

Clara hesitated. "I've been meaning to talk to you about that. I sort of promised my daughter and son-in-law I'd be available to help them, for at least a few days."

"No problem," Jake said cheerfully as he got up to help clear the table. He shot an affectionate look at his daughter. "Alex doesn't mind hanging out with us, do you, Alex?" Alex gleefully shook her head.

Jake looked at Jenna. "You don't mind if Alex comes with us this morning when we go look at the old carpet warehouse, do you?"

"Not at all." In fact, Jenna thought, there was safety in numbers. As close as she was beginning to feel toward Jake, it was best they not be alone if she could help it.

"What about Buster and Miss Kitty?" Alex asked as Jake put the butter and jam back in the refrigerator.

Jenna began loading the dishwasher. "We'll let Buster out before we go, and then crate him while we're gone. He'll be fine," Jenna reassured Alex warmly. "But just to make sure she feels all nice and safe, why don't you go to the laundry room and play with Miss Kitty for a while before we leave?"

"Okay." Alex skipped off, chattering all the while. Clara followed her.

Jenna smiled as she heard Alex say to Clara, "It's my turn to tuck you in."

HALF AN HOUR later, the pets all set, the kitchen cleaned up, Clara already asleep, they were on the road to the warehouse. The agent met them there and walked them through it, then, sensing they needed time to talk, stepped outside to make a few calls on her cell phone. "What do you think?" Jake asked, looking around at the spacious interior of the large building with its cement floor.

"It's certainly big enough for what I had in mind," Jenna mused. Indeed, it was the size of a football field, with enough height to provide either a loft of offices and showrooms or a second floor. "But we're going to need a lot more light and I don't like the fact it's all one big area."

"How would you like to see it set up?" Jake tipped his hat back with one poke of his index finger.

"I'd like to paint the outside white, and have a showroom at the front, where my designs could be modeled. The sewing bays would need to be comfortable, and a lot more intimate. No more than three or four people to an area, with plenty of room for tables to lay out fabric."

He sauntered toward her with easy, sensual grace. He was wearing a gray sport coat and a tan Stetson. The first two buttons of his light blue oxford-cloth shirt were undone. His jeans were fashionably faded a medium blue. They hugged his legs like a second skin. His boots were equally comfortable and broken in. "I take it you don't want to do this assembly-line fashion."

"No." Jenna's decision about that was firm. She met Jake's eyes seriously. "The quality suffers when you do that, and I want everything that's made out here to be top quality."

"What are you going to make out here?" Alex asked curiously as she walked across the floor.

"Dresses," Jenna smiled, "although I still haven't decided what kind. I'm known most for my wedding and evening dresses—but I sort of like doing those one at a time, so I'll have to think about it."

"There's always business wear," Jake suggested helpfully, his admiring glance skimming over Jenna from head to toe, taking in her tailored sunshine-yellow sheath and matching blazer. "There's a big market for that."

Jenna nodded, and adjusted the sunglasses on top of her head. The only problem was, the idea of doing a lot of business suits didn't set her on fire. And she needed to have tons of enthusiasm for whatever she did if her first mass-produced line of clothing was to be the roaring success both she and Jake wanted it to be. "I'm sure inspiration will strike once I've had a little time to think about it," Jenna said, beginning to feel a little warm, given the intent way he was studying her. Her pulse racing at his closeness, Jenna edged away. "I just need to think about it a little bit first."

"Well, I'm still not wearing any dresses," Alexandra put in with a frown. "I don't care how pretty they are." Alex narrowed her eyes at Jenna. "Why are you smiling?"

Jenna ruffled Alex's wildly curling strawberry-blond hair. "I was just thinking how different you and I are," she replied affectionately. "When I was your age I would have given anything to be able to wear frilly little dresses. Instead—" Jenna made a face "—I had to wear jeans and boots and hats and go outside to help with the animals and the chores."

Alex sighed wistfully. "That sounds like fun to me."

"I think you'd look awfully pretty in a dress," Jake said.

Alex's jaw thrust out pugnaciously. "I'm still not wearing one," Alex said. "And even if I did, I'd just spill something all over it."

Jake's eyes darkened at his daughter's threat. His expression grew perplexed. Jenna thought she knew how he felt. Alex was definitely a strong-willed, feisty little girl with tons of energy and a mind of her own. But this continuing resistance seemed uncharacteristic of her sweet personality. Something had to be behind her continued rebellion. Something more than the other kids having mothers or Jake and Clara's willingness to let her be a tomboy, given Alex's delight at playing dress-up. Jake had said Alex didn't know how Melinda felt about Alex conducting herself in a more ladylike manner. Given Alex's nonexistent relationship with her mother, Jenna felt Jake was right in protecting Alex that way. Alex had enough to deal with on that score already. But something was making her act out her unhappiness or worry this way. Jenna just wished they knew what it was. Right now, Jake clearly didn't have a clue. And for the moment, neither did Jenna.

The real-estate agent was back.

"How are we doing? Do you think this will fit your needs?"

Jake looked at Jenna. One glance and they knew they were in agreement on this much—if they could make the business end of it work, they would look no farther for a factory. "We're going to need to see some facts and figures first." Jake smiled. "And the names of three first-rate contractors."

THE REST of the morning passed swiftly. Excited about the prospect of a job that big in a town as small as Laramie, the three contractors the agent recommended drove over promptly to walk the warehouse and speak with Jake and Jenna. Several hours later, all three had faxed preliminary bids to Jake's home in Laramie. Meantime, Jenna, Jake and Alex had stopped by Rylander's Western Wear to purchase a baby gift for Nathan James. While Jenna gift-wrapped the present, Jake and Alex tended to Miss Kitty and Buster. A late lunch followed. Exhausted, Alex fell asleep on the cushioned sofa on the screened-in back porch, the puppy and kitten curled up beside her as the ceiling fan whirred lazily overhead. Wanting to be within earshot in case they were needed, yet far enough away not to disturb any of the sweetly slumbering trio, Jenna and Jake sat down at the kitchen table to discuss business.

Briefly Jake laid out what he was prepared to spend to expand Jenna's business, then they went over the bids. "If we do everything you want to the inside of the warehouse, use only top-drawer fabrics, pay the kind of salaries you want to pay the seamstresses, emphasize the quality and limit the volume and price the line somewhat affordably, it's not going to leave much in the way of either profits or salary for you. The profits I can live without," Jake said seriously. "Your salary is something we can work on if you're willing to make concessions in other areas."

"That's just it," Jenna warned, meeting his eyes. "I'm not. But that's all right," she told him, pleased he was so concerned about her well-being. "I can live with less the first year or two. What's important to me is that we take the time to build up our operation slowly, so we can ensure quality and originality. I want my first mass-marketed line to be something I can proudly put my name on. Besides, if we're successful, the profits will come. If not, I'll know it's not for me, and I can always go back to working only out of my shop, on custom-made wedding and evening dresses and the occasional business suit or lounging outfit."

"And if we're as wildly successful as I think we're going to be, then what?" Jake asked, his gray eyes looking more pewter than silver in the afternoon sunlight. "Will you consider expanding even further?" He searched her face. "To a line of ready-made wear for men?"

"Maybe." Jenna sat back in her chair and took a sip of her iced tea. "But first, we've got to get the initial venture off the ground. With all we have to do, I figure it will be at least a year before we get the factory up and running, and a line of clothing ready to market to the department stores in Dallas.''

Jake looked her straight in the eye. ''Again, that timetable is a little slower than I had in mind.''

Given how much he was investing in the expansion of her business, Jenna didn't blame him for wanting a quick return on his money. ''Trust me,'' Jenna returned just as decisively, wanting as much time as necessary to develop her new designs. ''You'll be glad you didn't rush things.''

Jake frowned. Seemingly unable to take his eyes from her face, he allowed, ''When it comes to business, Jenna, I don't usually compromise my vision.''

Jenna smiled and guessed, ''But in my case you'll make an exception.''

Jake nodded. He reached over and clasped her hands in his. ''I realize there's only so much change you'll be comfortable with and I want you to be comfortable.''

Jenna stared down at their linked hands. ''I'm glad you feel that way,'' she said softly. Deciding this meeting had taken a far too intimate turn, Jenna extricated her hands from his, pushed back her chair and stood. As she stepped away from the table, she looked Jake squarely in the eye. ''Because I'm very territorial when it comes to my business.''

Jake smiled and stood as well. ''And I'm very territorial about you.'' The next thing she knew he'd clamped both his hands around her waist, brought her close and lowered his lips to hers, deliberately robbing her of breath. Jenna moaned, confusion sweeping through her. Again, he brushed his lips softly, insistently, against hers. Feelings swept through her, followed by a need that was soul-deep. Jake threaded a hand though her hair and using the arm anchored at her waist, pulled her closer still. Her breath caught in her chest as he kissed her, long and hard. No one had ever asked her to give so much, so fast, and a few more kisses robbed her of the ability to think at all.

Jenna kissed Jake back, drowning in the pleasurable sensations sweeping through her. She couldn't believe they had found each other again after all this time, couldn't believe the dreams she'd held for years were actually coming true. She wanted him to want her; he did. She wanted him to need her. Judging by the pressure at the front of his jeans, that was true, too. But wanting and needing did not necessarily translate into a future together. And it was a future—and a lasting relationship with a man who loved her as much as she loved him— that Jenna desired most of all. Not sure Jake could—or would—ever give her that, Jenna pulled away. Heart pounding, body yearning for more, Jenna stared up at him. They were very close to making love, she realized, shaken. Had they been alone, who knew what would have happened? But they weren't alone. Alexandra, Buster and Miss Kitty were all sleeping nearby. Clara was still upstairs.

Jenna released a shuddering breath, aware Jake looked very much like he wanted to kiss her again. And then again. She held up a hand to stop him. Stepped back. "Jake—"

He let her go. Though it was clear from the reluctant look on his face and the desire still gleaming in his dark gray eyes that this was not what he wanted, either.

"We can't—" Jenna started.

Jake looked at her as if to say: *Wanna bet?* Out loud, he said gently, "It was just a kiss, Jenna." One he obviously did not regret for a moment.

But he wanted so much more from her. She could see it in his eyes. She could feel it in her heart. The question was, Jenna wondered nervously, what did she *really* want from him?

JAKE HAD TO hand it to Jenna later that afternoon as she, Alex and he all got off the hospital elevator and walked out onto the maternity ward. Not only was Jenna pretty, talented, kind and loving, she was also nurturing, attentive and supportive to the nth degree. Alex had received a grandparent's love from both Clara and his folks. She was now receiving the closest thing she had ever had to a mother's love from Jenna. And

Alex wasn't the only one who was benefiting from the relationship. Jenna looked happier than he had ever seen her, walking along beside him, Alex's hand tucked into hers. At that moment, the three of them felt like the loving, contented family he had always wanted. Not just for himself but for Alex. And for Jenna, too, he realized. It did his heart good to see both of them looking so joyful and content.

"Do you like babies?" Alexandra asked Jenna.

"Yes." Jenna smiled over at Alex. "I love babies very much," Jenna said.

Alex's brow furrowed as if she were contemplating a particularly thorny problem. "How come you don't have one, then?"

Jake winced at that question, but Jenna didn't seem to mind as she answered, "I guess I just haven't gotten around to it yet. I've been too busy sewing pretty dresses and running my shop. What about you? How come you don't have a baby?"

"Because I'm too little, silly. You have to be a grown-up to have a baby."

"Ah," Jenna said, nodding solemnly.

"He's awfully small," Alexandra said, as she peered through the Laramie Community Hospital nursery window. "And red, too."

"That's the way newborn babies look," Jake said gently.

"Even me, when I was borned?" Alex asked. Her lower lip pushed out as she considered the infant, swaddled warmly in a pale blue blanket.

Jake nodded. "You didn't have dark curly hair, though. Yours was light brown and very fine and straight. And the nurses taped a little ribbon in it, right here." Jake pointed to the crown of Alex's head.

Alex giggled. "I must have looked funny."

"You looked precious." So precious he'd known all the grief he'd gone through, being married to Melinda, had been worth it.

Nathan James yawned and blinked at them and promptly fell back to sleep.

"He's as cute as Buster and Miss Kitty," Alex said, after a moment. She looked up at Jake, in that instant every bit as decisive and determined as her daddy. "I think I want one."

Jake arched his brow inquiringly, hoping he misunderstood. "One what?"

"A baby brother or sister."

As he thought about what would be required to make that happen—Jenna, a bed, and the time and opportunity to pick up where they had left off years ago—warmth shot through Jake, pooling at the front of his jeans. He shifted his stance slightly. Now was no time to be thinking about making passionate love to the woman of his dreams, he reminded himself firmly. Aware Alex and Jenna were both still waiting for an answer, Jake looked down at his daughter. He cleared his throat. "It's not that simple, honey."

Alex continued to regard him patiently, as she demanded with perfect child logic, "Why not?"

Because, though Jenna still loved him—he could see it every time he looked into her eyes—she wasn't sure she trusted him not to leave her again. Yet. She would, and soon, if he had his way, because Jenna was, and had always been, the only woman for him. With as much equanimity as he could muster, Jake explained, "Because you need a mommy and a daddy for that. Your mommy and I aren't married anymore," Jake said, as much for Jenna's sake as Alex's. He wanted Jenna to know no matter what Melinda did, he was not being sucked back into the self-centered maelstrom of her life.

Alex thought about that for a long moment before her next idea struck. Apparently, she didn't much want Jake and Melinda to have another baby together, either. "You and Jenna could have a baby, then," Alex told Jake enthusiastically.

My wish exactly, Jake thought, knowing he'd like nothing better than to have a baby with the woman he had loved from the first day he met her. But unfortunately that was something that was going to have to wait, too, Jake thought reluctantly. Casting an apologetic glance at Jenna—who looked just as aware of him as he was of her—Jake turned back to Alex. "Jenna and I aren't married, either, honey," he explained. Yet, Jake thought for the second time, studying the warm flush of awareness spreading across Jenna's face, if he had his way, they soon would be.

Alex's exasperation with Jake grew. She looked at him as if he were the densest daddy around. "You don't have to be married, silly. Remember Tommy Parker, back in Dallas? His parents are divorced, too, and his daddy had a new baby with a friend." Alex paused, looking hopefully from Jake to Jenna and back again. "Jenna is your friend, isn't she?"

The flush in Jenna's cheeks deepened, as did the pressure at the front of Jake's jeans. To heck with everything that was still holding them back. He wanted nothing more, at that very moment, than to take Jenna to bed and make her wholly and completely his. The way Jenna was looking at him made him think she wanted that, too.

Reluctantly, Jake tore his gaze from Jenna and looked back at Alex, who was still waiting somberly for his answer. "Yes," Jake told Alex in a low, serious voice, "Jenna is very much my friend. But that still doesn't mean we're going to have a baby."

"How come?" Alex frowned her disappointment.

Because I've got to get her to agree to marry me first, Jake thought. Given how their elopement had failed, that would be no easy task. "Because a baby is a big responsibility and right now we have our hands full with you and Buster and Miss Kitty."

"What about when Buster and Miss Kitty and me all grow up? Then will you have a baby together so I can have a brother or sister?" Alex asked.

"We'll see," Jake said, deciding they had talked about this way too much. If he had been fantasizing about making love to Jenna before, it was nothing to the way he was dreaming about it now. "In the meantime, though, there is a way you could enjoy being around a baby. 'Cause you know what? I bet Clara is going to be baby-sitting for little Nathan James from time to time. And he'll be coming over to visit us at the ranch. So I bet Clara will let you help look after him."

"Really?"

Jake nodded.

Meg Lockhart walked up, in her nurse's uniform, the supervisor badge pinned against her chest. Although she smiled at Jake cordially, concern radiated from her eyes. Clearly, she wasn't all that thrilled to see him with Jenna. Which, given what had happened years ago, was no surprise. Jake should have known better than to encourage the nearly eighteen-year-old Jenna to elope with him, no matter how much he loved her and wanted to help her or how fiercely she was grieving the loss of her parents and the family ranch. He should have realized his actions could have been considered to be "contributing to the delinquency of a minor," and not left Jenna facing possible charges for trying to run off and marry him without first obtaining her guardian's permission. If he hadn't been so wrapped up in the romance of it all and made that misstep, well, who knew how things might have worked out between them? Would he and Jenna be married now? Would the rest of the Lockhart sisters be welcoming him with open arms instead of discreetly pushing him away?

"Jake." Meg nodded at him cooly, then paused to hug Jenna warmly and protectively before drawing back to look into her younger sister's eyes. "What are you doing here?" Meg asked.

Briefly, Jenna explained about Nathan James's birth, then Jake introduced his daughter. Meg smiled and shook Alexandra's hand. She might have reservations about Jake, but she clearly had none about the nearly six-year-old Alex. "I have a son about your age, you know. His name is Jeremy, and we've just moved here, too. He had a lot of friends where we lived before this, but not so many here yet. But we're working on it. In fact, we're having a pizza and video party tonight for some of the kids he's met so far. Would you like to come?'' Meg looked up at Jake. ''It's from five to eight, at our house. You remember Annie Pierce and Travis McCabe?''

Jake nodded. ''I heard they got married not too long ago.''

''Right. Annie and Travis, as well as Annie's triplets—Teddy, Trevor and Tyler—are going to be there, as well as several little girls from their summer preschool class. It'd be a good chance for Alex to meet some other kids. If you don't have other plans.''

Jake turned to his daughter, leaving the decision up to her. ''What do you think, Alex? Would you like to go play with some other kids your own age?''

Alex nodded enthusiastically. Now all they had to do was replan the evening ahead of them, Jake thought. He and Jenna had been given some rare time alone. He didn't want to squander it.

JAKE CUT the connection on his cell phone and put it back in the pocket of his sport coat, relieved to be cleared of all familial responsibilities for a few hours, and free to concentrate on himself—a rare thing these days. He turned to Jenna to fill her in. ''Clara said she'll feed Buster and Miss Kitty, and make sure they are all situated before she leaves the ranch so they'll be okay until we get back around eight-thirty. That gives us three hours here in town,'' Jake noted happily. He and Jenna waved one last time to Alex and Jeremy and the other kids playing at Meg's. He started his truck and pulled away from the curb. ''What do you want to do?''

Tensing, Jenna turned and offered him a prim smile. ''I've got to go over to my shop and check on things there, make a few stencils, and so on.'' Her tone of voice made it clear she was expecting to do her errands alone.

Not one to be put off when he wanted something, Jake ignored the hint. ''I'll go with you,'' he offered genially, wondering what had gotten into Jenna. Was it the idea of spending time alone with him that had Jenna abruptly acting so cool and proper toward him? Or the fact she'd run into Meg, and been reminded of all the reasons why the Lockhart sisters thought Jenna should be holding Jake at arm's length, if she held him at all.

"I'd appreciate the ride over, but as for the rest of the three hours, you don't have to stay." Jenna looked at him levelly as color swept into her cheeks. "I'm sure you have other things to do."

Nothing more important than spending time alone with you, Jake thought. But not wanting to argue with her, he merely turned his vehicle toward her boutique and dropped her off at the curb in front of her shop.

When he returned thirty minutes later, with a bouquet of flowers, a pepperoni pizza and two take-out garden salads, the Closed sign was hanging on the front door and Jenna was still going through a huge stack of messages with her assistant, Raelynn.

"And last but not least," Raelynn was saying as Jake let himself in the back way, "Mrs. Patricia Remington called, from Dallas. She wants a private fitting with you tomorrow morning at nine. I told her I didn't know if you'd be available, because you had rescheduled all your appointments this week in order to take care of some personal business. But she insisted she'll be here in any case, and will wait all day for you if necessary. Apparently there's some big do that she's giving for her daughter-in-law, Melinda Carrington, day after next, out at their summer ranch, that she needs a dress for, pronto. And she's willing to pay through the nose for it, too."

Raelynn, an attractive young woman and newcomer to Laramie who had only worked for Jenna for a year, obviously hadn't made the connection between Jake and his mother. Jenna had. She wasn't pleased about it. Nor was Jake. He had purposely not told his parents he was seeing Jenna again, or that he was going to back her financially in a business deal, for just this reason. He didn't want his parents interfering in his life.

Oblivious to both Jake and Jenna's discomfort, Raelynn continued going through Jenna's messages. "Kelsey wants you to know she left this morning and is going to be out of town for a few days. She and Brady Anderson are off looking for horses and cattle for the ranch they just bought. She said to tell you thanks for letting her bunk at your place and she'll call you when she gets back. Kate Marten called. She wants a knockout dress for the major's homecoming next month. And a wedding dress for some time later this fall."

"Kate and Craig Farrell are finally going to tie the knot?" Jenna—as well as many other Laramie residents—had begun to wonder if the two former high school sweethearts, having dated off and on for the past ten years, and engaged for the last three, would ever make it official. Of course, Jenna conceded quickly, they hadn't had too many opportunities to even see each other, as Craig was an F-16 pilot for the U.S. Air Force, and often deployed overseas.

Raelynn nodded. "The major's coming home to set the date, book a church and decide where to hold their reception."

"I didn't realize Kate Marten still lived here," Jake interrupted, obviously remembering that Kate had been one of Jenna's best friends.

"She's a grief and trauma counselor at Laramie Community Hospital," Jenna said.

Raelynn continued, "Kate said she'll stop by to talk to you tomorrow. I suggested eight-thirty before the shop opens. Is that a good time?"

Jenna nodded. Kate was so down-to-earth and such a good listener. It would do her good to talk to her old friend.

"And that's it, as far as messages go," Raelynn said, handing over the stack of notes to Jenna.

"Thanks," Jenna said.

"Nice flowers," Raelynn said, smiling at Jake.

"Want to stay and join us for dinner?" Jake asked.

"No, I don't think so," Raelynn said, glancing again at the flowers. "My husband is cooking tonight and I want to be home to eat with my kids."

"Some other time then," Jake said. "With you and your family."

"We'd love it. Thanks." Raelynn grabbed her lunchbox and purse. "Remember, I can't come in tomorrow morning until ten. Tommy has his dentist appointment."

"No problem. I can handle it," Jenna smiled.

Raelynn departed. As soon as she had, Jake said, "I'll call my mother and tell her to back off."

Her shoulders stiff with tension, Jenna locked the door behind Raelynn and pulled down the shade over the front door. Turning on her heel, she ignored the dinner and the flowers and headed for the back of the shop. "You'll just make things worse if you do."

"She's got no business calling you or coming here. Never mind throwing Melinda a welcome-back party at their summer place."

Her head held high, Jenna stormed into the sewing room in the back. She plucked pattern paper off the rack, a ruler and a pencil. Pulling up a chair, she slipped off her sunshine-yellow blazer and began making stencil letters and numbers for Alexandra's alphabet dress. Head bent, Jenna concentrated on her work. "Obviously, she still thinks of Melinda as part of the family, and she wants me to know she and your father are intent on the two of you getting back together."

Jake stood next to the long rectangular table where Jenna sat and folded his arms in front of him. "It doesn't matter what my mother wants."

Jenna shot him a sharp look. "Doesn't it?"

Irked that Jenna just assumed everything had to be the same now as it had been in the past, Jake pushed away from the wall and reminded her calmly, "They don't run my life, Jenna."

Jenna went back to concentrating on her work. "Maybe not,

but they can sure do a heck of a lot to make us all miserable. I'm not going through that again, Jake. I'm not going to be made to feel like I'm not good enough simply because I don't come from some old-money background.''

Jake didn't want that for Jenna, either. In fact, he intended to do everything in his power to protect her from just such snobbery. Not that it mattered to him what people thought of what he did or did not do. ''Why do you care what others think about you?'' he asked curiously.

Jenna pushed away from the sewing table. She stalked past him with another lofty toss of her red-gold hair. ''I just do, okay?''

''No, it's not okay,'' Jake shot back, resenting her doom-and-gloom attitude. Achingly aware that the last thing he wanted to be doing with Jenna in their rare time alone was fighting, he closed the distance between them. ''Not,'' Jake continued sternly, looking down into her face, ''if it means you're going to let someone else come between us.''

Jenna whirled to face him. Her feet were planted slightly apart and her clear blue eyes were glittering. ''That's a funny thing for you to be accusing me of,'' she remarked silkily.

Jake drew a calming breath. ''I admit I let my parents pressure me into walking away from you before, but that's not going to happen again.''

Jenna regarded Jake thoughtfully, reminding him a little of a lioness on the warpath. ''Why not?'' she demanded.

''Because you're not underage,'' Jake answered, tearing his eyes from the snug fit of her sheath dress. ''And you're not in an emotionally vulnerable place. You're an adult with your own life now. And so am I. And so are your sisters.'' They didn't have to worry about any of the things they'd had to be concerned about before.

But once again, Jenna didn't see it that way. Sighing, she spun away from him in a drift of freesia perfume. ''There's a lot more to it than that, Jake.''

Jake clamped his hand on her shoulders and held her in

front of him when she would have run. "I don't care what my parents or anyone else thinks. I want to be with you, Jenna. That has never stopped. And it never will."

"Don't say it," she ordered, giving him a look that said if she had her way he would never ever get any closer to her than he was at that very minute.

"Why not?" Jake demanded gruffly, refusing to let anything, including her fear, drive them apart. "It's true."

"Jake—"

The next thing she knew their mouths were locked in a searing kiss. Holding her tightly, he continued until desire swept through her in dizzying waves, and she arched against him wantonly, no longer caring what common sense dictated, only caring that this never end. "You want to be with me, too, Jenna. I see it in your eyes. I feel it in your kiss."

Jake bent his head and kissed her again. The look in his eyes robbed her of breath. She had never seen such desire. "I don't want to be hurt again, Jake."

"I'm not going to hurt you, Jenna," Jake promised huskily, the vulnerability in his voice getting to her the way no smooth seduction technique ever could have. "I'm going to love you," he promised, brushing the hair from her face. "And you're going to love me. And this time no one, no one is going to come between us." Jake swept Jenna up into his arms and carried her upstairs to her apartment, not stopping until he had reached her bedroom and lowered her onto her bed.

"You say that now," Jenna protested, as he followed her down onto the bed and stretched out beside her.

"I'll say that the rest of my life." Jake's arms slid around her back. He brought her close so they were touching in one long, electrified line. "We should have had a wedding, Jenna. We should have had a wedding night. We should have made love." He framed her face with his hands and brought her head up to his.

"You don't think I've dreamed about that?" Jenna whispered as she trembled in his arms. "You don't think I've wanted that, too?"

Jake's gaze softened tenderly as he kissed her temple, her cheek, her lips. "I know you have. As much as I have."

"But it's not that simple," Jenna told him as her fears threatened to overtake her once again.

"It is that simple," Jake said firmly. "It's as simple as this kiss." He gently touched his lips to hers. "And this touch." He laid his hand against her breast, feeling the nipple bud beneath his palm. Again, he brushed his lips softly, insistently against hers. "It's as simple as the way you tremble, and the way I need you." He took her hand and pressed it against him, letting her feel the strength of his passion, the urgency of his need for her. "We let others keep us apart for a long time, Jenna," he said hoarsely as her hand closed around him, his warmth and hardness penetrating through the denim of his jeans. "Let's not let the mistakes we both made in the past, the hurts we suffered then, or the fear of what the future holds keep us apart now." His body trembling with the effort his restraint was costing him, he pulled her fractionally closer. "I want you. I love you. And I have always loved you, Jenna. Always," he said, meaning the words with all his heart and soul. He wove his hands through her hair and lowered his mouth to hers. "And I'm not going anywhere until you know it's true."

JENNA HADN'T EXPECTED any of this. Not his kisses, so hot and sweet and wild. Not his touches, so soft and gentle and urgent. And certainly not her own response.

She knew she wanted him. And had for a very, very long time, if the truth were told.

She hadn't expected her knees would go weak the moment she looked into his eyes and knew he intended to make love to her then and there. She hadn't expected the silky dampness between her thighs or the overwhelming warmth that coursed through her at the first touch of his hand on the uppermost curve of her breast. But she was trembling. She was quaking from head to toe as he slowly unbuttoned the back of her sheath, eased it over her shoulders, worked her arms free, and pushed it down so it fell around her waist. His eyes darkened as he took in the sensuous curves of her breasts, and the pink, jutting nipples, crowning against the transparent lace.

"I'm afraid," she whispered as he gently caressed the rounded curves, from base to tip, and back again. Over and over again, in a series of ever shrinking, ever more sensual circles.

"There's no need to be, Jenna." Jake's lips followed the path his fingertips had blazed, not stopping until his lips closed over the transparent lace and hot, aching crowns, one by one. "You will always be safe—and loved—with me," he whispered, the darkness of his hair nestled against her skin.

Jenna felt safe. And loved. Desired. Cherished. Even understood. But she had felt all those things before, only to have the rug pulled out from under her. "Jake—"

"Just trust me, Jenna. Trust me."

And as he bent to kiss her again, hotly, rapaciously, she did.

She might not know what the future held, but she knew about the present. She knew she wanted him more than life. She knew she loved the feel of his hands on her skin as he slipped off her dress and then her hose. She knew she had never felt anything more gentle than the touch of his hands on her skin as he caressed first the outsides, then the insides, of her thighs. She had waited so long for this. Too long. No more, she decided recklessly.

Jake's eyes darkened as he scanned her lovingly from head to toe, his eyes leisurely drinking in every inch of her. "You are so...beautiful."

She felt beautiful when he touched her and looked at her like that.

"So are you." Eager to see and feel more of him, Jenna unbuttoned the front of his shirt, spread the edges wide. His chest was broad, lightly suntanned and firmly muscled, and covered with a mat of thick velvety-soft hair.

Jenna ran her fingertips through it, loving the heat and satin-smoothness of his skin, the flatness of his stomach and the tautness of his flat male nipples.

Jake groaned as her hands swept lower still, to the waistband of his jeans. Pushing him back so he was lying on the bed, she knelt astride him. Clad only in lacey bikini panties and matching demi-cup bra, she unbuckled his belt and unzipped his jeans. Fingers trembling only slightly, she tugged off his boots, peeled off his jeans.

His legs were as firmly muscled and covered with enticing whorls of dark hair. But it was the hard ridge of arousal, visible beneath the plain white cotton of his briefs that caught her attention.

Jake caught her by the shoulders. The next thing she knew she was on her back. He was astride her. "I want this to be as wonderful as it can possibly be for you." Eyes dark with mischief and affection, he peeled off her bra. Dispensed with her panties. Kissed his way from breasts to tummy to thighs, then spread her legs wide. The next thing she knew his hands were beneath her, cupping her bottom, tugging her toward the edge of the bed.

He slipped to the floor and knelt in front of her, lips and tongue tasting the insides of first her knees, then her thighs. Higher still, until he found her, until she was arching off the bed. Moaning her pleasure, she gripped his shoulders, not sure whether she was trying to hold him at bay or bring him closer, only knowing she had never...ever done anything like this, felt anything like this. It felt so good to be wanted and touched. It felt so good to be held by him and against him. Desire trembled within her, making her go all soft and syrupy inside.

"That's it," Jake murmured as she whimpered and fell apart in his hands. "Let me love you the way you were meant to be loved by me."

And then he was joining her on the bed. Pushing her back, so she was lying across the bed. Shoving off his briefs, and draping his hot, virile form over her. Once again, his hands were beneath her, cupping her bottom and lifting her toward him, spreading her thighs. Her heart pounding, her body strung tight with anticipation, she expected him to enter her. Instead he pressed against her, poised to enter, and then he kissed her, until the world was spinning, her whole body quaking and yearning. "I want you, Jake." *Oh, how I want you.*

"Jenna…Jenna…I want you, too."

"Now?" Jenna's chest constricted, making it difficult to breathe.

"Now." Jake shifted her hips again, pushed inside.

Not easily, as she had hoped and he had seemingly expected, but slowly, with difficulty. Jake paused in midstroke, something akin to panic on his face. "Jenna?"

Not about to back out now, not when they'd come this far, Jenna kissed him hotly and rapaciously. "Deeper, Jake." Jenna tightened her arms about his neck and lifted her hips. "Go deeper," she pleaded, loving Jake the way she always had, with every fiber of her being. As he moved, so did she. The barrier was broken. Jenna felt a flash of pain, followed swiftly by a feeling of well-being. Then Jake was moving again, slowly, carefully, lovingly. Allowing her the time she needed to accommodate him. Taking her to new and wonderous heights. And when she urged him on, he followed, taking her with him, shattering her control even as he lost his.

"YOU DIDN'T TELL ME." Jake wrapped Jenna in his arms and buried his face in the fragrant softness of her hair.

Loving the way she felt in his arms, Jenna cuddled closer. "I didn't think you needed to know."

Jake's arms curved a little tighter around her bare shoulders. "That you were still a virgin?"

Jenna loved the way their naked bodies fit together beneath the sheets. "It wasn't for lack of trying to replace you in my life," she murmured, draping one of her slender, silky legs between his hair-roughened ones. "I...dated."

"But...?" Jake rubbed a hand up and down her spine.

Jenna traced patterns through the mat of hair on his chest. "When it came to more than kisses, it just never felt right." Her cheeks pinkened.

Jake sighed contentedly. "I know exactly what you mean. If it's not right, it's not worth it. I found that out quick enough. I only had to make that mistake once to realize it was not a mistake I was going to make again."

"You're saying...?" Jenna shifted her weight and rolled gracefully onto her stomach.

"Since my marriage ended, no one. In a lot of ways," he teased, waggling his eyebrows and exaggerating every syllable to comic effect, "I'm just as chaste as you are."

Jenna flushed with warmth as she propped her chin on her fist. He acted as if that were such a great thing. "You sure knew what you were doing just now," she teased.

"I've read up on the subject," Jake drawled, his voice sobering once again. "And dreamed. Of course, you were always the stars of all my dreams."

Looking into his eyes, Jenna believed that was so. It amazed her to find Jake had waited for her, almost the same way she had waited for him. Although maybe that shouldn't have surprised her, she realized slowly. Jake was the kind of guy who never had been willing to settle for second best when he could have the ultimate by just waiting. As far as Jake—and she—were concerned, the two of them together were the ultimate couple.

Jenna traced Jake's lower lip with her fingertip. "Why did it take you so long to come after me?"

Regret flashed in Jake's silver-gray eyes. "I convinced myself there was no going back, that you were better off without me. I felt I'd already hurt you enough."

Jake looked over at her. When their glances meshed, Jenna

saw the tenderness in his face, the love, and knew it was true. "What changed your mind?" she asked on a trembling breath.

"Seeing you on TV, being interviewed," Jake confided, his voice dropping another rough, husky notch. He shifted her onto her back and rolled so he was on his stomach next to her, looking down at her. He framed her face with his hands. "And finding out you were every bit as alone as I was."

Jenna's brows knit together. They hadn't said anything about her love life in any of the TV interviews she had done—she hadn't allowed it. "How did you—?"

Jake smiled and sifted his hands through her hair. "Lilah and John McCabe. I got in touch with them when I decided to move back to Laramie. I wanted a recommendation for a pediatrician for Alexandra. While they were giving me their new daughter-in-law's name, they also mentioned that you were just as lovely and sought-after as you had always been. Only problem was, you weren't interested in other men, and hadn't been since we broke up."

Jenna flushed, groaned and comically covered her eyes with her hand. Sighing her exasperation loudly, she dropped her hand and looked back at Jake. "I should have known that's what happened. Since all four of John and Lilah McCabe's sons got married, everyone in this town has had wedding fever. And everyone's gotten it into their heads that all four of us Lockhart girls should be next."

"Can't say I disagree with that," Jake grinned, as he bent to kiss the nape of her neck. "Especially since you waited for me all this time."

Jenna aimed a playful punch at his chest. She didn't want Jake thinking she was that ridiculously romantic because the truth was, she had lost all her starry-eyed naiveté long ago. "I did not do that." After the first…oh, three or four years, she hadn't held out any hope at all Jake would ever come after her again.

Jake grinned and shifted so he was on his back and she was draped over top of him once again. "Say what you want,

Jenna,'' he chided, the heat in his eyes telegraphing his intention to make her his all over again. "But the simple truth of the matter is you waited for me all this time." He rubbed his hands lazily up and down her spine. "You saved yourself for me. And I'm going to make sure you are never sorry you did."

Ignoring the tingles of awareness shimmering through her, Jenna pushed away from him and sat up. As much as she loved making love with Jake, she didn't want to go back to being the naive teenager she had been. She didn't ever want to be blindsided like that again, and the only way to insure against that was to keep their relationship in perspective and not have any unrealistic expectations about what the future held for them—the way they had done before.

Jenna sat up against the headboard and brought the sheet up to cover her breasts. She shoved the tousled layers of her hair off her face. "It's not simple, Jake. It is never that simple, especially between you and me. I agree, this lovemaking was probably fated. We always intended to make love—we just didn't get married to do it. But to translate these few hours of passion into something else, something permanent or lifelong, when all the old problems still exist, plus a few more new ones to boot..." Misery and fear rushed in. Jenna shook her head.

Jake sat up, too, but let the sheet fall past his waist. He rested an elbow against his raised knee. "I know my life is a mess right now, with Melinda back on the scene. But she won't always be here," he promised.

Jenna did not share his confidence. Jenna turned away. "And what if she is?" she asked wearily.

"Then we'll deal with it," Jake said quietly, taking her hand.

Jenna turned back and searched his eyes. "Will we?"

"Yes." Jake tightened his fingers over hers. "We will," he insisted stubbornly. A gentle, loving smile spread slowly across his face. His eyes glimmered with a sexy light. "In the meantime, the old sparks between us are still there, Jenna. I feel them in here." Jake took Jenna's hand and laid it over his heart. "And I know from the way you kiss me back that you feel them, too."

"I don't deny there's a very, very potent physical chemistry between us," Jenna allowed reluctantly, as the heat of his skin and the thudding of his heart were transmitted through her splayed fingertips. "It'll probably always be there, but—"

Jake shifted Jenna onto his lap. "It's more than physical chemistry, Jenna." Jake paused and looked deep into her eyes, the desire he felt for her as potent an aphrodisiac as the way he held her closer. "What we have is something special. Something that comes along maybe once in a lifetime. If you're lucky. We're lucky." His lips moved down her neck, eliciting tingles of fire everywhere they touched. "We've found each other again. And this time, I'm not ever letting you go."

Tears filled Jenna's eyes even as she hardened her heart against him. "I know you want it to be the way it was. So do I. But we can't go back to the way things were, Jake." She shook her head miserably, determined to be practical even when he was not. "Too much has happened. Too much has changed." She looked at him steadily. "Our lives are even more complicated now." And he was moving too fast. Expecting too much.

"Then let's go forward," Jake said softly, not the least bit discouraged. He shifted again, moving Jenna off his lap and onto her back. Then, stretched out beside her, he draped her with his warmth and his strength. "Let's pick up where we left off, deal with all the changes, and just go forward."

Jenna turned her head away from him. "You can't make something happen just by wanting it, Jake. It may work for you, but it doesn't for me."

Jake gave her a sexy half smile, even as his eyes glimmered with annoyance. "*Only* because you don't want it enough."

Stung, because he just might be right, Jenna shoved him away and shot back, just as fiercely, "You don't just get to do something like this over, Jake. There are no do-overs in this life. Especially do-overs of this magnitude.'' She vaulted from the bed and reached for her robe.

''Guess you're right about that,'' Jake stated, coming after her lazily.

''I am,'' Jenna repeated, just as firmly, as she slipped her robe on and belted it tightly at her waist.

''And that being the case,'' Jake said, ignoring Jenna's warning look as he took her resisting body back in his arms and slowly, surely lowered his head to hers to deliver another long, breath-stealing kiss. ''I reckon we'll just have to plunge on ahead.'' And plunge on ahead he did.

Chapter Six

"As much as I hate to say it, we better get a move on if we want to be on time to pick up Alexandra over at Meg's," Jake said as they finished off the pizza and salad he had brought for their dinner.

Still in her robe and nothing else, Jenna stood and carried her dishes over to the sink. Jake followed gallantly, his dishes in hand, too.

Like Jenna, he was still glowing from their second round of lovemaking. Which had been, to Jenna's amazement, even more tender and incredibly arousing and satisfying than the first. For years now, she had channeled all her passion into her work. Tonight, she had channeled it into her relationship with him. She was both amazed and a little unnerved at how good that felt. She hadn't expected to fall in love with him all over again, yet that was exactly what was happening. To them both.

Nevertheless, at least one of them needed to be sensible and she guessed, from the ardent look in his eyes, it was going to have to be her.

Ignoring how sexy Jake looked in jeans and bare feet, his shirt open to the waist, Jenna slid her dishes into the dishwasher. She straightened, looked him straight in the eye. Calling on every inch of practicality she possessed, Jenna told him softly, "I know what you want, but…I'm not going back to the ranch with you tonight."

She held up a hand before a frowning Jake could interrupt. "And don't give me that look," Jenna continued sternly, knowing she had every right to want some time to herself after all that had happened tonight. Tightening her robe around her, she padded barefoot back to the bedroom, gathering up their discarded clothes as she went.

Jenna thrust Jake's socks and boots at him, then watched as he sat down on the mussed covers of her bed to put them on. "Buster and Miss Kitty are sufficiently settled in for you to manage them on your own. Nor are you in need of any kind of chaperone or buffer tonight, since Clara will be there to sleep and Melinda will not. Besides—" Jenna sighed as she hunted around for her slippers. "I have to be here early tomorrow to open the shop. And I need to get more done on Alex's new wardrobe." Steadying herself by curling a hand around Jake's biceps, she slid her feet into her ballet-style terry-cloth slippers, one at a time. Finished, she looked up at him, wishing he didn't look and smell so darn sexy. "For some reason," Jenna said. "I don't seem to get a lot of work done when you're around."

Jake smiled, and when she removed her hand from his arm, he caught it and brought it up to his lips. "You're saying I'm a distraction?" He kissed the back of her hand tenderly.

A mixture of longing and satisfaction shimmered through her. "So much so I think it's best if I sleep at my apartment tonight." She needed time to consider what she was really getting herself into here, and prepare for what was coming next.

Jake studied her, sensing there was more she was deliberately not saying. "You want to meet with my mother tomorrow morning, don't you?" He preferred she skip it. At the very least, put it off indefinitely.

Jenna sighed with a weariness and trepidation that cut clear through to her soul. "I admit I want to hear what Patricia has to say." Again, Jake appeared about to object. And again, Jenna put up a hand to stop him. "I have to know what I'm dealing with." She had to find out what his parents were thinking and feeling before she and Jake got any more involved.

"Then let me be here when you do talk to her," Jake said softly, taking her tense body in his arms.

Jenna shook her head, even as she rested her forehead against the solid warmth of his shoulder. "No. I have to handle her alone." Jenna looked up into his eyes. "I can't hide behind you, Jake. Not anymore. If this is going to work—at all—on any level, I've got to be able to stand up to your mother and anyone else who might not want us to be together."

Much as she could see he wanted to, Jake could not argue with that. "Alex will be disappointed," he said eventually.

"I'll see her later tomorrow. She's got to have a fitting for her alphabet dress, anyway. In the meantime," Jenna reminded as she buttoned his shirt for him and watched him tuck it into the waistband of his jeans, "you've got to go."

Aligning his length intimately with hers and cuddling her close, he kissed her brow, her temple, her cheek. "Just as soon," he said softly, pressing a hand to her spine, urging her closer, until her breasts were nestled against his chest, "as I steal one last kiss." And then his lips touched hers and he kissed her as she had never been kissed before, until the world fell away, and she felt that everything really was going to be all right.

"THANKS FOR SEEING ME on such short notice," Kate Marten said as she breezed into Jenna's shop at eight-thirty sharp the next morning.

"No problem." Jenna smiled at her old friend. "I hear you've got an Air Force hero coming home on leave next month."

"Actually, I think the whole town of Laramie has a hero coming home," Kate corrected with a slightly beleaguered smile. "Which is why we're spending the first night of Craig's leave alone, at a posh hotel in Dallas. We want to have some time to get reacquainted before we come back to Laramie and the welcome-home party my folks are throwing for Craig.''

"Smart move," Jenna said as she pulled out her tape measure, pad and pen.

"And romantic, I hope. Which is where the knockout dress comes in. When Craig steps off that plane I want to be wearing something that will really get his engines going, if you know what I mean.''

Jenna grinned. "I do indeed and I think I can manage that. Let's take a look at colors and fabrics and I'll show you some basic styles." Thirty minutes later they'd settled on a design that both Jenna and Kate Marten were sure would knock the major's socks off. Kate scheduled an appointment for a fitting in a couple of weeks and told Jenna she'd be in to look at wedding dresses as soon as they knew precisely when and where the wedding would be.

Kate thanked Jenna again and took off for her job at the hospital just minutes before the Remington limo pulled in at the curb.

Jenna watched as Patricia and Melinda emerged. Both were dressed to the nines in beautiful business suits and Italian leather shoes. Matching bags and expensive, elegantly understated jewelry completed their ensembles.

Squaring her shoulders for what appeared to be a surprise double whammy, Jenna went to greet them and usher them inside. Obviously they couldn't wait to do battle with her. Hence they might as well get it over with, Jenna thought as she summoned up a smile and put on her "game face." "Mrs. Remington. Melinda. How nice to have you both here," she said. For Jake's sake, she made sure she was extra-cordial. "Can I get you some coffee or tea?"

"That won't be necessary, Jenna, thank you. I'll get straight to the point." Ignoring Jenna's wish they sit comfortably on the sofa in her shop, Mrs. Remington and Melinda remained standing amid the wedding gowns and evenings dresses on display. "I think that it's best that you end this...fantasy that you and my son might someday pick up where you left off the night the two of you tried to elope."

Too late, Mrs. R. We already have, Jenna thought acerbically.

"The two of you are clearly from two different worlds," Patricia Remington continued gently but firmly.

"Not that Jake would ever be so uncouth as to point that out," Melinda added with an I'm-just-trying-to-be-helpful smile.

Patricia Remington sent a quelling look at her former daughter-in-law, then turned back to Jenna. "I wouldn't want to see you hurt again," Patricia said kindly.

"I don't want that, either, for either Jake or me," Jenna said.

"Good. Then we're on the same page," Patricia noted with relief.

Jenna studied Jake's mother. Much as Jenna was loath to admit it, Patricia did seem to have only Jenna's—and Jake's—best interests at heart. "Jake and I are going to be business partners," Jenna said eventually, figuring as long as Mrs. Remington was here they might as well get all their cards out on the table. "Did you know that?"

Worry lit Patricia's gray eyes. "I'd heard rumors to that effect," she said quietly. "I had hoped they were not true."

"Well, they are," Jenna said as the phone began to ring.

Jenna went to get it and quickly discovered the call was not for her. Covering the receiver with her hand, she turned to Melinda. "The personal secretary of a Count Something-or-Other is on the phone from Italy. He says the count would like to speak with you."

"It's Count della Gherardesca," Melinda said with a bored sigh and a steely look. "And you can tell him I said to forget it. Our relationship is over. I'm not coming back. I'm going to stay right here in Texas and concentrate on my daughter and getting to know my ex-husband again. And furthermore, the count knows that very well, as I made it very clear where we stood when I left Italy!''

Nerves jangling at the knowledge that Melinda indeed wanted Jake—and Alex—back in her life again, Jenna relayed the message. Listened again as that message was relayed and another sent forward again. ''The secretary says the count insists.''

An irritated look on her face, Melinda stalked over, took the phone and hung it up loudly in the cradle. ''There. That ought to take care of that. Now, where were we?''

''I think we've said everything there is to say.'' Jenna gave both women a look that let them know this meeting was over, then went to the door and opened it.

Patricia Remington looked at Jenna steadily. ''I'm not just thinking of you and Jake. I'm thinking of Melinda and Alex, too. For the first time in years, Jake has a chance to make his family whole again. I don't want him to let this opportunity pass him by, only to regret it later.''

Guilt and uncertainty flooded Jenna. She didn't want to stand in the way of Jake's happiness, either. It was obvious, at least to Jenna and to Jake, that Melinda was not and never had been the right woman for him. It was also obvious that Melinda resented and looked down on Jenna, and that Jenna's presence would likely cause problems for Jake—and perhaps Alex, too—as long as Melinda was around.

Her shoulders knotted with tension, Jenna held the door open. ''I appreciate your stopping by.'' The way she said it gave them no choice but to leave.

''Well, I never!'' Melinda fumed with a toss of her head as she stalked out.

''I'm sorry, Jenna,'' Jake's mother said. ''For everyone's sake, I felt obliged to let you know how Jake's father and I feel.''

''Well, you've done that, all right,'' Jenna shot back, just as honestly.

And it hurt, knowing Jake's parents wanted him back with

his ex-wife, both for Alex's sake and because they found Melinda more socially acceptable.

Jenna watched Patricia join her former daughter-in-law at the car. Jenna stayed at the window until the sleek black limo pulled away from the curb. With a sigh, Jenna turned and headed for the back of the boutique. She'd barely reached the storeroom when she realized she was not alone.

Her sister, Dani, and her brand-new husband, Beau Chamberlain, were standing there. Jenna had only to look at the distressed and worried looks on their faces to realize what had happened. "You heard that, didn't you?"

"Sorry." Beau said. "But we were across the street and saw them arrive. We didn't know whether you needed help or not, but we thought we would slip in the back and ride to your rescue just in case."

"Fortunately, you seemed to handle them just fine," Dani added.

"Mrs. Remington doesn't scare me the way she used to," Jenna said. In fact, she was beginning to feel a little sorry for Patricia Remington—she was so out of touch with her son. And yet she clearly loved Jake, and wanted only the best for him and Alex. Patricia was just wrong about what was best.

"As well she shouldn't," Beau interjected, protecting Jenna as fiercely as if he had been a part of their family since day one, instead of for just a few weeks.

Dani shook her head. "When I remember what Mrs. Remington said about you—"

Beau lifted a curious brow, prompting Jenna to illuminate, "Patricia and Danforth Remington were very upset when they found out Jake and I had been seeing each other for years, without their knowledge. Or approval." Jenna drew a breath, recalling how hurt and angry Jake's parents had been the night it had all come to an end. "They told Jake I was a social-climbing gold digger, that I was just using him to create a better life for myself."

"Only thing is, we Lockharts never cared a hoot about belonging to high society, and we were never poor,'' Dani said. ''At least not in any way that counted. Mom and Dad worked very hard to provide for us.''

''They just didn't count on a devastating tornado,'' Jenna said sadly, remembering how hard things had been for them financially after their parents' death. The ranch had still been heavily mortgaged. There were debts. Funeral expenses. The expenses of selling the ranch and moving into a much smaller place while saving every penny possible for the continuing education of them all. It hadn't been easy for Jenna or her sisters.

But not wanting to talk about that, or think about how little Mr. and Mrs. Remington really knew about her, Jenna turned to Beau and said, ''I saw your new movie, *Bravo Canyon.* And I hear it's still at number one for the third week in a row. That must feel pretty good.''

''It does.'' Beau grinned. He wrapped his arm around Dani's shoulders. ''But not as good as being married and having a baby on the way.''

They looked so much in love. Jenna couldn't help but be happy for them. ''So, how was the honeymoon? Or do I even have to ask?'' she said, taking in their glowing faces.

''It was romantic,'' Dani said with a heartfelt sigh.

''Very romantic.'' Jake smiled and kissed the top of Dani's head.

''Not that it's over yet,'' Dani continued.

''No.'' Beau wrapped his arms around his wife, bent her backward from the waist, and kissed her long and deep. ''We plan to keep this one going for a very long time.''

Dani sighed and wrapped her arms around Beau's neck and kissed him back. ''Infinity, even,'' she murmured dreamily.

''Stop!'' Jenna said. ''You two are making me jealous.''

''Really.'' Dani studied Jenna as Beau slowly set her on her feet once again. Dani teased, ''I could have sworn your cheeks had a telltale blush in them, too, when Jake's name came up.''

''But it hasn't come up,'' Jenna protested.

"It just did." Dani pinned her with a *gotcha!* look. "And see—you're blushing!"

Jenna rolled her eyes. "Only because you've embarrassed me."

Dani paused. "So you're not seeing him again, aside from business."

"Actually," Jenna hedged after a moment, "I am."

Silence fell between them. "Are you sure you know what you're doing?" Dani asked after a moment, concern in her eyes. "I don't want Jake to break your heart again."

Neither do I, Jenna thought. And yet there was no doubt she still loved him. No doubt, either, that the problems that existed back then still remained. If that wasn't a recipe for disaster, Jenna thought miserably, she didn't know what was.

"I remember the way he ditched you the last time when there was trouble with his family." Dani helped herself to some of the coffee Jenna had prepared for Jake's mother, then poured a cup for Beau, too.

"He's not going to do that again," Jenna said.

"He'd better not," Dani warned darkly as she stirred cream and sugar into hers. She lifted her cup to her lips. "Or he'll have the Lockharts and everyone else in Laramie to contend with."

"No, no, no, no! I am not wearing a dress!" Alexandra stamped her foot in the middle of Jenna's shop, several hours later. "I don't care how pretty it is! I hate dresses. I hate them all."

Clara, Jake and Jenna exchanged baffled looks. Alex was so worked up, and had been even before she got to the shop, that there was no calming her down now.

"Maybe we should take a break and go over to the hospital to see Nathan James for a few minutes," Clara suggested, clearly as much at a loss as how to fix this situation as Jake and Jenna. "And worry about your fitting later."

"Good idea," Jake said. He shot Clara a grateful look. "I'll be over in about twenty minutes to get her."

"Take your time," Clara said meaningfully. "I know you two have things to discuss." She and Alex exited the shop.

"What happened this morning?" Jenna said as soon as Clara and Alex had left. She hadn't seen Alex this upset since the first day she had come in to her shop.

Jake took his hat off and set it on the sales counter at the rear of the showroom. "Melinda came by with a whole carload of dresses that she bought in Dallas, all of them so frilly and expensive it's ridiculous. She and my mother came in and showed them to Alex, who was pretty overwhelmed just looking at them. I left for a couple of minutes—I had to put Buster in his crate and Miss Kitty in the laundry room, neither Melinda nor my mother are fond of animals of any kind—and when I came back Alex was in a full-fledged temper tantrum."

"And let me guess. *I* got blamed for it," Jenna said, wondering what was going to come next.

"Maybe initially." Jake closed the distance between them with easy, sensual grace. "But it quickly became clear, even to my mother, that the problem was really Melinda. Alex is— well, there's no other way to say it—she's afraid of Melinda."

Jenna drew a bracing breath and tried to still her racing heart. "I thought you said she barely remembers Melinda."

"Which is probably the problem." Jake sighed and shoved a hand through his hair. "Melinda storms in, acts all motherly and demands immediate, daughterly devotion in return. But Alex has spent very little time with Melinda over the years, so it's no wonder she feels threatened."

Given all they had going against them, Jenna had been determined to start regarding Jake with an unbiased, unsentimental view. It was easier said than done when he was standing in front of her, clean shaven and smelling of soap and man and his woodsy cologne, his inky-black hair agreeably tousled, his handsome face flushed with the heat of the Texas sun. "What are you going to do about it?"

Jake released a long breath and lounged against the counter. "What I would like to do is take it nice and slow. Get the two of them to get to know each other in a relaxed setting. See if we could get some kind of relationship going between them for both their sakes. Unfortunately, my idea of a relaxed setting and Melinda's are far from the same." His gray eyes radiated worry. "My parents think the way to fix everything is to bring Melinda back into the family as quickly and completely as possible. So they're hosting a welcome-back party for Melinda. They expect Alex to attend. It's a very dressy, catered affair, complete with a band for dancing. Right now the guest list is at five hundred, but they think they may expand it to include a lot of the prominent locals as well as their many business acquaintances and friends from all over the state."

Jenna's heart went out to Alex, just thinking how the nearly six-year-old child would react to such a glamorous, high-pressure, intensely social affair. No way was Alex ready for this. "And this will be where—in Dallas?"

His eyes never leaving hers, Jake shook his head and confided unhappily, "My parents are now back at their summer ranch indefinitely, I suspect at Melinda's behest. The party will be there."

A feeling of déjà vu swept over Jenna as she recalled another party—the only party she had ever attended with Jake—at his parents' summer ranch, shortly before their failed elopement. She had never felt so ill at ease or out of place. Mr. and Mrs. Remington had known it and, angry about Jake's insistence that Jenna attend as his guest, had purposefully done little to make her feel at home. Rather, they'd made sure she knew she didn't fit in with their family and friends. At seventeen, it had been a miserable experience she had never wanted to repeat.

He paused, seeming to know exactly what she was remembering, how his own efforts that night to put her at ease had failed, which had then led to their decision to just say the heck with it and elope. His eyes still holding hers, he went on in a gruff, unhappy voice, "It gets better. They've invited me, too, of course. And you."

A trickle of unease slid down Jenna's spine. "Me—or a date?" Jenna asked in a low, deeply cynical voice.

"My folks said I should bring a date. And it was all right if it was you. Meanwhile, they have invited Melinda to bunk with them and she's agreed, probably because they have a much more luxurious place in Laramie and a full staff of servants."

Sensing this was all some sort of trick, Jenna went to the storeroom and began gathering up her dressmaker's dummy, and several hatboxes. "When is this party?" she asked, knowing if they were going to accomplish anything they had to get busy.

"Tomorrow night." Jake leaned against the sales counter, his legs spread slightly, his hands braced on either side of him. He looked her up and down, then settled on her eyes. "I know I shouldn't be asking you this, but I really need your help. Clara is going home with her son-in-law tonight. She's going to get the house ready for when the baby and her daughter come home from the hospital tomorrow morning. I told her not to worry about us, to take a few days and just spend it with her daughter's family, and she agreed. Meantime, I've got to give Alex a crash course in young-ladylike behavior and figure out some way to get her into a dress for that party. Preferably one that Melinda bought for her."

Her lips pressed together thoughtfully, Jenna went back to the fabric room to get her portable sewing machine, a bag of cotton stuffing, several shades of green, red and brown velveteen and matching thread. She had a plan to get Alex to cooperate. She wasn't sure it would work. But it was better than nothing. And if there was any way she could help the little girl, she would. "And if you don't?" Jenna asked.

"Then it's almost a certainty, the way things are going now, that Melinda will try to get at least partial custody of Alex."

"Surely the court wouldn't grant such a motion," Jenna said.

Jake looked at Jenna soberly as he explained, "Whenever possible, the court feels it's better for a child to have ample contact with both parents. The judge who heard the case initially felt Melinda gave up her right to joint custody too quickly. So if Melinda were to go in now and put on a good show of being concerned and express her regret over her neglect, the court could very well decide to change the terms of our current custody agreement and give Melinda a second chance to be the mother Alex needs and wants." Jake paused, the worry in his eyes increasing. "I don't want the court involved if this is something Melinda and I can handle ourselves. And I certainly don't want Alexandra to have to go to court to testify. That would be far too traumatic."

Jenna considered Jake for a moment. His irritation with the situation aside, he seemed awfully confident. "You don't expect Melinda's interest in Alex to last, do you?"

Jake shrugged. "Experience tells me it won't."

As much as Jenna wanted to, she couldn't figure out Jake's ex-wife. *Not at all.* To her dismay, she sensed Jake was just as baffled by Melinda's actions. "Did Melinda make any other arrangements to see Alexandra again?"

"No." Jake shook his head wearily. "She said she would just see her at the party tomorrow night."

"Is she upset about the way Alex is reacting to her?"

Jake frowned. "Not in the deeply heartfelt way you'd expect from a mother who's threatening to sue for custody. There's certainly some surface annoyance, which you've seen for yourself. It's embarrassing to have a daughter who doesn't want anything to do with you. But other than that…" Jake's voice trailed off in confusion.

"Your mother indicated that Melinda is hoping to make you, Alex and her a family again."

Jake nodded. "I know that's what Melinda is telling them, but I don't buy it, not for a second," he said flatly.

Jenna quirked a brow. "We really tried to make our marriage work," he continued, "but without any real chemistry, well…it was pretty awkward and empty. I think, deep down, she was as disappointed as I was. She'd been looking for her Prince Charming, someone who would give her this fabulous, glamorous, jet-setting life. She married me, thinking I was it, then found out she'd married a workaholic homebody who had zero interest in living life in the fast lane. She wasn't very happy, and neither was I. Although in our defense we really did try that first year. For Alex's sake, we wanted and needed the marriage to work."

"But it didn't."

"No. Melinda found she had even less aptitude for motherhood than she did for being my wife, and she was supremely disappointed that our life together was not going to be some fairy tale romance. So she began to shop—incessantly—and when that failed to satisfy her, she began to cheat. When I found out, and it didn't take me long because she was being so indiscreet, it was over. I couldn't be married to anyone who was that disloyal to me and our relationship."

Jenna could understand Jake's hurt and disgust. She, too, was the kind of person who demanded absolute fidelity and loyalty from a mate. But she could also see why a woman like Melinda—who needed to be adored and admired—would look outside the marriage if she couldn't get what she needed within it. Jenna shrugged. "Maybe Melinda didn't really mean for it to go that far. Maybe she was just retaliating, trying to get your attention. Maybe that's why she's back now. Maybe she wants to start over, and just doesn't know how to go about it, except through Alex."

"With any other woman, I'd agree that was probably the case," Jake said, his gaze settling on Jenna's face. "But that's not Melinda. She's mercurial. She doesn't hold anything back. She's propelled by her emotions. Lives totally in the moment. And she's very impulsive, to the point of reckless self-indulgence. If it were really me she wanted, she'd still be staying at my place and she'd have already tried to seduce me." He shook his head in obvious bafflement as he tried to work the puzzle out. "She wants something here; I know it. But it's not me, and it may not even be Alex."

"Money?" Jenna guessed.

Again, Jake shook his head. "I've already made some phone calls, done some discreet checking. She's been investing very shrewdly for a number of years now. She's still got plenty of money, mine and her own. More than even she can spend."

"Social status, then?" Something was driving Melinda. Making her suddenly want to be in the thick of things here again.

Jake shrugged. "She's been living in Europe for the past four years, dating some Italian count on and off for the last two. Jet-setting all over Europe. Hobnobbing with royalty. Blue-blooded as it was, her previous life in Texas never compared with that on the excitement scale, so I can't believe she wants it back."

"Then what?" Jenna demanded, her frustration mounting at a pace with Jake's.

Jake lifted his hands helplessly. "I don't know. But there's something to be gained from her presence here, from her going after Alex this way," Jake said flatly. "That I can guarantee."

"We just don't know what it is," Jenna said.

"But we'll find out," Jake predicted, his expression growing more worried still. "Probably before the end of the week."

"YOU ABOUT READY?" Jenna asked Alex that afternoon.

Alex studied herself in the full-length mirror they had dragged into the playroom. She was wearing her usual overalls and a T-shirt, over which she had wrapped a length of pretty rose fabric toga-style from shoulder to floor. She had on a pair of Jenna's high heels, three necklaces, two bracelets and some clip-on teardrop earrings. "I can't decide which hat to wear." Alex turned her head this way and that, studying the full-brimmed straw garden hat, trimmed with bright blue silk flowers. Then exchanged it for a safari hat with a leopard print band. "Should I wear this one?" she asked, admiring herself with a grin. "Or the other one?"

"Whichever one you like," Jenna said cheerfully. She had on a long sapphire blue flapper dress, a fringed silk purple-and-pink-paisley shawl, a lady Stetson and dark green leather cowgirl boots, more suitable for ranching than an indoor tea party. She'd brushed her hair out and it fell over her shoulders in untamed waves. A heavy gold pendant swung between her breasts, and big bold hoops dangled from her ears.

"I think I'll wear the one with the flowers," Alex decided, confirming Jenna's hunch that Alex really did like girly things. She just didn't like admitting it. Maybe because Melinda did? Was it possible Alex was just being perverse here? Or was there something more to her stubbornness?

Jenna went back to the table set with real china and silver and co-ordinating linen tablecloth and napkins. Jenna had taken a quick turn in the ranch-house kitchen while Jake and Alex had seen to Buster and Miss Kitty. Her efforts had provided them with heart-shaped tea sandwiches, red and green grapes, and tea sets containing both real tea for the grown-ups and fruit juice for Alex. Pastel petits fours and flaky cheese straws from Isabel Buchanon's bakery completed the repast.

Now all they lacked was Jake, who had gone off to the master bedroom to dress and await his summons.

Alex settled her flower-hat on her head and put the safari one aside. "Should I call Daddy?"

Jenna nodded as she went down the line, situating their other guests. "Now, remember. He doesn't know much about tea parties in general, being a guy and all. So it's up to us to teach him some company manners. We wouldn't want to embarrass Miss Teddy and Mr. Panda and all the other folks now, would we?"

Alex giggled, getting into the spirit.

"This is going to be funny," she said. She clomped over

to the playroom doorway, being careful to keep Jenna's high heels on her feet. "Daddy!" Alex called. "It's time for our tea party!"

"Coming, ladies!" Jake called back.

Seconds later he charged in, acting like a five year old in a hurry and practically tripping over his feet in his haste. Seeing him, it was all Jenna could do not to laugh. He had exchanged his usual jeans for a pair of black tuxedo pants and his crisp shirt for a form-fitting, dove-gray T-shirt. Instead of wearing the tuxedo jacket, he had opted for a brown suede sport coat, and put his black satin bow tie around his neck. Two-tone Western boots and a top hat Jenna had brought over from the shop completed his ensemble. He hitched up a chair, and rubbing his hands enthusiastically, looped a leg over the top of the child-sized chair and prepared to sit down. "Great-looking grub, gals. Let's eat!"

"Whoa, whoa, whoa!" Jenna said, stopping him before his bottom could make contact with the seat. "You haven't met our guests yet, Jake. You have to come and say hello to everyone before we eat. And while we're at it, you need to make a better, more dignified entrance."

Jake scowled comically, which made Alex laugh, then stomped over to the door. He sighed, slumped his shoulders dramatically and skulked in slowly and with a lamentable lack of confidence. He hurried up as soon as he reached the table. He rubbed his hands together once again, "Hi, guys." He waved haphazardly at the stuffed animals. "Now let's eat!"

Jenna rolled her eyes and pretended to be aghast. "Jake!" she chided. "Surely you can do better than that."

Jake did not look confident. "You'll have to show me."

Jenna sighed. She went over to the door and stepped in graciously. Her head held high she glided across the room with quiet confidence, and then—when Jake continued to look a little confused—turned to Alex. "Maybe you should show him, too," Jenna suggested.

Alex went over to the door and carefully copied Jenna's

entrance. "See what a wonderful job she did?" Jenna said, praising Alex warmly. "Now that's a nice party entrance." Alex beamed at Jenna's praise.

"Okay, now let's eat!" Jake said, rubbing his hands together once again.

"Ah-ah-ah!" Jenna and Alex both moved to stop him before he could sit. "You've got to meet the guests first."

Jake sighed and thrust out his lower lip. "Do I hafta?" he complained.

Jenna and Alex nodded solemnly. "Miss Teddy and Mr. Panda's feelings, not to mention Mr. Zebra's feelings, will be very hurt if you don't greet them properly."

Jake shot Alex a look, hoping to get out of it, only to find she agreed with Jenna. "Daddy, my animals have feelings, too," Alex reminded Jake solemnly.

"Okay," Jake conceded somewhat reluctantly, sliding his lower lip out again in a childish pout. He sighed dramatically, slumped his shoulders comically and stuck his hands in the pockets of his pants. "I guess I can be polite."

"That's the spirit!" Jenna said. With Alex's help, Jenna demonstrated how to get through an introduction. Once again, Jake goofed up at every turn, but with Jenna and Alex's tutoring he finally got it right, meeting all her animals one by one.

Alex and Jenna clapped energetically when he was finished. "Now we can eat," Jenna said.

"But you gotta use your napkin, Daddy, and say please and thank you," Alex warned as Jake held out her chair and she slid into it. "This is a tea party, after all, so we gotta use all our table manners."

"Yes, ma'am." Jake tapped two fingers against the brim of his top hat in a dutiful salute. He helped Jenna sit, too, before joining them at the child-sized table. "I sure am glad I've got you two ladies to help make a gentleman out of me," Jake confided seriously.

Alex studied Jake, just as solemnly. "That's okay, Daddy, you learn quick."

If only, Jenna thought, all their problems were so easily fixed.

THEY HAD JUST carried the tea-party dishes downstairs to the kitchen when the phone rang. Still glowing from the success of their tea-party etiquette lesson, Jake picked up the phone. "Hi, Meg. How are you?" He listened intently. "I don't know. I'll ask." He pressed the receiver against his shoulder and turned to Alex. "Jeremy's mom said Jeremy can have a sleepover tonight and he wants you to come. Have supper. Go see the new Disney movie with the two of them. And then spend the night. What do you think? You don't have to if you don't want to."

Alex grinned at Jake as if he were being ridiculous and said quickly, "I want to."

Jake hunkered down so he and Alex were at eye level. "You're sure? You've never done this before. Spent the night elsewhere. I mean, except for Grandma and Grandpa's, and that's really not the same because—"

"Daddy, I'll be fine," Alex interrupted, rolling her eyes. She tugged on his sleeve. "Tell Jeremy's mom that I can come, 'kay?"

"You sure this won't make you too tired? You still have to go to the party at Grandma and Grandpa's ranch tomorrow night."

"I'll be fine!"

Reluctantly, Jake put the receiver back against his ear. "Meg, Alex wants to come. What time do you need her there? Does she need to bring a sleeping bag? See you soon." He hung up. "Jeremy has twin beds in his room."

Alex beamed her excitement. "I know, and they're both shaped like race cars. They're really neat. Don't worry, Daddy. It's going to be fun. Jeremy's really nice and so is his mom."

They'd certainly won Alex's heart, Jake thought. "I'll help you pack a bag."

Half an hour later, after numerous emotional goodbyes to Buster and Miss Kitty, Alex was ready to go. Jenna and Jake drove her into town and over to Meg's. "If you change your mind and want to come home, you can call me at any time," Jake said as he knelt to kiss Alex goodbye.

"Okay, Daddy, but I won't want to." Alex gave Jake one last hug, then ran off with Jeremy to the toy car and truck village he had already set up in the living room.

"First time for an overnight?" Meg asked, sizing up Jake.

Jake ran the flat of his hand along his jaw, said ruefully, "I guess it shows?"

"A little," Meg grinned, commiserating, one single parent to another. "You can call her here anytime and see how she's doing if it will make you feel any better."

"Thanks." Jake smiled, relieved. "I just might take you up on that."

Meg walked them to the door. "The two of you can also come over for Saturday-morning brunch tomorrow, with the kids. Say around ten? Dani and Beau and Kelsey are supposed to be here, too."

"Sounds good," Jake nodded. If he was going to be close to Jenna, he needed to be close to her family, too.

"For me, too." Jenna smiled.

Jake thanked Meg for her hospitality, they chatted a little more, then Jake and Jenna walked out to the car, a little stunned to find themselves free to just be with each other for the second night in a row.

"You still look a little shell-shocked," Jenna teased.

And with good reason, Jake thought, turning to Jenna as he climbed into the driver's seat of his truck. "It's the first time in years I've been absolutely free of parental responsibilities for the whole night," Jake said, amazed. "Even when I traveled, I either took Alex and Clara with me, or made sure I was back in time to tuck her in that night. If she spent the night with my folks, I was there, too.''

Jenna shot Jake an ironical glance. ''Don't know what to do with yourself, hmm?'' she teased.

Grinning, Jake turned to Jenna. He loved the sound of her voice, so soft and low and sexy. In a sleeveless sky-blue blouse and long matching skirt that brought out the blue of her eyes, with the evening sun turning her hair to shimmering fire, she had never looked more beautiful than she did at that very moment. Or more self-possessed. He wanted her more than any business deal, any personal achievement, he'd ever had. Not just in his bed, but in his life. ''Oh, I've got a few ideas,'' he said.

Chapter Seven

"Such as?" Jenna asked as her heart took on a slow, heavy beat.

Jake smiled at Jenna and looked into her eyes. "We've been so busy with my problems we haven't had much chance to talk about the expansion of your business. With Alex otherwise occupied, it's the perfect time."

Jenna did her best to hide her disappointment. She ought to be happy Jake was looking out for her best interests instead of disappointed that he hadn't suggested an evening of pure romance. Instead she just felt crushed. But not wanting him to know it, Jenna glanced over at the house next door to Meg's, which was now sporting a Sold sign on the front lawn. She wondered who had bought it. She supposed they would all find out soon enough. "There's not much we can do until I actually develop a line of clothes," Jenna pointed out as he backed out of the drive.

"I disagree." Jake turned his car onto the street and continued defending his position like the consummate businessman he was. "Now is the perfect time to pinpoint which department stores you'd like to pitch your clothing line to. I've got the figures back at the ranch. If you want to go back there with me, we could go over them tonight."

Jenna felt herself flush with an inner warmth and a private disappointment she could not contain. She had told Jake she had reservations about the two of them getting back together again—so very quickly. Of course, she hadn't really wanted him to stop chasing her. But, having apparently taken her pleas to slow down to heart, he was backing off.

"Sure," Jenna forced a smile, telling herself Jake was only giving her what she'd said she wanted. "If you don't mind talking while I sew," she continued. "I need to finish the alphabet dress for Alex. Given her hatred of all things frilly and feminine, the alphabet dress may be the only jumper we can get her into tomorrow night. Fortunately, everything I need to finish it is already back at the ranch."

"Tell you what," Jake suggested as they drove through the peaceful city streets of Laramie. "I'll cook dinner while you sew."

Jenna tore her eyes from the neatly kept houses and turned her attention back to Jake. "You can cook more than just scrambled eggs, the single man's staple?" she asked in surprise, her gaze dropping to the strong column of his throat and the crisp curling hair visible in the open collar of his shirt. When she'd known him he'd been lucky to know how to open a box of cereal.

Jake paused at a four-way stop and turned to give her a slow, thoughtful once-over. "You'd be surprised the things I know how to do now. I'm a pretty handy guy."

Trying hard not to be affected by the sudden intimacy of the situation, Jenna surveyed Jake. With his sport coat off, the first two buttons on his shirt undone, he radiated all the power and casual sexiness of a legendary hero. Unbidden, all sorts of romantic thoughts and fantasies came to mind. With effort, Jenna pushed them away. "Handy as in good with your hands, or handy as in you can actually fix things?" she teased.

He reached over to stroke her cheekbone with his thumb. "Har de har har." He favored her with a slow, sensual smile. "Steak, salad and baked potato sound good to you?"

Jenna shifted backward ever so slightly. Heat centered in her chest and then began to move outward in radiating waves.

"Sounds great." They could make this a casual evening. They could spend time together alone and work on business. And on their friendship. Just the way she wanted, and nothing more. All she had to do was forget the overwhelming sexiness of his kiss and touch—the fact that the side of her that still longed to be held was still very much there for Jake—and concentrate on building a rock-solid foundation of mutual interests, friendship and caring that would support their relationship for a long time to come, even if their romance faded. It could be done, Jenna told herself firmly. By golly, it *would* be done. Jake was fast becoming too important a part of her life to lose again.

They stopped by the grocery store on the way out of town, picked up a couple of steaks and the makings for a salad, as well as two nice plump baking potatoes and all the fixings, then headed back to the ranch. Because Jake wanted company while he cooked, Jenna brought her sewing machine down to the kitchen, set it up on the desk built into the wall, and got down to work while Jake scrubbed the potatoes and put them in the oven to bake. He had the steaks marinating and was halfway through with the salad when he began to mutter beneath his breath.

Catching the tense note of annoyance in his voice, Jenna looked up from the seam she was stitching. "What's the matter?"

Frowning, Jake pushed the kitchen faucet handle up, right, and left. To no avail. He was one hundred percent frustrated male. "There's no water."

Jenna's brows knit together in surprise. "Not any?"

Jake demonstrated again, more aggressively. The faucet rumbled and spurted and made all sorts of hideous noises. Nothing came out. "Maybe you lost all water to the house," Jenna suggested.

"One way to see." Jake strode off. He returned a second later. "We've got plenty of water in the guest bathroom. The problem is obviously in the faucet here."

Jenna felt for him—she hated it when she had problems of this nature at either her apartment or her shop. They were just so darn inconvenient and annoying. "You could call a plumber," Jenna suggested.

Jake glanced at his watch, noting it was already well after six. "It's Friday night. I'll just fix it myself."

Alarm bells sounded in Jenna's head. Jake excelled at many things. As far as she knew, plumbing was not one of them. "Jake—" She'd hate to have their evening—and their dinner—ruined by some domestic disaster.

"How hard can it be?" Jake asked, already opening up the cabinet beneath the sink and taking things out. He shot a look over his shoulder, caught the expression on Jenna's face. "Will you have a little faith?" he chided, already heading out to the garage.

Unable to shake her feeling of impending disaster, Jenna wrinkled her nose comically and muttered beneath her breath, "There's a difference between faith and common sense."

Jake trotted back, toolbox in hand. "I heard that!"

Jenna shot a skeptical glance at the wrench and pair of pliers he was taking out of the case. Mercy. This looked like a disaster waiting to happen. And Jake was too foolish—or self-confident—to see it. Taking a break from sewing for the moment, Jenna rested her chin on her upraised hand. Sighed. "I was hoping you'd take a hint."

"Nope," Jake said cheerfully. "But I will take a helping hand."

Jenna edged closer, trying hard not to let on what his low, sexy voice did to her. Her insides did *not* turn to mush just listening to him! If she was feeling a little funny, it was *not* because she was now standing so close to him, it was because she was almost afraid to see what was going to happen next. She wrung her hands anxiously. "You're really not going to try and take that apart, are you?"

Jake moved the salad fixings and steaks out of the way and, using both wrench and pliers, went to work on the end of the spigot. "I'm just going to take off the little thingamajig here on the end. There's a filter screen in there. Maybe it just needs to be cleaned."

"I don't think filters get clogged up that fast, Jake. A clogged filter is a gradual thing."

"Unless there's a big hunk of sediment in there, totally blocking it." Catching her incredulous look, he insisted, "It could happen."

"Uh-huh." Jenna wished she could think about something else besides kissing Jake when they were this close. "Maybe you should turn the water off under the sink first."

"Then how would I know if the water was getting through?" Jake struggled some more, to no avail. "This darn thing is stuck. Give me a hand here, would you?"

Jenna elbowed in, even closer. She'd thought—hoped—the two of them could be just friends. At least for a while. But she was beginning to see that was going to be much harder than she thought. Every time she was around him like this, she was reminded how good it had been between them, how happy he had made her when they were together. And then she would start wanting, and needing him, all over again. And she knew what a trap that was! Because if she let herself need Jake, and then things didn't work out—again—she would be devastated.

Aware Jake was still waiting for her to help him out, she said, "What do you want me to do?"

"Just hold the pliers steady while I—" He grimaced and put his weight into turning the wrench. All he succeeded in doing was scraping the chrome coating off the end of the faucet, revealing bare brass underneath.

Jake muttered something she was just as glad not to be able to decipher, then stood back with a frown. Bracing both hands on his waist, he stared at the faucet in total frustration. "I don't know why this thing is not coming off."

Reminded of her father behaving pretty much the same way when confronted with something manly he knew nothing about, Jenna shrugged. "Maybe it's not supposed to come off."

Jake scowled. "The end always comes off. You can see the seam between the two parts right here." Jake traced it with his fingertip, showing her what he meant.

Turning her attention from the gentle stroking of his fingertip, Jenna shrugged her shoulders helplessly. "Then maybe we're turning it the wrong way."

"Right." Jake gave her a sardonic look.

"At least try it the other way," Jenna persisted.

Jake sighed as if he had never heard such a lamebrained suggestion. Nevertheless, to humor her, he readjusted the wrench while she continued to hold the pliers steady. "See?" he said. "It's not—wait a minute—it *is* loosening. You were right. We were turning it the wrong way."

Remembering how her mother had handled such situations, Jenna suppressed the desire to roll her eyes and said, "Anyone could have gotten confused."

He looked at her.

"It was a simple mistake," Jenna continued.

When that attempt at diffusing the situation failed, Jenna fell silent.

Jake finished unscrewing the end. It came off in two pieces in his palm. One was a screen, the other an end cap with a hole in it for the water to stream out. There was nothing at all blocking either piece. "So much for that theory," Jenna said.

Jake merely scowled, put his head underneath the faucet, and looked up at the inside. "Anything blocking that?" Jenna asked, by now almost hoping something was blocking it, so he could fix it, feel victorious, and go back to preparing dinner.

"Nope. Not that I can see." Jake tried the faucet again. To their mutual dismay, not so much as a drip of water came out.

"We should call the plumber," Jenna said.

Jake turned the faucet on-off, on-off, on-off. Still nothing. "I don't understand this." He glared at the faucet, determined to emerge the victor. "It was working just a minute ago."

"Let's just put the filter and screen back together and put the thingamajig back on," Jenna said. Gingerly, working around and beneath his outstretched arm, she tried to put the end of the faucet back together before something really bad happened.

Ignoring her swift and timely declaration of defeat, Jake kept turning the faucet on and off. "Maybe there's something stuck in the pipe," he said as the pipes behind the sink wall continued to make funny gurgling sounds. "Maybe if I do this enough the water pressure in there will force out whatever's clogging it."

"And maybe," Jenna said, as Jake kept up his on-off approach and the water pipes gurgled and hissed all the louder, "all we'll really end up doing is making the problem worse."

"How can it be worse?" Jake countered. "We don't have any water in here now."

Prophetic words. And as it happened, so untrue, as the water rushed through the pipes with all the force of a breaking dam, spurting out the sides of the loose thingamajig and right up into their chests and faces. Jenna screamed and put up a hand to shield her face even as she tried to hold on to the end-cap of the faucet, lest it be washed down the sink and into the disposal. "Turn it off!" she yelled.

"I'm trying!" Jake shouted back. Frantically he moved the handle of the faucet up and down. To their mutual dismay, his actions had no effect whatsoever. He dropped to his knees and yanked open the cabinet doors. It took several more minutes of muttering and fumbling, but finally he located the shut-off valve. Seconds later, the water stopped. Jake popped back up. He took one look at Jenna's drenched face, hair and clothes and began to laugh. "I told you there was water in there," he said.

"You—you…!" Jenna sputtered furiously.

"Plumbing genius?"

Jenna dropped the thingamajig and the screen onto the

counter, pivoted and shoved him in the chest with the heels of both hands. "*Not* the words I would have chosen."

"Really." Grinning, Jake caught her wrists before she could shove him again. He tugged her all the way into his arms. "What would you have chosen?"

"Inept. Stubborn. Infuriatingly male!"

He turned her so her back was resting against the sink. "Keep going."

Jenna saw the determined, sexy glint in his eyes and ignored it just as resolutely. "Determined—"

"To have you." Jake's arms tightened possessively around her waist as his breath brushed her face. "True. So true."

"Jake—"

"And sorry." Ever so gently, he pushed the hair away from her face and tucked it behind her ear. The intensity of his dark, gray eyes mesmerized her. "So sorry that I ever let you go."

Jenna was sorry, too. She sighed softly as she searched his eyes. "But we did let each other go." She had to keep remembering that. She didn't want to be caught off guard if the same thing happened again.

"A mistake," Jake agreed firmly, as he lowered his head and slanted it over hers. He kissed her squarely on the mouth and pressed his arousal firmly against her. "One I don't intend to make again."

If only she could believe that, Jenna thought as his lips covered hers in a searing, sensual kiss. Heaven knew she wanted to, she thought, as the kiss deepened, turned more erotic yet. Needed to believe it. And yet, the past did exist. The heartache from years ago did remain....

Jake felt the change in her and lifted his head. "What?" he prodded, wanting to know why she had suddenly tensed in his arms.

Jenna fought her desire even as she shook her head, curled her fingers into the damp fabric of his shirt. Putting as much distance as she could between them, she splayed her fingers across his chest and felt his heart thud against her palm, its urgent rhythm marching in lockstep with hers. "We shouldn't," she whispered. "Not when everything else is still so uncertain." *Not when so many things can still go wrong.*

"Yes, Jenna," Jake said huskily as he tunneled one hand through her hair, tilted her head back and pressed his lips to hers. "We should." He pulled her closer and kissed her long and hard and deep. Unable to prevent herself from giving in, just a little, just for a moment, Jenna kissed him back the way she had wanted to kiss him all day, sweetly and lingeringly. It was so much easier to just follow the hidden wellspring of passion and desire Jake had unleashed within her than to fight. So much easier just to let herself be carried away on the sweet riptide of romance, so much easier to simply let their desire lead where it might. And yet, was a casual love affair what she wanted, what they both needed? Or was it the self-indulgent way out, a way to keep them from discussing and discovering all that they should?

Not sure of anything, except how much she wanted him, how much she had always wanted him, Jenna tore her lips from his. She had to be sensible here, she reminded herself firmly. And not let herself get hurt again. "Jake, I—"

He ignored her soft, muffled protest as his glance roved over her flushed face and diamond-bright eyes. As usual, he seemed exceedingly confident they would both get everything they wanted, and more. Because that was the way it had been for him his whole life. "That's it." He lifted her up on the counter and stepped between her thighs. With strong, sure fingers, he unbuttoned her sky-blue blouse, looked deep into her eyes. "Tell me what you want," he urged in a low, husky whisper.

"Not…this," Jenna whispered defiantly. But her head fell back and she arched her back as his hands slid beneath the lace of her bra and claimed her breasts.

"Then how about this?" His lips drew lazy patterns on her breasts, from base to tip. Sensations fluttered through her. Arrows of fire shot through her, turning her limbs to putty, and making her cling to him as if he were a life ring in a raging sea. "Or this?" He trailed kisses down her stomach. "Or this?" He pushed up her long skirt until it was bunched up around her waist and kissed her thighs. Jenna trembled uncontrollably, remembering how thoroughly and completely he had made her his the last time he had kissed and touched and loved her like this. But lovemaking, without a rock-solid relationship behind it, was no route to a safe and secure future. And that was what she wanted, Jenna told herself firmly.

"Stop." She caught Jake's hands before he could undress her further. Knowing she would be lost if they continued, she pushed her skirt back down over her knees.

Jake didn't look happy about it, but he did as she asked. Straightening, he braced a hand on either side of her and studied her face. "What's the matter?" he asked impatiently.

And it was the frustration in his face that made her feel pressured. "You always do this to me," she chided softly, as she drew the damp edges of her blouse together and rebuttoned it with trembling hands. "Make me lose sight of everything but you." Many more kisses, Jenna knew, and she wouldn't be remembering Melinda or his mother and father or the way all of them were seemingly determined to keep her and Jake apart. Many more kisses and all she would be thinking about was just how soon they could be upstairs and in his bed, instead of just how badly she and he could both be hurt if this didn't work out—again.

Jake let out a long, slow breath. For a moment, he looked as vulnerable as she felt. "And that's bad?"

No, just unnerving and dangerous, Jenna thought as she hopped down from the counter and buttoned her blouse. "I've vetoed any romantic entanglement for so long that now I'm not used to thinking about anything but my family and my business and…I don't want to have you disappear from my life again either. I want us to be friends. Lifelong friends."

Jake waited until she had finished fastening her shirt, then leaned closer, caging her in with his arms. "I want to be a helluva lot more than your lifelong friend, Jenna. I want it all.

Friendship. Love. The marriage we were going to have— should have had—if my parents hadn't interfered.''

Jenna wanted that, too. The problem was, his parents were still interfering, and now, so was his ex-wife Melinda. Plus, there was Alexandra to consider. Jenna didn't want to see Jake's child hurt, or caught in the crossfire between the adults, and it was very likely Alex would be hurt, in some way or another, if Jenna and Jake got any more involved. Jake had to know that. Whether he would admit it or not was another matter, though.

Still struggling for composure—not easy when her body was tingling and yearning for more of his incredibly exciting lovemaking—Jenna sighed and raked both her hands through her hair. ''The problem is, Jake, we can't always have everything we want in this life.'' *And I do want you. So much.*

Jake narrowed his eyes at her and retorted critically, ''Thinking that way will only ensure you don't get what you want.''

A mixture of fear and anger sifted through Jenna. She stared up at Jake, knowing now she, too, had crossed some imaginary line in the sand with him. ''You're angry,'' she stated, re- minded that he was a man who was very much used to getting exactly what he wanted, when he wanted it.

''Frustrated as all get-out,'' Jake corrected flatly. He cupped both her arms warmly, told her earnestly, ''Darn it, Jenna. We've wasted so much time already. Time we can never get back.'' Emotion shimmered in his eyes. ''I don't want to waste any more.''

Jenna felt tears gathering behind her eyes, a knot building her throat. Her heart was telling her to forget all her uncer- tainty and confusion and just be with him. Her brain was tell- ing her to slow down. Big-time. She swallowed hard, insisted stubbornly, ''I don't want to get hurt again, Jake.''

''You won't,'' Jake insisted passionately.

Jenna let out an exasperated breath as she remembered the

last time he had promised her that. "You say that now. You may even mean it."

"I do mean it, damn it," Jake interrupted hotly.

Jenna flattened her hands against the hard musculature of his chest and pushed away from him. She was tired of listening to his rosy, impractical view of the future. Tired of having her hopes raised impossibly high, only to have them dashed again. "You also said it before—and I *did* get hurt, Jake," she reminded him grimly, remembering how he had coaxed her into packing a bag, sneaking out of the house and meeting him at midnight so they could elope.

"We both got hurt." Jake agreed. "And it's too bad, but that's still no reason not to try again."

Confused, Jenna started to move by him. "This whole evening was a bad idea. We obviously can't be alone together without—"

Jake blocked her way. He took both her hands in his. "Yeah, we can. Stay and I'll prove it." His eyes searched hers as his hold on her gentled. "I promise I'll be a perfect gentleman the rest of the evening."

Jenna hesitated. The truth was, she didn't really want to end the evening on this note any more than he did.

"The least we can do tonight is continue rebuilding our friendship," Jake said.

"That's true." Jenna sighed. They both agreed on that— they did want to be friends again. So she relented. And stayed for an evening of platonic fun. The trouble was, that wasn't what she wanted, either. What she wanted was what he couldn't give her—what no one could give her—a guarantee that this time their love would work out, not just for now, but forever.

"IT WAS A BROKEN VALVE inside the faucet," the plumber said, an hour later when he'd finished the emergency call. "That's why the faucet suddenly quit on you. It's right as rain now."

"That's great." Jake paid the plumber, adding an extra fifty for his trouble, and shook his hand. "Thanks for coming out."

"No problem." The plumber grinned. "I was happy to get the double time. You-all have a nice evening, now."

"Thanks. We will." Jake walked the plumber out, then returned. "Ready to grill the steaks now?"

"To tell you the truth, I'm famished." Now that she'd calmed down and gotten her libido back in check, Jenna realized it had been silly to think she couldn't be with Jake—alone—without giving in to the passion flowing between them. They were doing just fine having a quiet, friendly evening at the ranch. True, they'd had a little kissing slip, but that didn't mean they couldn't get right back on track. All she had to do was keep the goal—friendship and a business partnership that was strong enough to endure with or without an accompanying romance—in mind and she would be fine.

Dinner went off without a hitch, as did the feeding and exercising of Buster and Miss Kitty. They spent some time going over business and reviewing the department stores Jenna should pitch her new line to. Then, when they were finished discussing that, more time just talking and catching up on the years they had spent apart. Throughout it all, Jenna continued sewing Alex's dress. Finally, the dress was finished—except for the hem, which Jenna was hoping to check on Alex before she pinned and whipstitched it. Jake touched the sewn-on letters and numbers as he admired the finished garment. "Alex is really going to love that dress."

"Thanks. I hope so," Jenna said.

The moment drew out. Jake was oddly quiet. Jenna studied his face, saw the parental worry he was too much of a man's man to admit. "Why don't I give Meg a call and see how Alex's doing?"

Jake shrugged. "If you think it's necessary."

Jenna grinned. She knew a put-on cool when she saw one. "I think we'll all sleep a little better if we know she's okay," she said, loving—and liking—Jake all the more because he did care so deeply about his daughter. "And I'll also see if Meg wants us to bring anything to the brunch tomorrow." Jenna picked up the phone and dialed. She got Meg on the second ring.

"Well?" Jake said, as soon as Jenna hung up.

"They had a great time. Alex ate like a stevedore. They loved the movie and now are both fast asleep and have been that way for an hour."

"Thanks."

"No problem. I know what it is to love someone."

They exchanged smiles as a feeling of deep, abiding intimacy descended between them.

Much more of this cozy tête-à-tête, and they really would end up making love again, Jenna realized. Her pulse accelerating at the unprecedentedly amorous nature of her thoughts, Jenna glanced at her watch, saw it was nearly ten-thirty. She feigned a yawn, stretched. "I hadn't realized it was so late," she fibbed as she gathered up her sewing supplies. "I'd better head on home."

"There's no reason for you to go back to town, especially when you're so tired. You already have an overnight bag here and probably at least one clean change of clothes. Stay here tonight."

He was so persuasive, Jenna thought, averting her eyes from the tempting proximity of his lips. Too persuasive. Jenna knew she should leave, and yet she found herself saying, almost before she could think, "All right. I guess I could stay here tonight." She closed her sewing kit with a snap. "Isn't it time to let Buster and Miss Kitty out again?"

Jake grinned as he took her hand in his and looked down into her face. "I'm sure they think so."

Buster whimpered enthusiastically when he saw them, then wagged his tail so hard he fell over. Miss Kitty purred as Jenna picked her up and cuddled her close. When she placed her on the ground again, she ran back and forth in the grass with Buster, then came back to play with the hem of Jenna's long, summery skirt and paw at the laces on her shoes, while Buster chased a ball with Jake.

When they tired of that, Buster and Miss Kitty scampered round and round in the yellow glow of the porch light while Jake and Jenna watched and held hands and laughed. Finally worn out, Buster and Miss Kitty ventured over to drink water from their bowls and then flop belly-first on the ground.

"I think I'll put Buster's crate in my room, like I did last night, so I can hear him if he wakes up and needs to go out," Jake decided. He gathered Buster in one hand, the portable pet carrier in the other, while Jenna picked up Miss Kitty and carried her to the laundry room, where her litter box, water, scratching post and cat bed were set up. "Then, when he gets a little older, and is thoroughly house-trained and able to sleep through the night," Jake decided, "he can sleep in Alex's room."

"That will make Buster one happy puppy." Jenna smiled and explained, "Dogs are pack animals. They want to sleep with the rest of their pack or family."

Jake followed Jenna up the stairs. "What about cats?"

"Cats are more aloof—when they want to curl up on your lap, they do, and when they want to be alone, they find a nice quiet place. Kittens, on the other hand, are more sociable. But they also need to be in a warm, safe place with easy access to their litter boxes when they aren't being watched, because there is just too much for them to get into that could hurt them. Houseplants, electric cords, household chemicals."

"I can see I still have a lot to learn." Jake paused outside her room, Buster and his crate still in hand.

"I can help you. You and Alex will be pros in no time. You'll see."

Jenna reached for Buster, taking him from Jake. She held the fluffy golden puppy cuddled against her chest. Buster sighed and looked up at her with sleepy, liquid brown eyes as she scratched behind his ears. Jenna looked over at Jake. "You don't have to get up with Buster tonight. I'll do it since I'm here." She had the feeling she wouldn't be sleeping that well, anyway, remembering how Jake had kissed and caressed her earlier, knowing he was just down the hall.

Jake regarded her skeptically. "You're sure you don't mind getting up in the middle of the night with Buster? Last night, his bladder only held out until around 4:00 a.m., then it was out to the backyard for a run."

Jenna gave Jake a mock-stern look. "I don't mind. I really miss having animals in my life."

Jake gave her a sexy wink. "And here I was, hoping you were doing it to be nice to me."

Jenna couldn't help but grin at his aw-shucks drawl. She gave him a playful punch in the arm. There was no denying it—he was just dying to take her to bed again. "You just never give up, do you?" she drawled right back.

"This time I won't." He gave her a look that said he meant it.

Her heart pounding, Jenna tried to push him out her bedroom door. "Good night, Jake."

Being careful not to squish Buster, Jake grabbed Jenna, kissed her breathless. When he drew back, all the love she had ever wished for was in his eyes. "Good night."

No DOUBT exhausted from his midnight run and all the activity the past few days, Buster settled down in his crate and went right to sleep. Jenna was a different matter. Even after she washed her face, brushed her teeth, put on her nightgown and climbed into bed, she was no more ready for sleep than if she had just completed an invigorating six-kilometer run. Still tingling from Jake's brief but oh-so-sexy good-night kiss, not to mention their earlier unfinished lovemaking, Jenna was restless. Edgy. Dissatisfied.

Fearing she would wake Buster if she kept tossing and turning, she finally slipped out of her bed, grabbed her matching robe and went downstairs, sketch pad in hand. In the kitchen, she poured herself a glass of milk, took it into Jake's study and settled on the sofa.

There was only one solution for nights like these. Work. Realizing she still had a lot of dresses left to make for Alex if she were to live up to her bargain with Jake and satisfy Melinda, Jenna began to sketch. Quickly, she translated her vision into a drawing on the page, completing first one dress, then another, her ideas coming faster with every second that passed.

WHAT WAS TAKING so long? Jake wondered, a little over an hour later. He rose from his bed and went to the window. The backyard was still dark. No sign of Buster or Jenna out there.

So why had she left her bed?

What was she doing?

Was she hungry? Sick? Bored? Restless? As restless as he was?

Telling himself that as host it was his responsibility to make sure Jenna had everything she needed and wanted, Jake decided to find out where she had gone and why.

He found Jenna in his study, curled up on his sofa, her hair cascading thick and wild around her face and shoulders, her robe falling open, the curve of her breasts visible above the plunging V-neckline of her satin nightgown. Taking in the creaminess of her skin, remembering how soft and silky it felt to the touch and what a warm, giving lover she was, Jake's whole body tightened. He grimaced, doing his best to contain his erection. He had promised her he would be a perfect gentleman if she spent the night. It was a promise he intended to honor. "You okay?" he asked casually.

"Yes." As she continued to study him, taking in his loose cotton pajama pants and bare chest, a pleat appeared between her brows. "What are you doing up?"

Too late, Jake wished he'd thought to grab a robe. A T-shirt. Anything to put more clothes between them, and lessen the possibility of them making love again. Ignoring the lightning bolt of desire arrowing straight to his groin, Jake crossed the room to her side. "Just checking on you," he told her casually. Smiling, he sat down beside her on the sofa, and looked down at the half-finished sketch in her lap. It was some sort of dress, but beyond that, he couldn't tell much. "What's all this?"

Jenna turned toward him, excitement in her clear blue eyes. "Oh, Jake, I know what I want to concentrate on with my clothing line."

Jake grinned, unable to take his gaze from her face. She was one beautiful woman, even at this time of night, with her hair tumbling loose and unbrushed to her shoulders, her face scrubbed bare of makeup. "So what's it going to be?" he asked. "Evening gowns or wedding dresses?"

"Neither." Jenna scooted closer, her bent knee nudging his thigh in her eagerness to share her creative notion with him. Quickly, she returned to the front of her sketchbook and began flipping through it, showing him the rough designs. "I want to do a complete line of dresses for little girls Alex's age. I want to create frontier-style party dresses with a definite Southwestern flair, frilly Southern-belle dresses, casual school dresses and dresses that are so right-now and city-chic. I want to challenge Esprit and Gunne Sax and Guess for the little girl's market. I want them to have a dress for every mood. Every occasion. And I want to help out their moms, too. Every garment—even the dressiest—will be machine-washable."

Impressed, Jake studied Jenna's designs. No doubt about it, she was very, very talented. Even he—who knew very little about women's or children's clothing—could tell that from her off-the-cuff designs. "Sounds good. That'll be a big help to a lot of parents trying to find something for their daughters to wear that is also easy and inexpensive to care for. But what about wedding gowns and evening dresses?" he wondered out loud. "That's where you've made your name." And Jake was unwilling to take any of Jenna's hard-won success from her with any new opportunity he gave her.

Jenna frowned. ''I want to keep doing those, but on an individual, custom-made basis. I don't want to mass-produce any of those designs. This way, I can have the best of both worlds.''

With Jenna leaning over his shoulder, Jake continued flipping through the pages of her sketchbook. ''You did all this in the past hour?'' he asked, completely amazed.

Jenna nodded. ''When I get an idea for a series of related dresses, it usually comes in the middle of the night. It usually all happens pretty quickly. Probably because my subconscious has been working on the problem for days.'' Jenna paused and narrowed her eyes at him. She propped a fist on her hip in mock indignation. ''How did you know how long I've been down here?''

Jake shrugged and tried not to notice the way her nipples were suddenly beading against the satin fabric of her gown. Whether because she was cold or as aware of him as he was of her, he couldn't tell. With difficulty he returned his gaze to her face and answered her question. ''I heard you go downstairs. I didn't hear you come back up. After a while, I began to wonder if you were okay or had run out on me.''

Laughter curved the edges of her soft, bare lips. ''Now, you know I'd never run off and leave Buster in the middle of the night,'' Jenna teased. ''So why aren't you snoozing away, Mr. Remington?''

''The truth?'' Jake said playfully before he could stop himself, tightening his hand on her own.

''Nothing but,'' Jenna shot back with a wry look that seemed to imply she could handle anything he could dish out. And more.

Deciding he and Jenna had played games long enough, Jake looked deep into her eyes and confided, ''I can't stop thinking of you.''

As THE IMPACT of Jake's words sank in, Jenna found her heart was pounding. She had that funny, fluttery feeling in her tummy, the feeling she'd had every time Jake had kissed her. Trembling, Jenna extricated their hands and pushed herself to her feet. Jake had barely stated his intention, and already her mind was filled with fantasies of Jake making love to her right here in his study, on the sofa, in the chair.... "Now, Jake—" she warned, flushing, as she edged away from him.

Jake followed her around the back of the sofa, lazily matching her pace for pace. When she stopped, so did he.

To her relief—keeping some distance between them—Jake stopped, legs braced apart, arms folded in front of him, and regarded her with serious gray eyes. "I've got to be honest with you, Jenna. I don't like having to hobble myself when it comes to romancing you."

Her emotions in turmoil, Jenna studied Jake silently for several moments, liking the way the soft light in the study highlighted the masculine planes of his face, and brought out the inky darkness of his hair. Finally, she swallowed hard, asked, "Is that what you think you're doing?"

Jake nodded and kept his eyes on hers. "In not pursuing you full-out, yeah, I do."

Jenna inhaled deeply, but retained her composure. "I thought you weren't going to pursue me any more tonight."

Jake pointed to the clock and grinned, the morning beard on his face making him look all the more dark, dangerous and alluring. "Actually, it's past midnight. Hence, it's morning. A new day. New opportunities—"

"—to be shot down," Jenna interrupted.

Jake tried but couldn't quite suppress a grin as he added, "Or welcomed with open arms."

Jenna took a couple of steps back. Safely out of reach, she pushed aside the tide of sensual longing she felt whenever he was near. "What on this earth could ever give you the idea that would happen?"

Jake inclined his head, taking her in from head to toe, before slowly...slowly returning his gaze to her face. "Oh, I don't know," he drawled with exaggerated seriousness. "Maybe the fact you can't sleep any more than I can. Then again, maybe it's the way you've been looking at me all evening long. Like you want nothing more than for me to take you in my arms and kiss you again.''

Jenna flushed with anticipation. ''You're dreaming.''

Jake merely grinned. ''Am I, Jenna?'' He took her in his arms. ''Then prove it to me.'' Giving her no chance to argue further, he ducked his head and gave her a slow, gentle kiss that turned her world upside down. Her response was immediate and just as filled with emotion and desire. Unable to resist his insistence, her arms moved from the defensive position against his chest, to wind around his neck. She felt his arousal pressing against her and she trembled from head to toe.

''Oh, Jake—''

His lips moved to the sensitive place just behind her ear. He rained kisses down her neck, across her collarbone, to the uppermost swell of her breasts. ''I know we've had rough days, and we may have even rougher days ahead, but I want to make you mine, Jenna, not just temporarily, but the way I should've made you mine years ago,'' Jake whispered as he kissed his way back up to her mouth.

Reason disappeared; feelings took over.

He threaded his hands through her hair and tipped her face up to his. ''I want you to love me, Jenna,'' he whispered hoarsely, kissing her as if the chance would never come again, ''the way I love you, with all my heart and soul.''

''Oh, Jake,'' Jenna whispered again as the scent of his cologne filled her senses, and everything around her blurred except the hot, hard pressure of his mouth.

''Just love me, Jenna,'' Jake coaxed as he backed her up against the wall, putting his arms on either side of her, his body against hers. Holding her tightly, he showered her with hot, passionate kisses that had her heart swelling and her body quaking with unmet need. ''Love me the way we were meant to love each other,'' he whispered.

Longing swept through her in undulating waves. Her robe, gown and panties were off in seconds. So were his pajama pants.

Naked, he held her against the wall. His mouth covered hers, demanding and receiving a response she hadn't realized she could give as she pressed against him, savoring his warmth and his strength, even as she stroked the powerful muscles of his back, shoulders and waist. Her breasts crushed against the powerful muscles of his chest, she was throbbing all over, inside and out. She wanted to yield to him and the need that drove them both. And she wanted him to surrender to her, too.

Her hand curling around his biceps, she guided him around so his back was against the wall. "My turn to be in charge," she teased, dropping to her knees. Jake groaned as her hands learned every male inch of him, then moved to the smooth, velvety hardness, and the depth of his need, a need she could ease.

Hand on her shoulder, he brought her to her feet. He kissed her again, until their hearts thundered together and she, too, trembled with the need to hold back her own release. He moved between her legs, nudging her thighs wide. He lifted her against him and surged inside. With an exultant sigh, she closed around the hot, hard length of him. And this time, as he loved her, they were pledging not just the moment, not just the sating of their desires, but their futures, too.

JAKE AND JENNA had barely stopped shuddering when Jake swept Jenna into his arms, carried her upstairs and dropped her into the mussed covers on his bed.

"I'm still not sleepy," Jenna protested.

"Funny," Jake drawled as he climbed in beside her, switched on the light and stretched out beside her. "Neither am I."

Jenna rolled toward him, a combination of anticipation and excitement in her blue eyes. Her fingers slid through the silky mat of hair on his chest. "But we—"

"Already made love once," Jake read her mind. "I know. But that was fast—"

"And good," Jenna sighed contentedly, as amazed as Jake at how hot and fast she'd reached fulfillment.

"You're right," Jake agreed lazily. "It was good. Damn good. Still, there are times to go fast. And times to go slow." He bent his head and kissed her again, until there was no question about what he wanted or what was coming next. Only passion so hot it sizzled. He swept her mouth with his tongue, circling, dipping deep in a rhythm of penetration and retreat. When she was trembling with excitement, stretching sinuously beneath him, he drew back, determined to make this time last. "Guess which one this is?" he asked wryly.

Jenna eyed him, a mixture of desire and laughter in her eyes. "We just finished five minutes ago!"

Jake acknowledged that was so with a lift of his head. "The advantage of going slow," he allowed wickedly as he ran his thumb across her lower lip, "is that it takes you a long time to get where you're going." He was pleased to be the one introducing her to the many pleasures of sex.

Jenna, already helplessly aroused from just their kiss, regarded him with hesitation. "Jake, I don't think I can go...that slow."

His gaze traveled sensually over the flushed pink curves of her breasts and taut, rosy nipples. "Worried about me catching up?" Jake teased, as Jenna shifted restlessly beside him "Well, don't be."

"Can't help it." Jenna's flush deepened. Shyly, she dipped her head. "I don't want to..."

"Outdo me?" Jake guessed, his humorous grin widening.

Jenna nodded with relief. She let out a gusty sigh. "Exactly."

"Well, don't worry about it," Jake winked playfully, aware he was already feeling a renewed rush of heat and blood to his groin. "This is one area where I don't mind lagging behind. One area where it *pays* to be the fairer sex."

"Jake—"

"Feels good, does it?"

Jenna moaned as Jake's lips and tongue blazed an erotic path across her breasts, paying tender attention to each nipple, laving the peak with his tongue, blowing it dry with his breath. "Too good," she moaned as he angled his body across hers and his lips returned to hers.

"How about this?" Jake probed the soft lining of her mouth with his tongue, kissing her until she sighed, soft and ragged.

"Also…exceptional." Jenna's voice sounded strangled.

He made his way down to her parted thighs, caressing her dewy softness, moving up, in. "And this?"

She practically soared off the bed. "You're too…kind."

"Told you I'd be a perfect gentleman," Jake whispered as Jenna shook uncontrollably again.

"I thought that was yesterday," she whispered as he stroked her, over and over again, until she was coming like lightning in his hands.

"It applies today," Jake said.

"Gentlemen…don't…do…this," she said, as Jake's lips and tongue replaced his hand.

"This gentleman does," he replied, continuing until she clasped the muscles of his shoulders and dug her fingers in, the pleasure gripping her, sending her spiraling over the edge. Satisfaction poured through Jake as Jenna climaxed wildly, wantonly in his arms. His own body now humming with pent-up desire, Jake held Jenna and kissed her. A wave of tenderness rushed through him as he realized how lucky they were to have come together again, this time for keeps. Jake brushed the hair from Jenna's cheek as he studied the flushed color in her cheeks. "What are you thinking?" he asked softly.

"In a word?" Jenna's whole body softened contentedly as she searched his eyes—and his heart. "That you're going to spoil me."

Jake grinned, happier than he could ever remember being.

"Don't mind if I do," he drawled. He reached for her again. Only, to his surprise, to be pushed gently but firmly away.

"Hold on there a moment, cowboy," Jenna said as she sat up and sent him a wickedly playful glance. "This isn't a one-way street we're on." Blue eyes twinkling, she said, "If I have my way—and I will—more than one of us is going to get spoiled tonight."

Curious as to what she was going to do, Jake lay back while Jenna knelt between his spread legs. She put a hand on the insides of his thighs, caressed them with exquisite pressure, covering all the erogenous zones except one. Jake groaned, her aptitude for loving him no surprise. Not being able to keep up with her was no longer the problem. In fact, if she continued her sensual teasing, their problem was going to be exactly the opposite. Gruffly, Jake caught her hands, only to have Jenna replace them with her lips. "This wasn't part of the deal here," he groaned, as his body turned to fire under the delicate ministrations of her mouth.

Jenna wrested her hands from his light, detaining grip. Mischief on her face, she rose to her knees and moved her fingertips over his flat male nipples and the indentation of his navel, her hot skin brushing his with maddening intensity. "It is now."

Jake throbbed as she knelt again and kissed him all the way to his ankles. "Jenna—" What she was doing was sensual and outrageous. And far too compelling to stop. He wanted to be touched now, the way he knew she would eventually touch him. Seemingly in no hurry despite the throbbing in his groin, Jenna lazily kissed her way back up his thighs, rubbing the tips of her breasts against the hard muscles. Her hot breath and the silk of her hair floated across his skin. He sucked in a ragged breath as she cupped him reverently between her palms.

"Jenna," he groaned. Much more of this love-play and he was going to explode.

Jenna touched him, ever so lightly, ever so carefully with

the tip of her tongue, then to his frustration, drew away. "Let me get where I want to be, Jake."

Jake shuddered as her hands replaced her lips, arousing him with slow, patient strokes. "You're certainly getting where I'd like you to be."

Jenna looked up at him with such love and intensity he caught his breath. "Glad to hear it," she said softly.

"Jenna—?" Jake didn't think he had ever experienced a more tender, thorough loving in his life.

"Hmm?" Once again, Jenna found him with her lips and tongue.

"Where'd you...learn all these things?" Jake gasped as she tried a particularly unexpected—and stunningly erotic and effective—move.

"You aren't the only one who can read—and dream," Jenna murmured, obviously delighting in the fact he was giving her free rein to do absolutely anything she pleased. "Just so happens I haven't had anyone to try any of it out on until now." She paused, sat up and looked into his eyes, her delight in her sensual explorations obvious. She wrinkled her nose at him playfully. "How am I doing?"

Figuring he'd been patient way long enough, Jake grabbed her by the waist and shifted her so she was astride him. The strain of holding back beaded his entire body with perspiration. "Too good, as a matter of fact."

"No such thing as too good when it comes to the bedroom," Jenna declared, as she settled onto his lap and eased down, slowly and surely, taking him inside her.

"You're right," Jake agreed as Jenna closed around him, hot and tight. And then got even tighter. "What you are doing is just right. But so," he said as he thrust even deeper, sparing nothing when it came to making her his, "is this."

Jenna took off like a rocket. "I'm ahead of you—again," she groaned.

"I'll catch up," Jake promised.

And he did, merging their climaxes as irrevocably as they

were beginning to merge their lives. Afterward, Jake held her close. Bliss consumed them, rendering them warm, cozy and totally unmoving. "Now what are you thinking?" he whispered in her ear.

Jenna's lips curved against his skin. She snuggled even closer, for the first time in their lives holding absolutely nothing back. "That I've never been able to resist you." She sighed wistfully, shook her head. "I couldn't then. I can't now."

"That goes two ways, you know," he said, looking deep into her eyes. "I've never been able to stop loving you, either." He pressed a kiss in her hair, on her temple, her cheek, her lips. "You're the woman for me, Jenna," he said seriously, holding her tight. "The only woman for me." He paused, shook his head. "Which makes us sneaking around this way, stealing time to be together, all the more ridiculous. Marry me," he whispered urgently, "just as soon as we get this whole mess with Alex and Melinda straightened out. Marry me so we can spend our whole lives together."

Joy filled Jenna as she saw all the love and tenderness in Jake's face. She loved him, too, so much. "Yes, Jake, yes."

Chapter Eight

"Well. Don't you two look like the cats that caught the canary," Dani Lockhart said when Jenna and Jake walked into the kitchen of Meg's home the next morning, where all the adults were gathered while the kids played on Jeremy's swing set in the backyard.

"As well as lacking in a little sleep, wouldn't you say?" Dani's husband Beau remarked. He waggled his eyebrows at them. "Late night? Out painting the town?"

Dani shot Jenna a look of sisterly concern even as she elbowed Beau. "Behave yourself." Dani stood on tiptoe and kissed Beau's cheek. "Just because we're still on our honeymoon doesn't mean everyone else is."

"Oh, I don't know," her husband drawled, giving Jenna and Jake a knowing wink. "There are more ways to honeymoon than you can list and...I think they look pretty head-over-heels in love." Beau opened his satchel and took out Old Faithful, the perfectly seasoned black cast-iron skillet that had traveled the world with him. He set his pan on the stove. "You forget, I knew Jenna before Jake came back into her life. She might have been doing well in her business life, but she wasn't nearly this happy before." Beau began laying thick slices of bacon in the bottom of the skillet as he added, "And I'd wager, neither was he.

"Of course, since for now I'm the official man of the family, I have to look after all these women.'' Beau looked at Jake. ''It's my job to kick butt should anyone get out of line with any of them.''

Jenna sucked in a breath at the warning in Beau's low tone. But to her relief, Jake didn't take offense. Instead, he wrapped his arms around her and tugged Jenna close. ''You don't have to worry about me,'' Jake told her family. ''I love this woman with all my heart and soul, and if I have my way,'' Jake paused to press a kiss into her hair, ''we'll be married soon, too.''

''Jake!'' Jenna chastened. They had specifically agreed they wouldn't tell anyone about his proposal to her last night, until things had calmed down on his home front, and they could go about it in a more official manner. And yet here he was, declaring his intentions to one and all, as if their union was pretty much already a done deal! But then that was Jake for you—if he wanted something, he pretty much felt it was his for the claiming. Right now, that was her.

Kelsey studied them, with a taunting grin that seemed to say: *Not so fast there, cowboy—you haven't dealt with me.* Shooting Jake a sly, assessing glance, Kelsey continued making coffee and tea for everyone. ''Well, maybe she's only seeing you again to get revenge for the way you treated her before.''

Shock reverberated throughout the room. Jake turned to Jenna, letting his eyes trail over her from head to toe. ''That so?''

Jenna raked a hand through her hair and flushed self-consciously. Nothing like running the gauntlet of the Lockhart sisters' love and protection. Especially when they were determined, it seemed, to smoke out any false or selfish note in Jake's attitude to her. Pronto.

''Did you really make that declaration?'' Jake continued mildly.

''Uh. Well.'' Jenna's chin shot up a notch. ''Actually. Yes. I did.''

"Good move." Jake nodded at Jenna approvingly. "I would have been disappointed in you had you done anything less."

Jenna's jaw dropped in shock, as did everyone else's.

"'Cause loving someone is always the best revenge." Confident and at ease, Jake turned to the rest of the family. "Jenna can deny it all she wants, but our feelings for each other are still there, and they're hotter than ever. The past couple days have proved that."

Meg studied Jake as she began mixing up the blueberry pancake batter. "Passion's great but it takes a lot more than that to sustain a marriage—or even a relationship—over the long haul," she said.

"You're right. It takes commitment. Loyalty. A determination to weather the storms, no matter how bleak things look. Or how much you have to overcome. I've pledged my devotion to your sister." Jake looked at Dani, Meg, and Kelsey in turn. "Jenna knows I won't abandon her again. All she has to do is stick with me through thick and thin, too."

Dani frowned worriedly as she began cutting up fresh strawberries and dropping them in a bowl. "Unfortunately, that's not what your parents are saying. They're dropping hints all over town that a reconciliation with Melinda is afoot."

"That's odd," Jake remarked, "since I'm dating Jenna."

"Word around town is they've got an explanation for that, too," Kelsey said, as she began setting the table. She looked at Jake steadily. "They're telling everyone that this fling you are having with Jenna now is really just 'unfinished business' between the two of you, and that it'll soon dissipate once reality sets in and you realize your backgrounds and very different outlooks on life can't easily be overcome. They're also saying that you already have doubts about the relationship. Otherwise, why would you be taking such pains to hide it?"

"I haven't hidden anything!" Jake fumed.

Refusing to back down now that she had Jake on the spot,

Kelsey lifted a brow. "Did you or did you not rent out an entire inn?"

"So we could talk privately, without all of Laramie gossiping and looking on!"

Dani turned to Jenna. "Has Jake taken you anywhere public?"

"You mean besides here—today?" Jenna asked, flushing. Too late, she realized how it had looked. "No. We've just seen each other at my place or his ranch. But that wasn't by design." Or had it been, she wondered nervously, hating to think Jake still might be too ashamed of his relationship with her, and his friend's and familys' reaction to it, to make it public.

Jake scowled, not liking the implication any more than Jenna did. "If it will make you all feel better, I'll take Jenna to lunch at the Wagon Wheel restaurant, and then hit every establishment in town, introducing her as my woman. We could even take out an ad in the paper, announcing our plans to get engaged as soon as possible."

"Don't be silly," Jenna murmured, beginning to feel a little like they had been ambushed, too. She took two dozen eggs out of the refrigerator and began breaking them into a mixing bowl.

"That's really not the point," Meg agreed.

"Then what is?" Jake demanded, reaching over to give Jenna a hand.

Meg paused in the act of stirring blueberries into the pancake batter. "We're just all wondering if we should be as concerned about Jenna getting hurt by you again. You know your parents, Jake. They've never really been ones to confide in the townspeople. They've always sort of drawn the line between us and them and just used their ranch as a tax write-off and a place to send you when you were a kid and have parties in the summer. But for the past few days, your mother has been running around town, talking nonstop to everyone who'll listen." Meg paused, looking as if it hurt her just to repeat it. "She's saying you're using Jenna to fan the flames of Melinda's jealousy and that the only thing standing between you and Melinda and Alexandra being a family again is Jenna."

Jake looked as stunned by that revelation as Jenna felt, but—in the end—not at all surprised. "My parents have always been scared I'd end up at the mercy of some fortune hunter," he explained as he addressed the group. "They wanted me to marry someone with means, so I wouldn't have to worry about that. But they forgot the most important part of any equation between a man and a woman is love."

"Our parents certainly knew that," Kelsey said softly. All the rest of the Lockhart women nodded.

Dani looked at Jake quizzically. "I'd think your parents would too. After all, they've been married a long time."

"That's true," Jake said as he watched Beau transfer sizzling strips of bacon from the skillet to paper towels to drain, "but since my folks both came from families of inherited wealth, theirs was essentially an arranged marriage. They were fortunate it's worked out. I love them a lot, and I know they love me and Alex and each other, but I don't think they've ever known passion. Not the kind I share with Jenna, anyway. The passion in their lives has been for things and activities, not necessarily each other."

"That's sad," Kelsey said, as everyone contemplated what a different kind of life that would be.

Jake shrugged. He had given up trying to explain how he felt about Jenna to his parents a long time ago. "It's how they were brought up."

"Then what happened to you?" Dani teased.

Jake grinned. "I imagine my folks are asking themselves that question at this very minute. 'Where did we go wrong? Why doesn't Jake value a Louis XV chair more than the woman he loves?'" With a wry grin, he continued, "The truth is, I understand them. I know why they think the way they do. I just don't share their beliefs. For instance, I'd never go off and leave Alex for an entire summer, the way they did me. I build companies up. My father tears them down. Our differences are many and far-reaching. I have no doubt they think they are helping me and Alex by championing a renewed relationship between me and Melinda. I just hope Melinda doesn't end up hurting them and or Alex in the process. Because, bottom line, even though they've made mistakes—we all have—they're still my family, and I don't want to see them hurt, either.'' Jake sighed tiredly. ''Given the way things are going, I just may not be able to prevent it.''

''What about this party your parents are throwing tonight?'' Kelsey asked curiously. ''We've all been invited. So have all the McCabes, everyone else important in town, plus dozens and dozens of your parents' socially prominent friends from around the state.''

Jake paused. ''Officially, they're throwing it to welcome Melinda back to Texas.''

What about unofficially? Jenna wondered. And why had they invited her sisters? So they'd be sure and have Dani's movie-star husband Beau in attendance, too? Or so she'd have someone to leave the party with other than Jake?

Meg frowned as she began ladling pancake batter onto the griddle. ''I hate to say this, Jake. I know they're your parents. But I wouldn't put it past them to try and use this gala affair to push the two of you apart forever.''

''Exactly why we're going to attend,'' Jake said confidently, wrapping his arm around Jenna's waist. ''To show them, once and for all, that they can't intimidate Jenna or push us apart. We're together whether they like it or not, and we want everyone to know it. Because the sooner they do, the sooner we can get on with our lives without any more familial interference.''

Jenna pivoted toward him, to better see his eyes. ''I don't know, Jake. That's sort of an in-your-face way to go about things, isn't it?'' Jenna remarked. Wasn't there an easier, less confrontational way to bring her into his family?

Jake tightened his arms around her possessively. "I'm not running anymore, Jenna," he vowed passionately. "I'm not hiding or sneaking around or covering up our relationship from my folks and anyone who might clue them in as to what was going on, the way we did when we were teens. And neither should you. We have nothing to be ashamed about and everything to be happy and proud about. It's not every day a love as special and wonderful as ours comes along."

"Jake's right," Dani said, beginning to relax again now that Jake was passing the cross-examination with flying colors. She set the bowl of sliced strawberries on the center of the table. "Mom and Dad always loved him. They always thought you two would end up together. I know this is what they would want, too. You're just going to have to weather the storm. And we'll be right there with you, helping," she promised emotionally. Beau, Kelsey and Meg—finally convinced of what Jenna had known all along, that Jake was not out to hurt her—also offered promises to help.

"Thanks." Jake said gruffly, relieved. He turned to her, for a moment looking overcome by the unconditional acceptance he and Jenna were receiving from her family, now that all their questions had been answered satisfactorily. "That means the world to us, doesn't it, Jenna?"

Jenna nodded, abruptly feeling a little choked up herself. She lifted her glass of juice. "To a quick resolution of all our problems," she toasted.

"Here, here," everyone said in unison and then drank to that.

"Okay, now I've got a question," Kelsey said as the emotional moment passed, and the earlier, easygoing mood returned. Everyone groaned. Kelsey was such a wild card. There was just no telling what she was going to say. Kelsey marched up to Jake and slapped her hands on her blue-jeans-clad hips. "Who is this guy Rick and why is he asking so many questions about you?"

"Rick who?" Jake asked. He hoped he was wrong, but his

gut was telling him this was trouble. Otherwise, Kelsey wouldn't be asking.

"I don't know." Kelsey shrugged and filched a piece of bacon from the serving tray before Beau could swat her hand away. "He wouldn't give me his last name. I saw him in town a few minutes ago at Isabel Buchanon's bakery."

Feeling both curious and baffled, Jake accepted the coffee Meg handed him. "What did he look like?"

"Tall, dark, handsome. Very well dressed. Not a Texan. At least I don't think so, since he didn't have any accent."

"What did he want?" Jake lounged against the counter while Kelsey tried—unsuccessfully this time—to sneak more bacon.

"He asked me if I was from around here." Kelsey settled for a strawberry instead. "I said yes. He wanted to know if I knew you. I said yes. He asked me what you were like."

"And you said...?" Jake queried while everyone waited for Kelsey's answer with bated breath.

"Exactly what you'd think," Kelsey volleyed back. "That you were rich, successful. But known to cut and run from the women in your life."

Jake winced at that reasonably accurate description—up until now, anyway. "Did he accept that?" Jake asked.

"He agreed with it, actually." Kelsey paused to pour herself a cup of coffee. She lounged against the counter, sipping it. "He also wanted to know if it was true that you had never stopped loving Jenna Lockhart, even though you went on to marry someone else and have a child with her."

Tension rebounded in Meg's kitchen once again.

"And you said...?" Jake asked. He could hardly wait to hear Kelsey's answer to this one!

"That it was my considered opinion that you were still carrying a torch for Jenna, and always had been, but that in any case you were currently chasing her again."

For forever this time, Jake amended silently, giving Jenna a glance to testify to it. Reluctantly, Jake turned back to Kelsey. "How did Rick react to that?"

"He didn't." Kelsey sighed, disappointed. "He just…walked away from me, got behind the wheel of his sports car and drove off. Oh. Wait." Kelsey snapped her fingers. "He asked me one more question."

"What was it?" Once again, everyone waited with bated breath.

"He wanted to know if you were one of the good guys."

"And you told him…?"

"I said I hoped so, I really hoped so."

Silence fell. "What do you think that's all about?" Jenna turned to Jake, her clear blue eyes alight with curiosity.

Jake shrugged. "I haven't a clue."

"Do you know who it was?"

Again, Jake shook his head. "I know dozens of Ricks but none that would be prying into my private life like that."

"Maybe he's a private detective," Beau theorized.

Jake turned and gave his brother-in-law-to-be a man-to-man glance. He could use Beau's unemotional assessment of the situation. "Checking into me for what reason?" Jake asked.

Beau took the last of the bacon from the pan and set his skillet aside. "Your ex is threatening to challenge the current custody arrangement for your daughter. Maybe she hired this Rick guy to dig up dirt on you. Maybe Melinda and Rick are going to use the party—and all the locals in attendance—to loosen a few tongues, see what they can scout out."

Jake frowned. "My parents wouldn't be part of that," he said firmly.

To Jake's dismay, Jenna was not so sure. "It wouldn't be the first time they've used blackmail to keep you away from me," she said quietly. "Last time, they had my best interests and those of my sisters at heart. This time they have Alex's, yours and Melinda's."

"That's not it," Jake said firmly. His parents would never help Melinda take Alex away from him.

"Then what's this all about?" Jenna pressed, as she cooked the eggs.

"That's just it," Jake said, uncomfortably, wondering once again who the mysterious Rick was. "I don't know."

"Well," Dani said eventually, "we'll all be there tonight, so I guess we'll find out then."

"Except me." Meg frowned, looking glad to change the subject, too, as she signaled to the kids—who were playing out back—that it was time to come in and wash up for brunch. "The new chief of family medicine is coming in tonight. As head of nursing, I'm supposed to show him around."

"Who is it?" asked Kelsey, who was always looking for someone new to date.

Meg shrugged. "All I know is that John and Lilah McCabe handpicked the guy to take over, he used to live in Houston, Texas, a long time ago, and he's really anxious to get started over at the hospital."

"Still, it's a Saturday night, Meg," Dani protested, looking as if the new guy could have waited until Monday morning to start putting demands on Meg.

"Maybe he doesn't have much of a social life. I don't know. I've been really busy, too. Trying to get things organized my way and recruit and hire nurses for the new wing of the hospital that's set to open next spring." Meg sighed as she carried a platter filled with scrumptious-looking blueberry pancakes to the table. "Filling Lilah McCabe's shoes is going to be no easy thing."

"You're up to the task," Jenna said firmly as she warmed the syrup in the microwave. Everyone promptly agreed.

"Thanks." Meg blushed at the vote of confidence. "Anyway, the appointment was made by the department secretary. The new chief said it would only take a couple of hours, so I should be able to hit the party at the Remingtons' ranch a little later in the evening and provide some family support for you."

"Great." Jenna sighed as the kids came barreling in the back door and she slid the piping-hot eggs on a platter and set it on the table. "I have a feeling Alexandra, Jake and I are going to need all the moral backing we can get."

TO JENNA'S RELIEF, the rest of brunch was a lighthearted event, full of love and laughter. By the time it ended, she was very glad she, Jake and Alex had accepted the invitation, fraught with ulterior motives as it had been. And she wasn't the only one who was happy to be there.

"I had the bestest time here ever," Alexandra declared to Jenna and Jake as they got ready to leave Meg's. "Can Jeremy come and spend the night at our ranch some time soon?"

"Sure," Jake smiled, ruffling Alex's hair.

"And maybe Buster and Miss Kitty can visit here, too," Alex continued enthusiastically as Jenna and Jake helped her gather up her belongings. "Jeremy likes animals. He doesn't have any of his own."

Jake knelt to help Alex zip her overnight bag closed. "Jeremy can come to our ranch to visit Buster and Miss Kitty."

Alex persisted with a frown, "But he wants them to come here, Daddy, to his house."

"Maybe we can work something out," Meg interjected easily. "They can come over for a play date, or we can pet-sit for you or something sometime."

Alex and Jeremy cheered.

"You are a generous woman." Jake grinned.

Jenna seconded the notion with a kiss and a hug. "Thanks for brunch." *And for giving me time alone with Jake last night.*

Looking every bit as happy and content as her daddy, Alex chattered nonstop on the ride back to the J&R Ranch. Jenna was less relaxed. A glance at her watch told her she had less than seven hours to get Alexandra into a dress. Jake was counting on Jenna. Jenna knew how important it was to him to have the tomboy issue taken off the table, where his parents and Melinda were concerned, and Jenna didn't want to let him down. First though, the pets had to be fed and cuddled and let out for a run, and as soon as they arrived, they were. Afterward, she and Alex went up to the playroom where Jenna had set up her sewing machine and dressmaker's dummy, while Jake stayed downstairs to make some business calls regarding their new business venture. Impatient that things weren't moving faster, he was determined to set up a full roster of appointments for Jenna and he the next week.

To Jenna's relief, Alex stopped dead in her tracks and grinned in surprise when she saw the alphabet dress on the dummy. "You finished it," she said, eying with delight the colorful letters and numbers Jenna had appliquéd on the dress.

"Almost." Jenna picked up the bottom of the dress and showed her. "It's not hemmed yet. I wasn't quite sure about the length, but it's hard to do that on a dressmaker's dummy. It's really better to do that on a live person. I asked your dad if he'd do the honors but..." Jenna rolled her eyes in obvious exasperation, "he seems to think he wouldn't fit in it."

Alex giggled at Jenna's clowning around. "He wouldn't, silly," she told Jenna seriously. "He's way too big."

"Oh." Jenna pretended to be disappointed and perplexed. "Well, if you think of any little girls who might be willing to do that for me, let me know. In the meantime, I'm going to work on my other project."

With difficulty, Alex tore her glance away from the dress and followed Jenna over to the playroom table. "What project?"

Jenna spread out the pieces of green, brown, red and yellow velveteen she'd already cut out. "I thought I'd make a stuffed frog for one of my very favorite people."

Alex stood on one foot. "Who's that?"

Achingly aware how good it felt to be mothering this child, if only by default, Jenna slanted her a playful glance. "Three guesses," she teased.

Alex looked hopeful as she pointed at her own chest. "Me?"

"You're right," Jenna praised Alex warmly. "And on the first guess, too." Her heart pounding, Jenna paused, knowing this next mission was integral to her plan to get Alex involved in more ladylike indoor activities as well as all her rambunctious outdoor pursuits. "Would you like to help?" Jenna studied Alex's face for any sign of resistance, and to her relief saw only bright-eyed interested. "I have a special machine that's perfect for someone your age to learn to sew. In fact, I learned to sew on it."

"Really?"

Jenna nodded, recalling what a happy time that had been in her life. "My mom taught me," she said.

Unable to help herself, Alex looked back at the dress. "What about the alphabet dress, though? Aren't you going to finish that?"

Jenna nodded, distracted. "As soon as I get somebody to help me with it," she promised.

"I'll help you," Alex volunteered quickly.

"You sure?" Jenna frowned consideringly. "I mean I wouldn't want to put you out or anything."

Getting more excited by the minute, Alex stood on one foot, then the other. "I wouldn't mind trying it on. Just for a few minutes."

"Okay. That'd be great."

Jenna helped Alex out of her T-shirt and denim overalls. Minutes later, she was standing on a dressmaker's pedestal while Jenna knelt in front of her, pinning and measuring the hem.

Jake walked in.

He, too, stopped dead in his tracks. "Wow." He let out a long, low wolf whistle that had his daughter blushing with delight. Hands braced on his hips, Jake walked around Alex and surveyed her from every angle as if unable to believe his eyes. "You are one heck of a pretty Texas lady. You look great in that dress, Alex. I mean really great!"

Alex beamed. Then, remembering her avowed dislike of anything feminine, she quickly tamped down her enthusiasm and said, "I'm jus' helping her out, Daddy."

"I can see that," Jake said solemnly, promptly tamping down his enthusiasm. "It's very nice of you." Apparently realizing they were in a very delicate moment, he turned to Jenna, once again all business. "Dillard's, Foley's and Bealls department stores all want to meet with you. Next week, if possible. Think you can have preliminary sketches ready to show?"

"Maybe by Thursday or Friday."

"How about one Wednesday, one Thursday and one Friday?"

"That's a lot of driving back and forth."

"They're coming here to Laramie. They want to meet at your shop, see the warehouse we're going to turn into a factory. Maybe Alex could even model a dress or two as a favor. If…" Jake paused, looking unwilling to impose "…she wouldn't mind helping you out."

"I like to help," Alex said.

"Then it's settled?" Jake said, looking back at Jenna. "I can tell them yes?"

It would mean she would have to work very hard, starting tomorrow, Jenna thought, but it was a small price to pay for what Jake was offering. And, if truth be told, she was a little anxious to get moving on this project too, not just because it was the fulfillment of her personal, professional dreams, but to further cement their involvement as a couple. Aware Jake was still waiting on her answer, Jenna nodded. "Tell them yes."

Jake kissed his daughter, told her again how pretty she looked, thanked Jenna for helping her look that way and kissed her, too, then went back downstairs.

Finished measuring the hem, Jenna helped Alex out of the alphabet dress. Alex climbed back into her play clothes. "What are you going to do now?" she asked.

Jenna smiled. "Help you make the frog, then whipstitch the hem of this dress."

Alex frowned. "Are you going to the party at Grandma and Grandpa's with Daddy and me?"

Jenna looked at Alex's face and realized she wasn't the only one feeling the heat as far as that particular party went; Alex needed moral support, too. "Yes."

Alex scooted closer. "What are you going to wear?" she asked anxiously.

Jenna smiled. "A pretty dress." *A drop-dead gorgeous dress that would leave no doubt in anyone's mind that Jenna could be just as high-society as the next woman.*

Alex sat down on Jenna's lap and wrapped both her hands around her neck. She peered into her face with childlike intensity. "What do you think I should wear, Jenna?"

Aware she was treading on dangerous ground, Jenna sighed and said, "Honestly?"

Alex nodded solemnly, clinging to Jenna all the more.

Gently, Jenna said, "I think you should consider wearing one of the dresses your mommy bought for you in Dallas." Such an action would please everyone, which in turn would lessen the pressure on Alex.

Alex rolled her eyes in exasperation. "But they have all those bows and ruffles and pouffy skirts."

Not to mention fragile fabric and thousand-dollar price tags, Jenna thought. "Not really your style, are they?" Jenna sympathized, stroking Alex's long, strawberry-blond hair.

Alex ducked her head. "Nobody dresses like that here."

"True," Jenna agreed. "You wouldn't see a dress like that on the street in Laramie. But I have a feeling everybody at your grandparents' party is going to be wearing very, very fancy dresses. So you won't be out of place. But that's not why you should wear one of those dresses to the party." Jenna paused and looked deep into Alex's eyes. "You should wear one of those dresses because it was a very special present from your mom, because she cared enough to go all the way to Dallas to buy it for you, and because it would make her very happy."

JAKE DIDN'T HAVE to ask where Jenna and Alex were. All he had to do was follow the sound of Disney music, being played at full blast. Pausing only long enough to check on Buster and Miss Kitty, who were both happily ensconced on the back porch, he headed for the second floor, strode into the playroom, then blinked and blinked again. Jenna and Alex were seated at the table, their heads bent together, working on something. Both looked breathtakingly beautiful. Alex in a pink organza dress, black-patent leather shoes and tights. Jenna in a very simple, midnight-blue evening dress. "Wow," Jake smiled, as the two stood and pirouetted for him. "I have never in my life seen two such incredibly beautiful ladies." Fresh from her bath, with her hair curled and combed, Alex looked like a little lady. More important, she was happy as could be.

As for Jenna...in the elegant off-the-shoulder gown that gently molded her slender body and ended just above her knees, her red-gold hair swept up into a sophisticated topknot, she looked like a million bucks.

"Thank you," Jenna smiled, taking him in from head to toe. If the gleam in her eyes was any indication, she very much liked the way he looked in his tuxedo. "You look pretty good yourself," Jenna drawled.

Alex sat back down and pulled Jenna down with her. "Yeah. Thanks for the compl'ment, Daddy, but we're busy." Alex picked up some white cottony material and began stuffing it in a small, oddly shaped pillow.

"I can see that." Jake pulled up a chair and sat down opposite them. "What are you doing?" Whatever it was, it was taking a heck of a lot of concentration.

"We're making a frog named Freddy for Alex to play with," Jenna said as Alex crammed the last of the stuffing inside the green velveteen frog. "All we have to do now is sew his tummy shut and we're all done."

"Yeah, Daddy," Alex continued excitedly, "and we're going to do it on the sewing machine like we did the rest of it. Jenna showed me how to use it."

Jenna's brow furrowed. "We've got time, haven't we?" she said, consulting her watch.

Jake nodded. 'We don't have to leave for another half an hour." He didn't want to be early. This evening was going to be long enough.

With Jenna's help, Alex fit the frog into the machine. Concentrating fiercely, Alex began to sew.

She was nearly done when the rhythmic clicking of high heels sounded in the hall. "Well, here you are! I was wondering why no one answered the door." Melinda grimaced and held a hand to her ear as if she could shut out the lively sounds of the children's record that way. "Now I know."

"Sorry." Jake turned to his ex-wife. She was wearing a stunning white evening gown that looked like two separate dresses, worn one over-top of the other. The dress nearest to her skin clung to her body seductively. The dress over that was looser and made of transparent material. It swirled more loosely around her and had a jagged hem that fell to mid-calf. Jake had never seen her look more beautiful. Or smoothly calculating. "We didn't hear the bell."

Melinda strode to the stereo as if she were gliding down a fashion runway and turned the music down. Stepping back to Alex's side, she asked, "What are you two doing?"

Once again, Alex explained. To Jake's dismay, Melinda dismissed the activity with a curt smile and a nod. "Honey, I was hoping you'd wear the ice-blue satin dress tonight. The one with the cute little petticoat. Not the pink organza."

Jake held his breath. Melinda had no idea how much finesse it had taken him and Jenna to get Alex into that dress.

"We can put it on in a minute," Melinda added pleasantly, as if it were just that simple. She looked down at her daughter. "In the meantime, why don't you run downstairs, honey, and wait for me there?" she instructed Alex matter-of-factly. "I'll help you change. Right now, I want to talk to your daddy and Jenna."

"It's okay," Jake said, when a suddenly tense Alex seemed

disinclined to move. ''You can take your frog. We'll all be down shortly.''

Her previously happy mood shattered, as well as her confidence in her appearance, Alex gave them a half-hearted smile that broke Jake's heart and went downstairs.

As soon as Alex had gone, Melinda went over and shut the door to the playroom. ''What's going on here?'' Melinda cast a glance at the sewing machine, then glared at Jake. ''Did you give permission for this?'' Not waiting for his reply, Melinda continued curtly, ''I don't care who you're currently dating, Jake. I don't want my daughter turned into a seamstress.''

Jake grimaced. If it hadn't been for the fact that Melinda was Alex's mother and he didn't want an ugly scene...

Jenna looked from Jake to Melinda and back again. ''Maybe you two should talk about this without me present,'' she said quietly, as eager to get away from this ugliness and tension as Jake.

''No. You stay right here.'' Melinda blocked her way to the door. ''This concerns you, too. This is a family affair tonight. There are going to be so many people there that we know, looking to us to set an example.'' Melinda turned to Jenna, ''You wouldn't mind going alone, would you? I think Jake, Alexandra and I should arrive as a family.''

Jake had suspected Melinda was going to pull something. He just hadn't known what, until now. Ten to one, this opening gambit was merely the tip of the iceberg for what she had planned tonight. ''I think it would be better for Alexandra if all four of us arrived together,'' he said. ''That would be a good way for us to show we're all friends.''

''But we're not really all friends, are we, Jake?'' Melinda shot back acerbically, clearly furious he wasn't immediately bowing to her wishes, even if only to avoid a fight and any unpleasantness for Alexandra. ''Just like we're not all family. And for propriety's sake,'' she continued unpleasantly, ''I think—''

Jake frowned, and held up a hand, cutting Melinda off in

midsentence. "What is that?" he demanded, every parental instinct in him suddenly on full alert. He turned to Jenna and Melinda. "Do you hear barking?" *And squeals of laughter from Alex?* he added silently.

The three of them rushed to the windows overlooking the backyard. Looked down. "Oh, no," Jenna said, clapping a hand to her mouth to stifle her sigh of dismay. "No!"

Chapter Nine

Alex was running across the back lawn, garden hose in hand, Buster chasing after her and nipping at her heels while Miss Kitty romped in the sidelines. "We've got to get down there before they all get soaked!" Jenna said.

"Brilliant deduction!" Melinda snapped. She glared at Jake. "This is all your fault, do you hear me? Bringing your—your *girlfriend* here and installing her in this house. No wonder Alexandra's upset!"

If Alexandra was upset, it had nothing to do with Jenna's presence, but rather, everything to do with Melinda's. But not wanting to waste time standing there arguing when disaster was looming, Jake rushed to the door of the playroom. He yanked it open and sprinted through the upstairs hall, down the back stairs, into the kitchen, across the screened-in back porch, and out to the lawn.

By the time he reached Alex, it was too late. Her hair, so beautifully curled, now hung in wet tangles around her head. Her dress was muddy, ripped and wet. She had streaks of grime across her face, arms, legs and hands. Worse, the trigger on the sprayer nozzle on the garden hose was apparently stuck in the open position, because it was still spraying water full force even as Buster and Alex played tug-of-war over the wildly undulating length of green hose.

Jake trotted forward and picked up the hose. Buster grabbed

it back with his teeth. The nozzle hit Jake square in the face and chest, sending a stream of water soaking through his tuxedo. With difficulty, he got ahold of the wet, muddy, squirming puppy with one hand, wrested control of the hose with his other just as Jenna reached the spigot next to the house and cut the water at the source.

As soon as the water was turned off, and Buster under some modicum of control, Melinda charged forward, screaming like a shrew. "Alexandra Remington, you are a very, very bad girl!"

Alexandra jerked upright. Her eyes widened in shock, then just as quickly filled with tears as she stepped back out of her mother's reach.

Realizing a lot of damage could be done in very little time, Jake put himself between Alex and Melinda. "Jenna, take Alex upstairs now and get her cleaned up."

"That's it?" Melinda fumed, the moment Jenna and Alex were out of sight. "That's all you're going to do, Jake Remington?"

Jake held on to the squirming, barking Buster with effort, while Miss Kitty, who'd taken off for the shrubs when things got really wet, emerged headfirst from the top of a bush, then bounded down to the ground in a single leap. Jake looked Melinda straight in the eye. "What would you have me do that wouldn't make things worse?" he demanded harshly.

Melinda smiled at him in a brisk, impersonal manner. "Try a little discipline, for once."

"Alex's upset," Jake replied, communicating all that and more in a single glance.

"Well, so am I, Jake," Melinda shot back, just as harshly. "And you don't seem to be going out of your way to comfort me!"

Jake wanted to point out that Melinda was a grown woman, and Alex a child, and that as Alex's parents, they ought to let Alex's needs take precedence over theirs. But Melinda hadn't gotten that nearly five years ago, when Alex was born. There was even less chance now in the heat of temper and disappointment. His patience with his former wife exhausted, Jake turned away with Buster still in his arms.

"Look, we can still go to the party together," Melinda murmured huskily.

Jake hadn't thought it was a good idea five minutes ago. Now he *really* didn't think it was a good idea. He sighed and uncomfortably aware just how wet he was, set Buster down on the ground, well away from Melinda. The puppy immediately began to sniff the ground intently. "Maybe Alex just shouldn't go tonight," Jake said.

"No," Melinda shot back defiantly. She walked slowly over to him, holding his eyes all the while. "Alexandra has to be there with you and me tonight."

"Why?" Jake narrowed his eyes at Melinda, wondering what destructive, self-serving scheme she was cooking up now. "What are we trying to prove?" he demanded, "And to whom?"

"I want people to see we are still a family," Melinda insisted as Buster moseyed off to relieve himself, and Miss Kitty circled around them.

But that was just the problem, Jake thought, as every protective instinct in him went on full alert. The three of them never had been a family. Or would be in even the loosest sense of the word given the way things were going. "People know we are divorced," Jake reminded her calmly. "They know we both love Alex." Or should. At this point, Jake wasn't sure Melinda was really capable of loving anyone but herself.

"That's not enough—" Melinda shot back, uncertainty in her eyes, as Miss Kitty sat down primly right behind her.

"Then what would be?" Jake demanded impatiently as Miss Kitty suddenly bounded up on her hind legs. Her front paws batted the handkerchief hem of Melinda's chiffon dress. Melinda frowned as she felt something tugging on her hem, then turned around and let out a shriek that would wake the dead.

"Oh, for pity's sake! Shoo-shoo!" Melinda tried to wrest her gown free. The action only served to embed Miss Kitty's claws in the fabric. Melinda jerked back, taking her gown with her.

"She's shredded my dress," Melinda screamed. "I can't go to the party like this!"

"Just take off the outer dress, and wear the one beneath," Jake said, beginning to feel very irritated that Melinda, who had more clothes than Neiman-Marcus, was more concerned about what she was going to wear to the party than the well-being of their daughter.

Melinda spun around and glared at Jake as if he'd lost his mind. "What is wrong with you? Can't you see this is an utter disaster?" Kicking the cat away with her foot, she brushed past Jake. "I've got to go change. I can't let people see me like this."

Not really all that sorry Miss Kitty had altered their arrangements with Melinda for the evening, Jake followed lazily. "What do you want me to do about the party?" he called after her.

"Just show up." Melinda whirled, the hem of her shredded dress dragging behind her. She glared at him pointedly. "And I'm warning you, Jake, there had better not be any more trouble."

Jake hoped there wouldn't be, too. Though, strangely enough, Melinda seemed to have the most riding on tonight...

ANXIOUS TO GET to Alex—he was sure his daughter wanted to talk to him as much as he wanted to talk to her—Jake dried Buster off as best he could, put him back in his box, found Miss Kitty and took her back to the laundry room, then went in search of Alex and Jenna. They were in Alex's suite. Alex's wet and muddy clothes were in a pile on the floor, and she was cleaned up and wrapped in a warm, fluffy robe. She sat on Jenna's lap, her small arms wrapped around her neck. To Jake's dismay, Alex was holding on for dear life and sobbing like her heart would break. When she saw Jake, she jumped up immediately, went to him, still crying hard, and hugged him fiercely, too. "I'm so s-s-s-sorry, Daddy. I didn't mean to get in trouble."

That was just it, Jake thought. He was pretty sure Alex did mean to get in trouble just now—at least on some subconscious level. Otherwise she wouldn't feel so darn guilty for all the trouble she'd been causing everyone the past couple of weeks.

Aware—until recently anyway—that it wasn't like Alex to misbehave at all, he sat down on the bed beside Jenna and shifted his still-sobbing daughter up onto his lap. "What's going on here, Alex?" Jake asked gently, determined to get to the bottom of all this calamity, whether Alex wanted to talk about what she was doing and why or not. "You're a pretty smart little girl. You know better than to play with the garden hose when you're all dressed up and we're about to go to a party. So why'd you do it?" Jake took the tissues Jenna handed him and wiped Alex's eyes.

For a second Jake thought Alex wasn't going to answer him. Then she looked up at him and said, "Because I don't want Mommy to take me away with her."

Shocked speechless, Jake looked at Jenna—who also didn't have a clue what was going on, either—then back at his daughter. "What do you mean—*take you away?*" he demanded.

Alex sniffed and rubbed her teary, red eyes. "If I wear pretty dresses and do everything Mommy wants me to do, she's going to take me to Europe or somewhere way far away, and I won't never get to see you hardly at all."

Jake tightened his arms around Alex protectively. "Alex, no one is taking you away from me," he assured his daughter firmly.

"Mommy wants to," Alex protested.

"How do you know?" Jake waited until Alex looked at him. "Has Mommy told you that?"

Still clinging to Jake with all her might, Alex shook her head. "I heard you talking to your lawyer on the phone when you thought I was asleep. You said if I started acting like a little lady and wore dresses Mommy was going to try and take me away."

Regret washing through him like a tidal wave, Jake shook his head. "No. I said if you *didn't* start wearing dresses and acting like a little lady Melinda might do something rash, like sue for custody." Jake continued gently but simply, "I was just worried your mommy thought I let you be too much of a tomboy."

"But I like being a tomboy!" Alex protested. "Playing with animals and chasing frogs and stuff. And it's even better now that I've got a kitten and a puppy!"

Jenna grinned, as did Jake. At least he'd done one thing right, bringing more love into Alex's life. Through the pets, and through Jenna.

"I know, honey."

"So if I like those things, why doesn't my mommy like to do those things, too?" Alex persisted.

Jake stroked his hand through the tangled dampness of Alex's hair. "Because Mommy likes other things better," he said, pressing a kiss to the top of Alex's head. "It doesn't mean one way is right and one way is wrong. It just means you and Mommy are different. Different is okay."

"Oh." Alex thought about that as Jake and Jenna exchanged another soft, sad, mutually worried smile. Alex clutched the damp, muddy fabric of Jake's tuxedo shirt. "Then why is my mommy trying to take me away?" Hurt Jake would have given anything to take away radiated in Alex's young eyes.

"That's not going to happen," he told his daughter firmly.

Alex studied him suspiciously, looking suddenly so much older than her almost-six years. "How can you be sure, Daddy?"

Because she doesn't have a maternal bone in her body and

can't be bothered to spend even five minutes with you, never mind have the tenacity to weather a long drawn-out custody battle. And that was what it would take, because Jake had no intention of letting Melinda come in and take Alex away from him. But unwilling and unable to say anything that would hurt his daughter more than she had already been hurt, Jake said solemnly, "Because I won't ever let it get to that. Because I would see that your mommy and I worked together to solve our problems and do what's best for you." And he would enlist the court's help in that, too.

"But what if Mommy won't cooperate with you?" Alexandra asked worriedly.

Out of the mouths of babes, Jake thought as he caught the increasingly worried look in Jenna's eyes. "Then I'll work harder," Jake promised Alex as he pushed the hair from her face. "And I'll fight for you. And I'll never stop. Because that's what you do when you love someone as much as I love you, Alex. You don't let anything come between you," he told her fiercely. "No matter what happens, you don't walk away. You hang in there and let them and everybody else in the world know that you love 'em with all your heart and soul and you're never going to stop."

To Jake's relief, Alex finally seemed reassured that everything was going to be okay. Just as Jenna began to look all the more distressed. Why, he couldn't figure.

"Daddy?" Alex demanded his full attention once again.

"Hmm?"

"I don't think I want to go to the party," Alexandra said, cuddling closer.

Downstairs, a door slammed. Seconds later, footsteps thudded on the stairs. Clara appeared in the doorway. Her glance fell to Alex's muddy party dress and shoes. "Whoa, cowgirl! Looks like I got back just in time."

"What are you doing back?" Jake's brow furrowed. As much as they needed Clara, he wanted her to have all the time she needed with her daugher, son-in-law and new grandson.

Clara shrugged and stuck her hands in the pockets of her jeans. "Nathan James's other grandparents are in town. They're going to be here for the next few days. I thought I'd let them have some privacy."

Alex hopped off Jake's lap and went over to give Clara a big hug. "Clara, will you baby-sit me tonight so I don't have to go to the party?" Alex asked.

Clara looked at Jake, seeming to say: *It's okay with me, if it's okay with you.* "What do you think?" Clara asked Jake. "Should Alex go or stay?"

HE HADN'T MEANT IT, not the way it sounded. Jenna was still telling herself that half an hour later, as she and Jake turned into his parents' summer ranch. Just because he hadn't fought for her years ago, the way he was now pledging to fight for Alex, did not mean he hadn't didn't love her then, or loved her now. It just meant he was more mature now. To think otherwise, well…she was making too much out of this, that was all.

Although it was still early, dozens of cars lined the grass on either side of the drive. Lights and white catering tents had been set up on the green lawn. A country-and-western band was already playing in front of the dance floor that had been erected. Flowers and ice sculptures were everywhere. The scent of the finest Texas cuisine money could buy filled the air. "You okay?" Jake asked as he drove up to the ten-thousand-square-foot country manor house that served as Patricia and Danforth Remington's "summer place."

Jenna shot Jake a glance. "I'm fine," she fibbed, noting without wanting to how handsome he looked in the Armani tuxedo the gala affair required. Lucky for him he'd had three more of them hanging in his closet at home. Which just went to show, she thought wearily, how different they were. The only reason she had gowns galore to choose from was because she made them for a living—for other people.

Aware Jake was still waiting for her answer, Jenna turned

to him and shot him a careful smile, "Why wouldn't I be?" She hadn't had to change clothes. Her evening dress had come through the fracas back at the ranch just fine.

"Oh, I don't know," Jake said, after he had turned the truck and keys over to one of the ranch hands serving as valets. Bypassing the path to the yard, he guided her in the opposite direction from the party, behind the barns. "Maybe because you don't want to be at this shindig any more than Alex did."

Unable to help but note that they were running off to "hide" again at Jake's behest, Jenna sent Jake a challenging glance and shot back angrily, "Can you blame me? The party is in honor of your ex. And I'm not exactly on your parents' Most-Wanted-Guest list. Why would I be eager to attend?"

Momentarily, Jake seemed shocked by Jenna's sarcasm.

Jenna was a little shocked herself. It wasn't like her to complain. Even when she had something to complain about.

Looking as desperate to comfort her as he had been to comfort Alex, back at the ranch house, Jake took her hand in his and squeezed it reassuringly. "You'll have your sisters for moral support."

And maybe go home early with, if all went as Jake's parents hoped.... "I'm surprised your parents invited my sisters."

"So was I, frankly, but maybe they think it's time we all put the past behind us and moved on."

His attempt to soothe her did little except irritate her more. Jenna knew Jake's family did not like scandal. But right now they were championing Jake and Melinda, hoping the two would reunite and become a family again for Alexandra's sake.

Beginning to wish she had begged off, too, and stayed home with Alex and Clara—it probably would have been more fun and a lot less nerve-racking—Jenna withdrew her hand from Jake's. "Yes, I'll have my sisters," she parroted wearily. Thank heaven for her sisters—she didn't know how she would have managed the past seven years without them. "Except Meg, of course, who won't be arriving until later." But even her sisters wouldn't be able to protect her from Melinda, should Melinda decide to make a scene or some major public play for Jake, Jenna thought.

Accurately reading Jenna's fears, Jake reiterated firmly, "Melinda knows we're a couple."

"Right. She just doesn't want anyone else to know."

Jake regarded Jenna stonily. "I don't think it is as simple as that."

Simple. Complicated. What did it matter? Jenna wondered dispiritedly. Having Melinda here in Laramie with them still meant trouble. Having Melinda at the party meant even more. "I think we should join the party before someone starts to talk," Jenna murmured.

Jake nodded. Again, he took her hand in his. "It's going to be all right," he promised firmly.

If only, Jenna thought, she were so certain. As they approached the crowd on the lawn, she felt more than a few curious glances coming their way.

Kelsey made her way to their side. Brady Anderson—Kelsey's newfound business partner—was with her. He looked about as happy to be attending the party as she was. Kelsey inclined her head in the direction of an exceedingly handsome, dark-haired man, dressed all in black—black tuxedo, black shirt, black tie. "There he is," Kelsey told Jake in a voice slightly above a whisper. "That's Rick, the guy who was asking all the questions about the two of you this morning in town."

Jake studied the mystery man with a frown. "I've never seen him before in my life." He turned to Jenna. "Have you?"

Jenna shook her head. Try as she might, she couldn't place the stranger, either. Not only did she not know him, she couldn't recall ever having seen him in Laramie, either. "I haven't a clue who he is."

"Probably a guest of my parents, then," Jake said, "although what he'd be doing asking questions about me is a definite mystery.''

''Unless,'' Jenna murmured, ''he's a private detective.''

Jake frowned at her. ''Don't start.''

''About time you got here.'' Melinda sashayed up to join them. ''Where's Alexandra?''

''She was too tired to come,'' Jake said. He gave Melinda a look only she could see, daring her to disagree.

Jenna expected Melinda to throw another fit.

Instead, acting as if he had just given her a stunning compliment, Melinda linked arms with Jake and smiled as if she were still very much the woman in Jake's life. ''Perhaps that's just as well,'' Melinda said, looking for all the world as happy as could be.

Jenna saw the shock in Jake's eyes. The confusion.

''We have something very important to discuss,'' Melinda murmured mysteriously. She ran her fingertips across Jake's chest in an incredibly intimate gesture. ''Inside the house. Away from all this.''

Jake caught her hand, lifted it away from his chest, and held it—firmly—in his. ''Surely it can wait,'' Jake countered, just as insistently. Letting Melinda know with a look to knock it off.

''I'm afraid not.'' Melinda lifted her other hand and, ignoring the silent warning in his eyes, touched Jake's cheek affectionately, smoothing away an imaginary smudge. ''If you care about our daughter at all, meet me in the library in five minutes.'' Standing on tiptoe, she kissed his cheek, gave his arm a final affectionate pat and, ignoring Jenna and the rest of them completely, glided off.

''Whoa!'' Kelsey said beneath her breath to Jenna. ''Is that woman a real operator or what?''

''She's something, all right,'' Jake pushed the words through his teeth. He had a smile on his face that did not reach his eyes.

Jenna knew Jake did not want a scene. She couldn't blame him. She didn't, either.

"If you'll excuse us, we're going to dance," Jake said politely.

Ignoring the stiff resistance of her body, Jake took Jenna's wrist and led her through the crowd onto the dance floor. "Shouldn't you be running off to meet your ex?" Jenna asked with a bantering smile meant to disguise how she felt.

Anchoring his arm around her waist, Jake tugged Jenna closer and pressed his cheek to her temple. His gray eyes darkened ardently as he looked down at her. "I want to dance with you first."

Jenna warmed to the possessive feel of Jake's arms around her, even as everything in her screamed a warning to be careful. Trying not to notice how much she liked the woodsy fragrance of his aftershave, she shrugged and avoided Jake's eyes. "What will dancing with me prove?" she murmured around the tightness in her throat, trying not to care how good it felt to be in his arms again, or have his hand splayed so proprietorially across her bare back. *Especially when my heart is about to be broken all over again? Only this time it'll be worse, because I'll know what a wonderful, tender, insatiable lover you are.*

Jake leaned closer, pressed a light kiss to her flushed cheek and whispered in her ear, "I'll tell you why we're dancing like this. Because when everyone sees us like this they are going to know—" Jake drew back to look into Jenna's eyes "—how very much I love you."

Jenna couldn't deny that everyone was looking at them. Which wasn't surprising considering how close he was holding her. New-love close. Wishing their steps didn't fit together quite so well, Jenna said, "Sometimes love isn't enough."

"It's always enough," Jake countered meaningfully. "It's when you stop loving someone, or try to, that the trouble starts."

Jenna angled her chin at him and insisted stubbornly, "Melinda is not going to let us be together.'' In fact, Jenna bet that Melinda was going to be just as much of a burr under their saddles as his parents had been, years ago.

Jake pressed his lips together firmly. He looked more annoyed than guilty now. ''Melinda doesn't have anything to say about it.''

''Maybe not,'' Jenna responded, wishing she could just leave the party now, before the situation between her, Jake and Melinda got any messier. ''But as her mother, Melinda does have plenty to say about Alex, even if she doesn't have custody at the moment, and that makes her a powerful opponent in this little domestic drama.''

Jake paused as the song ended and people burst into appplause for the band. ''Is that how you see this, as a domestic drama?''

''I see it as a...mess.''

''A mess that can definitely be cleaned up,'' Jake vowed as the next song began.

Heat started in Jenna's chest and welled up through her neck, into her face. ''How?''

Jake shrugged as he deftly kept time to the Tim McGraw tune. ''By giving my ex exactly what she wants, that's how.''

''And how do you plan to do that?'' she asked, feeling more frustrated than ever.

Abruptly, Jake took Jenna's hand and led her off the dance floor to a deserted spot next to his mother's rose garden. ''Look, Melinda says she wants us to be a family again. But I know her and that's not what she wants at all.'' Jake's eyes were hard and accusing. ''She is using Alex and me to get what she wants.''

''Which is?'' Jenna asked as all the breath left her lungs in one sudden whoosh.

''I don't know. But I'm tired of waiting for her to show her hand.'' Jake stared at Jenna in mute frustration, then seemed to come to some decision. ''It's time I called her bluff.''

Jenna's heart took on a slow, thudding beat. She knew that

dangerous look in Jake's eyes. It always meant trouble with a capital T. "And how are you going to do that?"

Jake's eyes darkened contemplatively. "By offering to give Melinda exactly what she *says* she wants," Jake told Jenna honestly and without apology. "And demanding she run off and elope with me. Tonight."

Chapter Ten

Unable to believe what Jake had just suggested, it was all Jenna could do not to slap his face. "Is that your solution to all your woman troubles?" she asked wryly. "Just ask the woman in question to elope!"

"Of course not," Jake retorted, annoyed Jenna could even suggest such a thing. "But it is the solution to this particular situation," he continued, more sure of himself than ever.

Jenna's temper, on slow burn all evening, exploded. "Fine. Then by all means, go right ahead," she muttered, throwing up her hands.

"She'll refuse, of course," Jake continued.

Jenna stared at Jake, her heart pounding. This felt like such a bad dream. And yet, Jenna counseled herself sternly, just because it felt the same as it had before—with the two of them seeing each other only in quiet, private settings—did not mean it *was* the same. After all, this time, there was nothing secret about their romance; his parents knew they were seeing each other. And this time, even though they still didn't approve of her relationship with Jake, they had invited her to be here with Jake—and at a party to honor his ex-wife, no less. Yet even though Jenna was Jake's date for the evening, it was Melinda who was commanding Jake's attention. Melinda who Jake was going after now. Jenna swallowed hard and pushed her doubts away. Jake loved her, she loved him, that was all that mattered.

"What happens if Melinda *doesn't* refuse?" Jenna countered as calmly as she could. She couldn't even bear to think about Jake marrying someone else again. That had hurt enough the first time.

Jake continued to regard her with an intensity that was both casual and unnerving as he took both Jenna's wrists in hand. "She will."

Jake was so sure of himself. So certain everything would work out exactly the way he wanted. Jenna did not share his optimism. Worse, the implacable expression on his face right now reminded her of the way he had looked at her on that fateful night so long ago, when she'd refused to duck his parents and run off and get married anyway. Thwarted in what he wanted, he had promised her it wasn't over between them, he had promised her he would call her and come back for her. Jenna had looked into his eyes, and she had believed him with all her heart and soul. Only to find out the hard way that he wasn't going to call her again or come after her, that he wasn't going to marry her the way he had promised.

And now, here they were again. Their renewed relationship just publicly revealed, with Jake's parents—and now Melinda, too—doing their best to get between them and break them up. Here they were again, with Jake telling her privately that he wanted nothing more than to be with her every day of his life and marry her as soon as possible. And yet, when push came to shove, here he was leaving her in the lurch and walking away from her. To do what? To propose to Melinda!

"It sounds like you've made up your mind what you want to do," Jenna said numbly.

Jake looked at her pointedly. "I have."

"Why even tell me, then?" Jenna demanded angrily, as every uncertainty she'd ever had about the two of them came back to strike her with blinding force. Already, she felt like he'd made a fool of her. And once again, he'd done it right here in Laramie, in front of everyone she loved and cared about.

Jake's touch gentled and he continued to regard her earnestly. "Because I want your permission," he said softly, persuasively.

That, at least, had not happened before, but the fact it hadn't was no comfort to Jenna, who'd spent more than six years living down her failed elopement to Jake. Anger flared within her. "Well, that's new," Jenna muttered sweetly, hating the jealous, insecure way she felt—the way only Jake and his family could make her feel. "Asking the current girlfriend to give permission to elope with the ex-wife."

Jake sighed, dropped his hold on her, stepped back. He regarded her patiently, obviously irritated to have his integrity questioned. "I won't do it unless you agree with the plan."

"And if I say that I don't?" Jenna countered.

Jake shrugged as if it no longer made a difference to him and predicted grimly, "Then we wait until Melinda shows her hand, which could mean days, even weeks, of being at her mercy. Not just for us, but for Alex, too."

As much as Jenna hated to admit it, that sounded ten times worse than what they were already enduring. With a beleaguered sigh, Jenna tilted her face up to Jake's. She folded her arms in front of her and for a moment stayed where she was. "You really think if you put Melinda to the test she'll reveal what she is really up to?"

Jake nodded gravely and continued to hold Jenna's eyes with his. "I'd stake my life on it," he said bluntly.

Jenna shoved her hands through her hair and released a quavering breath. "All right."

Jake paused. "You're sure?"

His hot gray gaze raked her up and down.

Jenna nodded, doing her best to hide her hurt. Determined to get this over with as soon as possible, she said, "She's waiting for you. You better go. You don't want to be late."

"Jenna—" Jake caught her arm as she turned away from him.

As gently as possible, Jenna pried his fingers from her arm

and pushed him away. "Just go. We'll talk later." Jenna made her way blindly to the bar. She helped herself to a glass of champagne and when she turned around, ran smack-dab into John and Lilah McCabe. Since their retirement from Laramie Community Hospital and the renewal of their marriage vows, the couple had never looked better. Trim and fit, they practically glowed with good health and familial concern.

Lilah was the first to reach her. Admiring Jenna's off-the-shoulder gown, she kissed her cheek. "Jenna, darling, you look lovely tonight."

Jenna smiled, glad to see a friendly face. "Thanks. So do you."

John looked at Jenna fondly. "We'd heard you were seeing Jake again."

Lilah splayed a hand across her chest. Leaning forward, she confided emotionally, "It did our hearts good. The two of you should have been married years ago."

Suddenly, Jenna was not so sure. Especially since every time they turned around something or someone was coming between her and Jake. Jenna took a small sip of champagne and tried to concentrate on the lively country-and-western music emanating from the band instead of her own melancholy feelings. "We were awfully young."

"But so in love!" Lilah reminded her happily. "Trust us, that's something that doesn't change."

"Not that it will be easy for you two to build a life together," John warned with paternal concern. "Jake's parents are very protective of their son."

Not to mention, Jenna thought wearily, their money and family name.

"But it can done," John continued confidently.

"Don't forget, now that we know you're the next of the Lockhart sisters to get married, we expect to be invited to the wedding," Lilah added.

Jenna flushed, feeling they were a long way from that ever happening. "That's a little premature," Jenna protested, embarrassed by the enthusiasm the McCabes were showing for her and Jake. "We're a long way from setting a date. We haven't even talked marriage, at least not in any official terms." A proposal in the heat of passion, meant to take effect only after all their current problems were solved, really didn't count. How well Jenna knew that. But to Jenna's chagrin, John and Lilah felt differently.

"Trust us. We saw the way he was looking at you when you came in tonight. He will propose, and soon." The McCabes moved off, and Dani and Beau moved in. Jenna greeted her sister and brother-in-law, noticing he looked movie-star handsome in his evening wear. The three of them walked over to the tent where the buffet tables were set up.

"Let me guess," Dani drawled, taking in the distress Jenna was doing her best—and failing mightily—to hide. "John and Lilah have you in their matchmaking sights."

Pretending to be absorbed in deciding what to eat, Jenna picked up a plate and cruised the table that was groaning with delicious appetizers. "They approve of me and Jake as a couple," Jenna admitted, as she added spinach dip and some crispy tortilla chips to her plate.

"So does everyone else in town," Dani said cheerfully, as she helped herself to some chicken-and-cheese quesadillas. "It's all people are talking about tonight." Dani added sour cream and guacamole to her plate. "Everyone knows you two were meant to be."

Then why, Jenna thought, did she feel as if everything were falling apart? Why did she suddenly feel so left in the lurch, unsure if Jake was actually coming back or not?

Jenna watched as Beau filled his plate with Gulf Coast shrimp and spicy jalapeno-pepper barbecue sauce. "'Meant to be' and actually *being* are two different things," Jenna said, and right then, with Jake off somewhere conferring with his ex-wife, she felt alone, bereft, excluded. All the things she had promised herself she would never feel again.

Their plates piled high, the three of them threaded their way through the well-dressed crowd and moved to a quiet spot, beneath the trees. As intuitive as ever, Dani seemed to look beneath Jenna's surface composure and guess something was indeed wrong. "Trouble between you and Jake?" she asked bluntly, while her husband looked on, concerned.

"Trouble between Jake and his ex," Jenna explained.

Dani and Beau exchanged looks that were even more concerned. "Is that where he ran off to?" Dani asked as she cut into a quesadilla.

Jenna nodded. She cast a glance toward the house, and told herself that Jake knew what he was doing, and that everything would work out. Jenna swallowed, her mood turning grimmer and less optimistic with every second that passed. "I just hope he knows what he's doing."

JAKE FOUND MELINDA just where she said she'd be, in the ranch-house library.

Cheeks bright with color, she immediately closed the distance between them and curled an elegant hand around his biceps. "This isn't a good place to talk. Someone might come in."

It was all Jake could do not to knock her hand from his arm and step away. "So?"

"I want more privacy." She took his hand, looked outside furtively, then headed up the stairs, in plain view of a dozen or so guests, as well as his parents. Figuring he would find out sooner what she was up to simply by playing along, Jake gritted his teeth and followed her up.

Melinda sashayed down the hall as if she owned the place until they got to her bedroom. She led him inside, not bothering to close the door behind them.

Jake had to admit he felt a little easier leaving Melinda's bedroom door ajar.

She moved in on him, her expensive perfume dominating the air around them. "It's clear Alexandra is in need of a mother."

"I couldn't agree with you more," Jake said quietly. He just didn't happen to think it was Melinda she needed—biology aside. Jenna was the woman Alex now turned to. It was Jenna who had shown Alexandra more love in one week than Melinda had in his daughter's whole life. "That's why," he said, turning the tables on Melinda and taking charge, "I think we should get married again. Tonight."

Melinda blinked, clearly stunned. "I agree we ought to think about it, but—"

"Why think at all?" Jake backed Melinda all the way to her antique four-poster bed. "Let's just skip out of the party tonight—we can leave without being seen, go to J. P. Randall's Bait and Tackle shop and get married within the hour. I hear they give free nonalcoholic champagne and your choice of either nacho chips or chocolates with every wedding."

Melinda put out a hand to steady herself, curling her fingers around a bedpost. "You're joking."

"Nope." Jake looked at his ex-wife like a prosecuting attorney facing a hostile witness. "It's obviously what you want, so let's just do it."

"I want to be married again," Melinda sputtered as red blotches moved across her white face. She tilted her head back, said in a low, throaty tone, "But not like that."

"Why not, if it's best for Alex?" Jake prodded with a speculative smile. "You can move in and start cooking and taking care of Alex and me immediately. I gotta tell you, I really could use some help with those pets. They, along with Alex, are a handful."

Melinda swallowed and looked about to protest. Jake was sure she was going to cry uncle. The next thing he knew Melinda was in his arms, trailing wet, passionate kisses along his neck, then his jaw, toward his lips. Not about to let her kiss him on the mouth—no matter what she was up to now—he caught her by the arms, drew her back. And just as suddenly, felt a hand at his back, closing around the material of his tuxedo jacket.

"That will be quite enough," a man's low voice growled fiercely in his ear.

Melinda gasped. The lack of real surprise in her eyes told Jake this was exactly what his ex-wife had been wanting all along. She turned to the interloper, a hand splayed across her chest. "How dare you!"

Jake turned, to see the man Kelsey had identified as the mysterious Rick.

"You had your chance with her, cowboy," Rick told Jake calmly but furiously. "You will not get another one."

Like the heroine in some B movie, Melinda placed herself in front of Jake. She spread her arms wide on either side of him, and squared off with the handsome stranger. "That, Riccardo, is not for you to say."

Riccardo took Melinda into his arms. "Isn't it, darling?" he said in perfect English.

"Who the hell are you?" Jake demanded, annoyed beyond belief. And what was this guy's connection to Melinda? Why was he here at Jake's parents' summer ranch?

Riccardo let go of the preening Melinda to introduce himself and shake Jake's hand. "Forgive me. I am Count Riccardo della Gherardesca—"

"From Italy," Jake guessed, beginning finally to put it all together.

"That is correct." The count puffed out his chest like a strutting peacock. "I see you have heard of me." Shooting another glance at Melinda, he looked very pleased.

"Only in passing," Jake acknowledged with a sigh, realizing he should have put this all together much sooner, would have if he'd been paying a lot more attention to Melinda, and a lot *less* attention to Jenna. Even so, he wouldn't do any of it over for anything in the world—the days and nights with Jenna had been the best in his entire life!

Determined to sort this out once and for all, Jake looked at the handsome Italian count. "What are you doing here?"

Riccardo slipped his arm around Melinda's waist. "I have come to claim my woman."

Melinda lifted her chin haughtily and pushed Riccardo away like some odious piece of trash. "I told you. It's over. Completely." She taunted Riccardo with a haughty look and physically aligned herself with Jake. "I'm getting back together with Jake, for our daughter's sake."

Riccardo remained both unimpressed and disbelieving—as was Jake. "You do not love him, darling," he said, giving Melinda a coaxing glance. "You love me."

Ain't that the truth, Jake thought, not sure whether to be amused or just annoyed by the drama unfolding before him.

Melinda's chin lifted even higher as she informed her former suitor coldly, "Jake has offered to remarry me."

Riccardo scoffed. "That is what it will take to get you to return to Italy?" he demanded. "Marriage?"

Melinda gave Riccardo a wickedly derisive look. "That, Riccardo," she said sweetly, "is the only way I will ever go...."

HALF AN HOUR later, Jenna had endured all the suspense she could handle when Melinda suddenly swept through the crowd of revelers, glided up onto the outdoor stage, grabbed the microphone off the stand, and stopped the band in midsong. As the music faded abruptly, the crowd turned their eyes to her. She beamed out at them joyously. "Everyone! I have an announcement to make!" She waved to the tall, dark and handsome man Kelsey had pointed out earlier, grasped his hand and tugged him onto the bandstand with her. "We are very honored to have a member of the nobility here with us tonight. I'd like to introduce Count Riccardo della Gherardesca from Italy. And I would also like to tell you that he has asked me to marry him tonight and I have said yes!"

For a moment, everyone stared at them in stunned disbelief, including Jenna. Most shocked of all, though, were Jake's parents. Hurt, embarrassment and disillusionment flickered across their faces in rapid succession. At last they seemed to realize they had put all their faith in the wrong person. But whether or not that meant they would accept Jenna as the woman in Jake's life was another matter entirely, Jenna thought worriedly, as she joined in the polite ripple of applause following the announcement.

"Can you believe it?" Melinda asked one and all, beaming. "I'm going to be a countess by Christmas!"

Smiles frozen on their faces, Patricia and Danforth Remington continued to stare at Melinda with obvious disappointment. Clearly, this had caught them as off guard as it had everyone else. Jake had been right, Jenna realized. Melinda had had another agenda—one that had nothing to do with him and Alex—all along. She had used his parents to get what she wanted, perhaps even more heartlessly than she had used him and Alexandra.

Relief flowing through her now that they knew what Melinda had been up to, and that she would soon be out of their lives—hopefully for a long time—Jenna watched as Jake finally emerged from the ranch house and threaded his way through the crowd to her side.

He looked happy and relieved, and not the least bit jealous or distressed by his ex-wife's announcement. Which was odd, Jenna thought, suddenly feeling even more upset than his parents were at that very moment, given the incriminating stains on the starched white collar of his tuxedo shirt.

"I told you my plan would work," Jake said, taking Jenna into his arms and leading her back onto the dance floor as the music and revelry began once again.

"Perhaps better than you thought?" Jenna prodded furiously, unable to take her eyes from the faint but distinct stains trailing from his collar, across his throat and jaw, all the way to his lips. She did not want to imagine how all that pale rose lipstick had gotten there. Never mind how or why Jake had allowed such a thing to happen!

Oblivious of the evidence on his own face, Jake frowned at

the sarcastic note in her voice. Staring at Jenna in frustration, he tugged her close and whispered in her ear, "She just told me she thought Alex would be better off with me, now that she's going back to Italy to marry Riccardo."

"Congratulations. I'm sure Alex will be very sad—at being abandoned again—and relieved that the threat of a custody fight for her is over." And for that much, Jenna was grateful, too. It had been wrong of Melinda to put their little girl in the middle of any of this. But as for the rest... How Jake could come back out here, reeking of Melinda's expensive perfume, his face and neck smudged with her lipstick, and act as if nothing had happened was beyond Jenna. Way beyond her!

Jake frowned as Jenna stiffened in his arms. He studied her as he deftly kept time to the Clint Black tune, "I thought you would be happy, too."

"Oh, really happy," Jenna agreed. Unable to bear looking at the lipstick stains on his face one second longer, she moved away from Jake. "I'd like to go home. Now, Jake."

Jake continued to study her unrepentantly and with a little annoyance. "Fine," he said eventually. "I suppose our business here has been done anyway. Just let me tell my parents we're leaving—"

Jenna put up a hand to stop him. Her pride was already smashed to pieces. Much more of this and her heart really would break. "You don't have to leave the party on my account," she said tersely. "I can leave by myself."

"You don't have a car."

"I'll get one of my sisters to take me."

Jake's gray eyes darkened to pewter. His expression grew all the more worried. "I want to go with you," he said softly.

Jenna did not have the patience to argue further. "Fine. Give me the keys. I'll ask the valet to get your truck and bring it around while you say good-night to your parents."

His expression still concerned, Jake wordlessly did as she asked. By the time he caught up with her again, Jenna was already in the passenger seat. His mouth was grim as he got behind the wheel. The faint but distinct smudges of lipstick that had been on his face were no longer in evidence—obviously someone had told him about them and he had wiped them off—but he said nothing as he drove, not toward his own J&R Ranch, but toward Laramie.

Jenna told herself his silence was fine with her. What she had to say to Jake would only upset him, upset them both. It was best they not be driving somewhere when she did so. Best they not be back at his ranch, where Clara and Alex could overhear.

Finally, they reached her shop. "I can take it from here." Jenna slammed out of his truck as soon as it stopped.

"No doubt," Jake countered dryly. "I'm still coming up with you."

Jenna gave him a withering look and swept up the exterior stairs to her second-floor apartment. "Don't bother."

"It's no bother." Jake's voice was calm, very calm.

Jenna's hands shook as she let herself in. She flipped on the lights, but barred his way inside. "I think it's best if you and I don't see each other again."

"I had a feeling you were going to say that." Jake took her elbow and steered her inside. He took off his bow tie and dropped it into the pocket of his tuxedo jacket. "I don't agree."

"That is just too, too bad." Jenna dug in her heels and squared off with him. She refused to notice how sexy he looked with his jacket open and the first couple of buttons of his shirt undone. "Because this is what I want and in this situation what I say goes."

Jake removed his jacket and dropped it over the back of Jenna's sofa. He went to her refrigerator and helped himself to a bottle of water. "I understand you're upset about the lipstick on my face."

Jenna shook her head. "No joke, Sherlock."

Jake twisted off the cap in one smooth motion. "You could

have told me about it, instead of leaving it to my mother to point out.''

Jenna's heart pounded as Jake strode closer and took a long, thirsty drink. ''Why would I, when it made such an attractive and telling clue to your recent activities?''

Jake frowned as he put the half-empty bottle down on the counter with a thud. ''I know what it looks like,'' he said evenly, keeping his eyes on hers.

Jenna backed up until she felt the counter against her hips. ''That makes two of us then.'' She folded her arms in front of her militantly.

Jake braced his hands on either side of her. He leaned in close, so his head was slanted just above hers and there was no avoiding the heat or the calm determination in his eyes. ''I didn't kiss her.''

Jenna tore her eyes from the intent set of Jake's lips. ''She kissed you.''

''Yes.'' Jake clenched his jaw and continued to look deep into Jenna's eyes. ''And not on the mouth, either, just exactly where you saw.''

Jenna flattened her hands on Jake's chest and shoved; he was about as movable as a two-ton boulder. ''That is so lame,'' Jenna muttered. Unable to budge Jake an inch, she dropped her hands and once again folded them at her waist.

Jake continued to loom over her. ''She was using me to get to Riccardo, to make him jealous enough to propose. Our so-called clinch precipitated their reconciliation.''

Jenna did her best not to breathe in the compelling, woodsy fragrance of Jake's aftershave. Her overwhelming attraction to him was what had gotten her into this mess in the first place! Jenna tilted her head back, putting some distance between their lips, and continued to glare at him furiously. ''And if he hadn't come along and saved the day for you, then what?''

Jake shrugged his broad shoulders and edged back just a little. ''She still would have turned my proposal down.''

"Or seduced you to make Riccardo even more jealous," Jenna suggested sarcastically.

Jake's jaw tightened. "That wouldn't have happened."

Jenna wished she could have been so sure! But it had happened before, just weeks after she and Jake had broken up. "And yet you were in Melinda's bedroom this evening, were you not?"

Jake frowned. This, he had apparently not planned to tell her. "How do you know that?" he demanded unhappily.

Jenna sighed as misery rushed over her anew. "A dozen guests saw you. It was all over the crowd, long before you even came out of the house." She just hadn't wanted to believe it. And hadn't, until Jake had shown up with smudges of lipstick on his face.

Apology radiated from Jake's gray eyes. "I'm sorry," he said softly. "I didn't mean for you to be humiliated."

"Just like you didn't mean for me to be humiliated when you told me that our elopement wasn't cancelled—just postponed, that you were coming back for me. And then never showed?"

Jake's face tightened with chagrin. "I explained to you why that happened."

"And you explained to me why you had to go to Melinda and propose tonight, too." Tears stung Jenna's eyes. "Neither incident stopped me from being hurt, Jake."

Jake spread his hands wide and stepped back, his frustration with Jenna evident. "I told you I didn't kiss her!"

Shaking her head in futility, Jenna slipped past him. "That's not even the point," she retorted sadly. "Although the evidence does suggest you let yourself *be* kissed. Which in my point of view, for the record, is just as bad." Her eyes shot accusing daggers at him. "The point is that our relationship will always take second place for you. Whether it's the welfare of my sisters or your parents or heaven knows what else, you will always choose to protect others rather than preserve our relationship."

Jake clamped both his hands on her shoulders and forced her to face him when she would have turned away. "I'm not going to apologize for what I did tonight—especially given the results!"

"I didn't expect you to," Jenna muttered contemptuously, as tears of abject misery slid down her face. "I know you think you're right now, just as you did then. And I also know the bottom line is you don't love me enough for this to work, Jake. You never have, you never will. Because otherwise we wouldn't have been putting others first and sneaking around, hiding what we feel for each other from everyone else. We would have been proclaiming our love to anyone who would listen from the very beginning."

"You know why we did it that way when we were kids!" Jake said, desperation edging his low voice. "I was trying to spare you the grief you would have gotten from my parents."

"And last week you were trying to spare me the grief I would have gotten from Melinda! Don't you see?" Jenna dashed the tears away with her fingertips. "It doesn't make any difference," she said bitterly, painfully aware that had Jake's instincts been wrong tonight, had Melinda accepted instead of rejected his proposal that they elope, her heart would have been broken again. "The only time our relationship works is when it's completely separate from everything and everyone else. Well, I'm tired of indulging in a backstreet affair, Jake! I'm tired of feeling like I'm someone you have to ignore in public or hide away!"

Jake's pewter eyes gleamed with hurt. "I took you to my parents' ranch tonight. I walked in proudly with you on my arm."

"Then ditched me and went to an upstairs bedroom with your ex-wife and returned with lipstick on your face."

Jake was silent, unable to deny that had been a public-relations disaster for him and Jenna, even if it had ended with Melinda joyously announcing her engagement to Riccardo.

Jenna sighed miserably and pushed both her hands through

her hair. After just one week with Jake she had gone from being one of the most creative and respected businesswomen around to an object of pity and a hopelessly romantic idiot. "Once again, Jake, we're the talk of the town." Everyone was going to be saying she had made a complete fool of herself over Jake Remington. Again. And, as usual, they'd be right.

Jake leaned against the opposite counter and kept his eyes on hers. "We can turn this negative into a positive."

Jenna was tired of viewing their romance through rose-colored glasses, only to get slammed back to reality again. She regarded Jake with a weariness that went all the way to her soul. "Is that really the way your parents will see it?" she asked softly, fighting for serenity. Or were Patricia and Danforth Remington one more stumbling block she and Jake would not be able to overcome?

"I guarantee you after the way Melinda treated them tonight they won't be championing her anymore."

Jenna pushed away the mental image of Melinda kissing Jake in an upstairs bedroom of the Remingtons' summer ranch house. "So then they'll be championing someone else in your blue-blooded social set."

Jake scowled at her unhappily. "You don't give yourself enough credit." He pushed away from the counter and started toward her.

"No, Jake," Jenna replied, "you don't give me enough credit." She could see the future as it was going to unfold, even if Jake couldn't or wouldn't. As long as his parents disapproved of his relationship with her, there would never be a happily-ever-after for the two of them. Having lost her own parents, she couldn't see herself willfully separating Jake from his. "What was it you said to Alex? 'I'll fight hard for you and I'll never stop, because that's what you do when you love someone as much as I love you. You don't let anyone come between you. No matter what happens, you don't walk away. You hang in there and let them and everybody else in the world know that you love 'em with all your heart and soul and you're never going to stop.' Well, that's what I want. I want you to feel the same way about us!''

"I *do* feel the same way about us!''

"No, Jake. You don't." And sadly, Jenna had known that ever since she had heard Jake talking to Alex about the potential custody fight earlier that evening. She just hadn't wanted to admit it to herself. But once Jake had left her and gone off with Melinda she'd had no choice but to see the situation the way it was, instead of the way she wanted it to be.

Feeling like her heart was breaking, Jenna continued hoarsely, "I do feel that way about you—but you don't feel that way about me, you never have. And you can't build a relationship by yourself." Jenna blinked back a fresh flood of tears. "It takes two people to make a marriage. Two people, equally committed, to make the kind of long-lasting union that Lilah and John McCabe have, that my parents had and that even your parents have." Jenna knew she did not deserve any less.

Jake stared at her incredulously. "You really think that little of me?" he demanded, looking as deeply disappointed in her as she was in him. "That I would let anything or anyone come between us again?"

"You already have," Jenna whispered, wishing with all her heart that things were different. "And I can't live that way, Jake, always waiting for the ax to fall. Waiting for the next thing to come along and get in the way of our relationship. Waiting for another reason for you to once again abandon me or push me aside or ask me to wait until you come back, and never knowing whether or not you actually will!" She couldn't bear for him to make seemingly heartfelt promises to her, only to break them. It would be better not to have him in her life at all.

"Nothing is going to get between us unless you *want* it to," Jake retorted furiously, pushing the words between his teeth. Looking exasperated beyond belief, he planted his hands on his hips and regarded Jenna sternly. "But then maybe that's been the plan all along," he said slowly. Moving closer, he narrowed his eyes at her suspiciously. "What was it you told your sisters—that the only reason you were seeing me at all again was to get your revenge? That you wanted me to suffer the way you had suffered the last time, when you were dumped unceremoniously? Well, congratulations, lady," Jake growled as he stormed toward the door, grabbing his tuxedo jacket as he went, "you got your revenge."

Chapter Eleven

Jake had just parked in front of the old carpet-and-tile warehouse early Monday morning and cut the motor on his truck, when the convoy of three vehicles pulled in behind him and parked, too. Seconds later, Meg, Dani and Kelsey Lockhart all emerged from the drivers' seats, slammed their doors, and marched toward him purposefully. Meg in her nurse's uniform, Kelsey in ranch gear and Dani in a sophisticated linen pantsuit.

Muttering his own displeasure beneath his breath, Jake left his briefcase on the seat beside him, grabbed the travel mug of coffee he'd brought with him, and emerged from his vehicle, as well. He had only to look at the three Lockhart women's faces to know they were about to give him heck, whether he liked it or not. Jake glanced at his watch, noting it would be at least another fifteen minutes before the real-estate agent showed up. Plenty of time to get this dressing-down over with once and for all.

Jake drank his coffee in a leisurely manner meant to annoy. Since he knew why they were there, he said before they could get a word in edgewise, "You needn't worry. Jenna is still going to get her own factory and mass-produced clothing line. I always honor my business obligations."

Meg folded her arms in front of her and regarded him like a teacher facing a habitually truant student. "That's good to know," she volleyed back. "Now if only we could say the same about your personal ones."

Here they go again, Jake thought, swearing silently. Questioning his judgment. Trying to make him feel like he didn't know what he was doing. When was it ever going to end? First his parents, then Jenna, and now her sisters, too!

"You asked her to marry you, Jake," Dani reminded him.

"Yes, I did," Jake said bitterly. "And Jenna said yes. Not once. But twice." He narrowed his eyes, recalling the events that had followed. "And then she called it off the moment things got difficult, just like before."

Kelsey planted her cowgirl heels firmly on the pavement beneath her feet and smiled tightly at him. "Maybe the lipstick on your collar had something to do with that."

Jake suddenly knew what it was like to deal with a disapproving family. Then again, Jenna's sisters had warned him. If he hurt her, he would have the three of them to contend with. The only surprise was that Dani's new husband, Beau Chamberlain, wasn't there, too.

"Look, pleasant as this has been," Jake said, hoping to cut the impromptu confrontation short, "the real-estate agent for this place is going to be here any minute with the papers."

Dani shook her head. "Beau took care of that. Turns out she is a big fan of his movies. The two of them are having coffee at Isabel's bakery as we speak. She won't be out here until we give the go-ahead. And right now we're not finished with you, cowboy."

If his heart hadn't been aching so, it would have been funny.

Meg's expression softened abruptly. "We thought the six of you—if you count Clara, Buster and Miss Kitty—were going to be a family, Jake."

Jake had thought so, too. He and Alex had both been counting on it.

"But this is not what families do," Kelsey put in, picking up where Meg had left off. "Families stick together and don't let just anyone break herd."

Dani shook her head disapprovingly. "We saw the way you let your parents treat her. Not just way back when you were both still kids, but last week at her shop and at the party at their ranch. By not making a big show of welcoming Jenna instead of Melinda to that party, they treated Jenna like she's not good enough for you and Alex, and never will be."

That, Jake thought, even as he rankled at the way Jenna had been treated, had not been his decision. "As for what happened at the shop, Jenna wanted to deal with my mother on her own," he informed Jenna's sisters curtly. And he'd thought she, as a responsible adult, should have the opportunity to handle that difficult situation as she saw fit. It hadn't been the way he had wanted to handle the situation, true. But he hated being second-guessed himself, so he had put his own reservations aside, trusted in Jenna the way he wanted her to trust in him, and let her do what she felt best. Only, he thought grimly, to be derided for that, too. "I had no idea Melinda was going to be there that morning, too."

"Okay, we'll let you off the hook for that. What about the party?"

"I plead guilty. I should have taken Jenna over to speak with them the moment we arrived, but I didn't. Later, when I wanted her to talk with them before we left, she refused— probably because she was planning to break up with me again."

"Can you blame her?" Kelsey put in furiously.

"For running out on me the moment the going got tough? Yeah, I sure can." Jake wanted a love that would stand up to the pressures life presented, not collapse under the weight of them.

Meg sighed. "Look. There's no doubt she has handled your parents, and others like them, in the past and could do it again if necessary. The question is, Jake, should she have to?"

Jake sighed. There was no doubt that had been a mistake, letting Jenna meet with his mother and Melinda alone. But there was no point lamenting what couldn't be changed. Like it or not, they had to forget about it and move on. "Look, as much as I hate to admit it, the attitude of my parents—particularly my mother—is not likely to change," Jake said tiredly. The Remingtons would always want him to marry someone from the same monied background—it was the way they had been brought up.

Dani lifted a disapproving brow. "Then maybe your attitude should, cowboy."

Kelsey nodded, and joined in. "Jenna told us about the way your parents blackmailed you into staying away from her when you tried to elope, years ago. To a point we're even grateful. It was selfish, but we needed Jenna with us back then, we were all so devastated by the loss of our parents."

Meg finished, "We understand you were little more than a kid yourself, that you thought you were being noble, walking away from her the way you did. You didn't want social services to use your elopement as proof of our inability to be on our own. But you're not a kid anymore, Jake. And we are no longer in jeopardy. And what you did to her Saturday night at that party, abandoning her and going off with your ex-wife, was not noble."

"Whether or not she agrees—in retrospect—with what I did, Jenna knows why I did it. The two of us discussed it in depth on the dance floor before I acted." And as far as Jake was concerned that should be enough. "And you ladies are forgetting something." Jake angled a thumb at his chest. "I didn't call it quits this time around. Jenna did. As soon as the going got difficult—and let's face it, life will always be difficult—Jenna told me I was naive to think this was ever going to work out in the long run, and she bolted."

She had also accused him of wanting to love her only in secret, and damn it all, she had to know that wasn't true! From the beginning, Jake had wanted a heck of a lot more than a backstreet affair with Jenna. He had wanted it all—marriage, family, kids, pets—the whole shebang.

"So what?" Dani spouted right back. "You've got two legs. Go after her! Make her see the error of her ways."

As if it were that easy to make everything right again, Jake thought bad-temperedly. Jenna was the one who had taken one look at the lipstick on his collar and jumped to all sorts of unfair conclusions. She was the one who had accused him of using poor judgment on everything from buying Buster and Miss Kitty at the same time to the way he handled his ex-wife and his daughter. She was the one who had accused him of being ready to sacrifice their relationship again for the sake of other people when all he'd been trying to do was take charge of the situation. He'd had to force Melinda to play out her hand, whatever it was, so he would know how to deal with her and get her out of their lives, once and for all. So that he could marry Jenna! And his plan to take the bull by the horns, so to speak, had worked like a charm! He had smoked out Riccardo and revealed Melinda's true intentions. As well as gotten Melinda and the count together—permanently, this time.

But was Jenna grateful for the way he had accurately sized up the situation and his ex-wife? Jake fumed as he finished the rest of his coffee. Was Jenna grateful that he had been ready and willing to do whatever was necessary to clear the way for them to marry—even if it was a little unorthodox and meant temporarily playing one of Melinda's games? Was she happy he had decided to forget about the hurts of the past, charged back into her life, and done everything and anything to make her his again? No. Instead, Jenna had taken his hell-for-leather pursuit of her as the ultimate proof of their unsuitability and his lack of judgment. Instead, she had used the fact he had done his best to keep her away from his parents— and anyone and anything else that might keep them apart—as the ultimate proof that he was somehow ashamed of her. That he had never really loved her and never would.

And Jake didn't know how to counter that. Not after all he had done to show her how much he did love her. Not after all he had done to win her back. She was the one who didn't believe in them, he thought furiously. Jenna was the one who wouldn't give them another chance. Not him.

"It's not that simple," Jake said gruffly, as all three of Jenna's sisters continued to glower at him with a mixture of exasperation, disapproval and impatience.

Dani—still glowing with her own newly married happiness and pregnancy—scowled at him contemplatively. "It could be, if you love her even half as much as she still loves you."

Jake *wished* that were the case.

Meg leaned toward him urgently. "Bottom line, Jake, there's still a slim chance she'll take you back, but only if she's convinced the two of you have more than a backstreet, fly-by-night love affair this time, and that you really mean it when you say you want to marry her."

Kelsey nodded, fully agreeing with her two sisters. She gave Jake a sisterly slap on the arm. "Looks like you've got your work cut out for you, cowboy, if you're going to make this situation right again. Meanwhile—" Kelsey straightened the brim of her cowgirl hat purposefully "—we've got our own lives to live."

The Lockhart sisters left, as swiftly as they had arrived. His temper soaring, Jake watched them go. He still felt maligned as hell, and yet... He paused. Were the Lockhart women right? Was there still a slim chance? Or had he blown it all with his decisive, autocratic actions? Jake exhaled wearily as he climbed back into his truck. There was only one way to find out. But first, he thought, his lips compressing grimly, there was something he had to do. Something that should have been done years ago.

JENNA HADN'T HAD a Monday this bad in a very long time. Of course, that was not surprising considering the weekend she'd had, Jenna admitted as she brought out a beaded-satin wedding gown for a final fitting and hung it on an overhead hook. One minute she'd thought she had everything she had ever wanted, only to realize her romance with Jake was an illusion, and a heartbreaking one at that.

Sighing, Jenna continued bustling around the back of her shop, getting ready for her two-o'clock appointment with the fussiest bride west of the Pecos. Thank heaven it was Wendy Smith's last appointment. Or what she hoped was Wendy Smith's last appointment. With Wendy, you were never sure. She had already selected and unselected twelve different veils to go with her dress. Fortunately, she was a little firmer on the dream dress that Jenna had custom-designed for her, a process that had taken several months. Even so, Jenna wouldn't have been surprised to see Wendy change her mind at the last minute on that, too.

At the front of the shop a door opened and closed. A low murmur of voices followed as Raelynn greeted whoever had come in. "Don't you all look pretty today!" Raelynn said.

Then a striped gray-and-white kitten scampered in.

Followed by a fluffy golden blur, racing by in a tangle of fast-moving legs and a wildly wagging tail. Alex came next, peeking her head around the door of the fitting room. "Buster! Miss Kitty! You come back here!" Alex dashed in, followed swiftly by Clara.

"You two do look pretty today," Jenna echoed Raelynn's compliment. Alex had on the alphabet dress Jenna had made for her. Clara was wearing a neatly tailored-blue denim dress, her trademark red bandana tied jauntily around her neck. Both wore cowgirl hats and boots.

"Thanks." Clara smiled as she scooped up a squirming Buster, while Alex took charge of the more docile, for the moment anyway, Miss Kitty. "Alex insisted. She also suggested I buy my dress for Nathan James's upcoming christening here."

"I'd be honored to make a dress for you for your grandson's christening. When is it?"

"In three months or so."

"That gives us plenty of time, then."

"For that. Other things are a mite more urgent," Clara drawled, giving Jenna a significant look.

Jenna flushed self-consciously as Alex edged closer. Obviously, she was about to get the one-two punch here.

Still cradling Miss Kitty, Alex sat down on the edge of the pedestal in front of the three-way mirror. "My Mommy went back to Italy to get married to the count, and Daddy says that's good because he thinks Mommy will be happy now."

Jenna smiled and sat down next to Alex.

"Mommy also wants me to be the flower girl at the wedding and Daddy says I can do it if I want to but I gotta wear a dress—one Mommy picks out." Alex let out a big sigh as Miss Kitty leapt from Alex's lap to Jenna's. Purring, the kitten rubbed her back against Jenna's middle. "But he thinks it would be really nice if I did that," Alex chattered on, leaning over to pet Miss Kitty, "so I said okay, on account of I don't got to go to Italy to live. I can still live here in Laramie."

Noting that Alex was half on her lap, too, Jenna put her arm around her. "I'm sure that will make your mommy very happy."

Alex beamed, as if she thought so, too. She tilted her head to the side. "Were you ever a flower girl?"

"Yes, I was," Jenna said. "At a friend's wedding, a long time ago. It was fun. You'll have a good time."

"That's what Daddy says." Alex nudged closer. "Daddy also told me you don't want to go on dates with him no more."

"Anymore," Jenna corrected absently, as she tightened her arm around Alex's shoulders and held her all the closer. And that wasn't exactly true. She did still want to go on dates with Jake. She did still want to marry him, more than ever. She just couldn't bear to be loved in private and shunned in public any longer. She just couldn't bear to live her life, waiting for the next family catastrophe and resulting noble but ultimately heartbreaking action of Jake's that would end up ripping them apart. She was tired of being excluded and feeling like she wasn't good enough. She was tired of feeling like the only time she and Jake could really love each other—freely and without reservation—was on the sly. She wanted a man who would love her enough to brave even the most horrendous scorn and disapproval. She wanted a man who would fight for them no matter what, and who would include her—not exclude her—in that struggle to build a life together. Not just for now, or when it was convenient, but forever. And that just wasn't Jake, Jenna thought sadly. Jake hated familial discord and Jenna brought a double dose to his life.

Reading Jenna's expression, Alex frowned, looking all the more worried and distressed. She watched as Buster squirmed to get down until Clara released him, and then trotted over to look at his reflection in the mirror. "Does this mean we won't see you anymore?" Alex asked, as Miss Kitty bounded off Jenna's lap and went over to join Buster.

As much as Jenna wanted to protect Alex, she couldn't. "Probably not as much as before," she said honestly, "although we will see each other just because we all still live in Laramie."

"I don't mean like that," Alex protested emotionally, hurt welling in her eyes. "I mean like before. Does this mean you won't come out to the ranch and have tea parties and stuff with me?"

Jenna swallowed around the ache in her throat, and replied gently, "You can still have tea parties with your daddy and Clara and your new friends, like my nephew Jeremy."

Alex's chin quivered. She dashed at the moisture seeping from her eyes with the back of her hand. "It won't be the same without you."

No kidding, Jenna thought, doing her best to hold back her own tears. "You and Clara can come by my shop any time you want. The three of us could always have a tea party here, if your daddy says it is okay."

Alex gave Jenna another brokenhearted look and didn't reply. Jenna knew Alex felt abandoned. First by Melinda, and now by her.

"Honey, why don't you take Miss Kitty out to see Raelynn?" Clara said gently, scooping up the kitten and putting her in Alex's arms, "so I can talk to Jenna a minute?"

"'Kay." Looking as if she hoped Clara would miraculously fix everything she hadn't been able to, Alex stood and kissed Jenna's cheek. She left, Miss Kitty still cradled in her arms.

Clara closed the door after Alex, ensuring their privacy, then sat down on the dressmaker's pedestal, next to Jenna, and reached over to pet an increasingly concerned Buster, who sat at Jenna's feet. "Alex isn't the only one who misses you, you know," Clara said gently. "Jake needs you, too, even if he's too mule-headed at the moment to admit it."

Jenna stood and paced the room.

"Jake's a very private person, Jenna. You know that. He doesn't wear his heart on his sleeve. The fact he romanced you at all means an incredible amount."

Jenna wanted to believe that. She wanted to believe the two of them had shared something special. But bitter experience had shown her differently. Edgy, upset, Jenna leaned against the wall. "Years ago, he let his parents come between us, and he never explained to me why he left—he just did what he thought was best for me, with no thought to what I might have wanted to do. Which would have been, I'm embarrassed to say, wait a few more weeks until I was eighteen and legally of age and then run off and get married, come back and live close to my sisters. But Jake didn't give me that option. Instead he walked away from me completely for over six years. Then he came back and in one fell swoop offered me everything I'd ever dreamed about, and said he wanted to try again. And like a fool, I put my fears about being abandoned aside, and said okay." Tears of frustration stung Jenna's eyes.

Clara comforted Jenna with a look. "You weren't a fool for loving him," she said softly.

Wasn't she? Jenna sure felt like one. She shoved her hands

through her hair and began to pace as she continued to explain, "This time it was Melinda and his parents causing trouble for us. Okay, so he solved the problem with Melinda—possibly permanently. But his parents are still around and they still think we are all wrong for each other, particularly his mother. It's naive to think their dislike of me won't continue to be a problem for us."

Clara sighed. "I'd be the first to agree Mr. and Mrs. Remington can be very difficult people. But their disapproval and distrust of you is something you and Jake could overcome, given time."

Jenna knew there was a chance that was true. But there was also a chance it wasn't. Angry with herself as well as him, she sighed wearily. "For all their flaws, Jake loves his parents. Just the way I loved mine." If there was one thing Jenna honored with all her heart, it was family. She shook her head determinedly. "I won't be responsible for causing a permanent rift between him and his folks, Clara." She knew how much that hurt, and she wouldn't be responsible for it happening to someone else. Nor did she want Jake blaming her for it later.

Clara sighed, abruptly looking as frustrated as Jenna felt. "Have you ever thought it wouldn't be you causing the rift, but them, if it comes to that?"

Clara was making this situation sound so simple to resolve and it wasn't! "We've got to consider Alex, too. She's had a hard enough life as it is. You saw how sad she was just now because Jake and I have decided not to see each other anymore. I was only in her life a week! Imagine how hurt she'd be if Jake and I got back together, only to break up again!"

Clara sent Jenna a pleading look—one Buster promptly mirrored. "Which shows just how much you mean to her."

And she to me. Jenna swallowed around the growing knot in her throat. "I don't want to put her in the middle of a family fight between Jake and me and his parents."

"And yet," Clara said archly, "you'd deprive her the loving mother she wants and needs so desperately?"

Jenna flushed. This was not her problem, no matter how much others were trying to convince her it was. There was no reason she should feel guilty. "Alex has you and Jake and her grandparents, Clara. Now she even has Buster and Miss Kitty."

"There's a difference between having a housekeeper and a father, and a housekeeper and a father and a mother."

Guilt hit Jenna anew. She pushed it away. "Jake will find someone else. Someone his parents will approve of, someone he won't be ashamed to be with." And when he did, life would be so much better for all of them.

Clara shook her head and said disparagingly, "If you believe that, you really are fooling yourself. He has loved one woman in his life, Jenna Lockhart, and that's you."

Jenna studied Clara tensely. "He told you that?"

"He didn't have to tell me that. I know him and I love that boy like my own son." Crossing the distance between them, she took Jenna's hands in hers. "Forget about the mistakes Jake has made in the past and stop using Alex and his parents as an excuse. If Jake is really what you want, then for heaven's sake, go after him."

The tears Jenna had been withholding streamed down her face. "I'd fail."

Clara teared up, too. "Not if you really had your heart set on being with him, you wouldn't," she said in a low, trembling voice. Getting hold of herself, she swallowed hard and pressed on, "I've only known you for a short while, Jenna, but I see what you have built here, with this shop. I see the success you've made for yourself, and I'd wager there were dozens of people, from the bankers to the suppliers to your family and friends, who stood in your way, who told you it was too risky, you might get hurt, but you charged on ahead and prevailed anyway. Why? Because this shop—this dream of owning and operating your own business—meant something to you. So you didn't give up. You hung in there, weathered the bad times as well as the good, and made your business the success it is.'' Clara looked at her seriously. ''Well, families are the same, Jenna. They're hard to build, and even more difficult to maintain. But bottom line, they're worth the effort. Because at the end of the day, your family is what is going to be important to you. Not how many dresses you sold or what you achieved that day in the business world.'' Clara paused, shook her head, dropped her hold on Jenna and stepped back. ''No business deal ever kept you warm at night, or comforted you when you were sick, or gave you the kind of love and tender loving care all of us need.''

''I have my sisters,'' Jenna said fiercely, self-consciously wiping her tears away.

''And you're lucky to have them.'' Clara agreed as Jenna knelt to pet an increasingly concerned Buster. ''But you need to ask yourself, Jenna, are they enough? Or are you still wanting more out of life? Like a husband and children?''

''You think if Jake meant something to me I'd be going after him with the same kind of energy I've applied to my business, don't you?''

''I only know if my husband were still alive, bless his soul, that nothing, and no one, would keep us apart. I thought— hoped—you and Jake shared the same kind of love.'' Clara looked at Jenna steadily. Drew a breath. ''Now I've said what I had to, I'd better go.''

Clara picked up Buster. ''I want you to know I've never interfered like this before and I won't interfere like this ever again. But as I said, I love Jake like a son, and for both your sakes this had to be said.'' Clara cuddled Buster with one arm, squeezed Jenna's hand, and exited the fitting room.

Somehow, Jenna made it through the last fitting for Wendy Smith and helped Wendy select yet another veil that ''went even better'' with her wedding dress. Then Jenna paced and thought, and thought some more. By three-thirty, she knew what she had to do. Find time to talk to Jake, alone. So she called the ranch. There was no answer.

She got out the business card he had given her. Surely his

secretary at his Dallas headquarters would know how to get hold of him. Mustering up her courage, Jenna dialed and got through to Jake's personal secretary immediately. "This is Jenna Lockhart. I'd like to speak to Jake."

"I'm sorry, Miss Lockhart, he's not in today. He called a while ago and said he was going out to his parents' summer ranch, to spend some time with his folks."

Jenna's heart dropped. *Don't give up. Don't assume just because he is with his folks today that he doesn't want to be with you, too.* "I wanted to meet with him as soon as possible."

"Jake was very firm when he telephoned this morning. He said absolutely nothing else on his calendar until he tells me different." His secretary sighed. "He does still have you down for a meeting Wednesday afternoon."

"Is that with a department store?"

"It says here it's personal, and is supposed to take place at your shop in Laramie."

Disappointment surged through Jenna as she realized he was probably coming by to sever their business relationship, once and for all. "I see." Though her heart was breaking, Jenna worked to keep every ounce of emotion out of her voice.

"Would you like me to page him?"

"No," Jenna replied swiftly. She did not want to get the brush-off over the phone. Or worse, no return call at all. The least she could do in this situation was maintain her pride. "I'm going to see him Wednesday." Jenna injected the most cheery, carefree note into her voice she could manage. "That'll be soon enough."

Jake's secretary hesitated. "You're sure?"

"Positive." Jenna said. "Wednesday is plenty soon enough for what the two of us have to do."

ADDING INSULT to injury, all that day and the next, Jenna's sisters completely blew her off. Instead of throwing her a pity party, which Jenna felt was the very least she could have expected under the circumstances, Meg, Dani, and Kelsey all avoided her like the plague. There were no I-told-you-so's when she did manage to see them. Just absent hugs and vague reassurances that everything would be all right. It was almost like something was up. And yet nothing was up. Meg was very busy trying to avoid the new chief of family medicine—for reasons she never did satisfactorily explain. Kelsey and Brady Anderson had run out of start-up money already and were scrambling, trying to get additional financing for the revitalization of the just-repurchased family ranch. The very happy and newly married Dani was busy settling into her new life with Beau Chamberlain.

Only Jenna was at loose ends, and so lonely, miserable, and full of regret she didn't know what to do with herself. Which was why she spent so much time preparing for her meeting with Jake on Wednesday afternoon. Maybe it was silly, she thought as she spent an inordinate amount of time on her hair and makeup, and dressed herself to the nines, but this time she wanted him to know what he was giving up, and lament it with all his heart and soul!

Nevertheless, nothing prepared her for the sight of Jake coming in through the doors of her shop, wearing a tuxedo and looking more handsome and debonair and mouthwateringly sexy than she had ever seen him.

Suddenly feeling woefully under-dressed in her sage-green ultrasuede business suit and matching pumps, and very glad that Raelynn—who had unexpectedly asked for the afternoon off—wasn't there to see this, Jenna folded her arms in front of her. She didn't know what he was trying to prove by showing up here, but she didn't like it. Jenna planted her pumps firmly in the carpet and said contentiously, "If this is a joke, Jake, I am *not* finding it very funny."

Jake gave her a maddeningly lazy look that indicated he still felt the world was theirs for the taking. "We have business to do today, remember?"

Abruptly, Jenna was more wary of him than ever. She could

have sworn Jake Remington was up to something, though she had no idea what. She narrowed her eyes at him. Then said in a low, disbelieving tone, "With the department store reps?"

"Actually—" Jake threw her a casual glance over his shoulder as he ambled over to the rack of wedding dresses against the wall "—they're all at the warehouse waiting for us."

"Representatives from all three stores?" Jenna said, surprised.

"Yep." Jake nodded, looking distracted as he began thumbing through the various gowns with more interest than she would have expected. "As a personal favor to me—and you, I might add. The only thing is—" Jake slanted Jenna a deliberate glance as he went back to the storeroom where the rest of Jenna's inventory of evening and wedding gowns were hanging "—you can't wear that dress."

Beginning to feel more than a little irritated and very impatient, Jenna stormed after him. "What's wrong with this dress?"

Jake turned to face her. "Everyone is expecting to see you in a wedding gown of your own design. So pick out your favorite one and slip into it."

Jenna stared at him, not sure whether to laugh or slug him. "You're joking."

"Not in the least," Jake countered smoothly. "Come on. Time's a-wasting." Jake consulted his watch. "We are due out at the warehouse site in forty minutes. Even with the limo I've got waiting for us out front, we're going to be cutting it close."

"Have you lost your mind?"

"Not yet," Jake grinned, "but I will soon if you don't get into one of those dresses."

Jenna didn't know what Jake was up to, but whatever game he was playing, she was not joining in. "I am selling a line of children's clothing to the department stores," she reminded him, furiously. "Not wedding dresses."

"But you're famous for wedding dresses," Jake pointed out just as determinedly. "And since we don't have any children's dresses made—except Alex's alphabet dress, which is being washed because she now insists on wearing it every single day—and we didn't have time to get any models to wear your famous wedding dresses...well, we're just going to have to make do."

Jenna regarded Jake with mounting exasperation. "Let's just say I buy all that." She didn't. "That doesn't explain why you're in a tuxedo in the middle of a summer afternoon."

Jake shrugged, as if that were certainly no cause for pique. "I have a pressing social engagement later that can't wait."

The man was triple-booking her with business appointments without asking her, demanding she get into a wedding dress, and back to dating other society belles already! Not sure whether she wanted to deck him or grab him and kiss him, Jenna glared at him. Deciding anger was easier to act on than either love or lust, she grumbled, "It didn't take you long to get back in the saddle, did it?" And here she had been going to apologize to him! Ask his forgiveness. Ask him to take her back, to let them start over, start dating again. And here he was, already doing just that. With someone else!

Jake leaned down and leered at her sexily. "You ought to get back in the saddle as soon as possible, too."

Jenna ignored the mesmerizing twinkle in his eyes. "Thanks for the advice, but no thanks," she said sourly.

Jake straightened, looking no less determined to have his way. "Suit yourself." His hot-blooded glance scanned her from head to toe. "Need help picking out a gown?" he asked thoughtfully.

Jenna rolled her eyes. "Forget about me modeling a gown. No way am I doing that."

"You're going to have to if you want this afternoon to work out," Jake told her flatly, looking absolutely determined to have his way on this. "I've already promised everyone you'll be wearing one of your wedding gowns when you get there."

Then he could un-promise it, Jenna thought, since he hadn't checked with her first. "I understand why they'd want to see one of my gowns on a model instead of a hanger," Jenna allowed, forcing her mind off her failed romance and back to business. "And since there's no time to get a model, I'll call one of my sisters and ask them to do it." This deal was too important to blow. The success of her business might be all she had left.

Jake didn't look happy, but he waited patiently for her to make the calls nonetheless. "Well?" Jake asked when Jenna finally hung up the phone minutes later.

Jenna frowned, perplexed. "None of them are around, which is odd. I was sure Meg had to work today, but they said she had taken the day off from the hospital. Dani's off with Beau somewhere and Kelsey isn't answering her phone."

Jake went back to the rack and selected a long-sleeved beaded gown with a chapel train. "I think you ought to wear this one."

Aware time was running out on them—she had roughly five minutes to get into a gown if they weren't going to be late to their meeting—Jenna picked up a white silk-chiffon gown with a fitted bodice and full tulle skirt. "I look best in off-the-shoulder gowns."

Jake smiled in a way that said he remembered. "Don't forget a veil. Shoes." He looked pointedly at Jenna's display of sexy lace-and-satin garters. "All that girly stuff."

Jenna ducked back out of the dressing room to snatch up the necessary undergarments, including a form-fitting bustier, bikini panties, garter belt and hose. She passed on the lacy garter. "Forget it, cowboy! I'm not showing anyone my leg."

Jake grinned mischievously, as if he hoped to somehow convince her otherwise. "Then I'll just take one for show."

Jenna ducked back in the dressing room and closed the curtain with a snap. "This better be absolutely necessary."

"I am sure you'll think so afterward," Jake soothed from the other side of the curtain.

Jenna shucked her clothes and began struggling in to the appropriate undergarments. "You'd better *hope* I think so or you are dead meat."

Jake's chuckle was low and sexy and sent ripples of awareness ghosting over her skin. "I like it when you talk rough."

Jenna rolled her eyes and continued dressing. Short minutes and much muttering later, she stalked back out and stepped up on the pedestal in front of the three-way mirror. Flushing with frustration, and holding the off-the-shoulder dress firmly to her front, lest he get a bird's-eye view of her breasts, she turned her back to him. "You're going to have to help me with these buttons."

Jake grinned and got right to work. "My pleasure."

Still clutching her dress to her breasts, Jenna turned around and glared at him. "Just keep buttoning."

Jake shrugged as sexy mischief sparkled in his eyes. "I'd rather be unbuttoning, but—okay." He did his best to quell a smile.

Jenna scowled at his reflection in the mirror. "You are living dangerously, cowboy." And acting, to her chagrin, like someone who was much more interested in being her lover than her business partner.

Finished, Jake straightened. "Ready to go?"

Jenna slipped on her white satin shoes, grabbed her veil and picked up her portfolio of sketches of children's clothing. "I guess." Handing Jake the veil and sketches, she concentrated on lifting her skirts up off the ground. She didn't want them dragging on the concrete, lest the hem get dirty. Jenna hung the Closed sign on the door locked up and out they went.

"Looking good," the limo driver said, giving Jenna a thumbs-up when she climbed in and carefully arranged her skirt. He seemed not the least bit surprised to see her in a wedding dress, or Jake in a tux. "Thanks," Jenna said as Jake climbed in after her.

The driver put up the glass window between them and they were off, driving through the streets of Laramie, which were surprisingly deserted for that time of day, and toward the warehouse just outside the city.

Minutes later, they arrived at the old building. To Jenna's amazement, it had been painted white, just the way she had wanted. A beautiful white canopy shaded the entrance, which had been fitted with double doors more suited to a chapel than a warehouse entrance. And the building was surrounded by hundreds of neatly parked cars, many of which were luxury vehicles and limousines.

No sooner had their limousine parked in front of the building than another limo pulled up some distance away. Jenna saw Jake's parents step out and start toward them. "What's going on, Jake?"

Jake took her hand in his. "My parents have something to say to you." Jake squeezed her hand in his before she could pull away. "Hear them out, Jenna. It's the least you owe me and the least they owe you."

The Remingtons were dressed up. Danforth was clad in a tuxedo, Patricia in a mother-of-the-bride-style dress. The chauffeur shut the door behind them and moved away from the car.

The older couple exchanged a glance, then Danforth began to speak in a low, somber tone. "We owe you an apology, Jenna, and we're here to give it unreservedly. All these years, we've been championing Melinda, hoping that she and Jake would get back together and make things work."

Patricia admitted this was so with a troubled nod. "The party Saturday night showed us how wrong we were." She shook her head at the remembered hurt and humiliation in front of all their friends. "Melinda doesn't love Jake, and never has. You, on the other hand, have never stopped loving him, even when we did everything we could to push you away and keep you from Jake. But that's over now, Jenna," Patricia promised solemnly. "Jake's father and I are here to tell you we were wrong to try to break the two of you up, and that it's never going to happen again. In fact, we've promised Jake we'll do everything we can to help you two find your way back to each other. This time for good.'' Patricia's voice caught as she looked from Jenna to Jake and back again. ''We want you to be a part of our family, Jenna, from this moment on.''

Jenna had only to look at their faces, listen to the emotion trembling in their voices to know they were speaking from the heart. And that somehow the miracle she had always prayed for had occurred. Jake's parents had opened their hearts and minds to her. At long last, they were willing to give her a chance. And now they wanted her to give them one in return. Could she rise above the past, just as they were, and begin again?

''What changed your mind?'' Jenna asked, still struggling to get past the hurt.

''Jake made us realize that you are the key to his happiness—and Alex's.'' Tears glistened in Patricia's eyes. ''And that's all we've ever wanted for our son and granddaughter, for them to be happy.''

Danforth nodded, and continued thickly, ''We have a lot of making up to do.'' He looked at Jenna steadily, all the acceptance she had ever wanted in his eyes. ''But if you'll give us and Jake a second chance, we know we can be the happy family we were meant to be.''

Danforth turned to Jake. ''It's up to you, son.''

Patricia leaned over and kissed Jake's cheek ''We'll see you inside,'' she said as she and her husband started for the door of the warehouse.

Jake took Jenna's hands in his the moment they were alone. ''My parents aren't the only ones who owe you a Texas-sized apology, Jenna,'' he began gruffly. ''I've hurt you, too. Instead of just assuming my parents could and would never change, I should have gone to them a long time ago and poured my heart out to them. I should have made them see you're the only woman for me. Instead, I let them keep us apart—''

''It wasn't just you,'' Jenna interrupted tearfully, knowing she had to throw it all out and let the chips fall where they might. "I let them do it, too. I should have fought for you, Jake. I should have stood up to them years ago. Insisted they get to know me, instead of sneaking around, indulging in a romance I was sure was destined to end. But I didn't because I was afraid, Jake."

"Of what?" Jake drew back to look into her face.

"Everything," Jenna confessed on a ragged whisper. "That you wouldn't love me as much as I love you. That our backgrounds and life-styles were just too different for us to make this work."

"Differences can be nice," Jake interrupted, kissing her deeply. He looked at her with quiet confidence. "They can be very nice."

"Yes." Jenna sighed, relief and wonder flowing through her in waves. She kissed Jake back with all her heart and soul. "They really can." And it was wonderful that they all finally knew it. Curious, Jenna looked back at the building. "So what's really going on inside there?" she asked, her pulse racing with anticipation.

Jake's gray eyes softened seriously. "You remember promising not just to marry me but to elope with me?"

Jenna nodded, tightening her grip on his hands. "What does that have to do with what's inside the warehouse?" she asked cautiously.

"Well," Jake sighed, regret shimmering in his eyes, "you know when you accused me of only loving you when no one else was around, of loving you best behind closed doors?"

Jenna flushed. How could she forget how wrong she had been? "Yes—"

"Well," Jake drawled, using his grip on her hands to draw her closer yet, "I got to thinking, maybe you had a point." He looked at her steadily, everything he felt for her in his eyes. "Maybe I hadn't made it clear enough how I felt about you, Jenna. So to rectify that, I called up everyone we know, including all your sisters, and Beau Chamberlain, 'cause now he's family, too, and I told them all how I feel about you, and I asked them to meet us both here this afternoon.''

Her heart turning cartwheels in her chest, Jenna stared at the number of cars around the warehouse, noted the festive atmosphere, then turned her gaze back to Jake. ''This is what you've been doing the past two days?'' she asked incredulously.

Beau nodded solemnly. He lifted her hand to his lips and kissed the back of it. ''I needed time to talk to my folks, to make them understand what was in my heart and get everything worked out before I saw you again. Of course, I couldn't have done all this—'' Jake looked around approvingly and gestured at the gussied up exterior of the warehouse ''—without Beau's help. That brother-in-law of yours is one helluva guy. He's the one who got his favorite Hollywood set designer, Kiki Harrison, out here to work miracles on the interior. I saw it earlier, along with your sisters and brother-in-law, and she did one fantastic job!''

Jenna could hardly believe it, but at long last, it did seem that all her dreams were coming true. One thing about life with Jake, it would never be dull. ''So, inside that warehouse is...?''

Jake hugged her close, letting her know with the tenderness of his touch that they had their whole lives ahead of them and, this time, nothing would force them apart. ''The wedding of your dreams. Not to mention all our family and friends. So this is either going to be best wedding ever,'' Jake predicted, gray eyes twinkling happily, ''or the biggest public breakup in Texas history. So here's your chance, Jenna,'' Jake said softly and solemnly, ''to pay me back for every hurt I have ever bestowed upon you and make the biggest fool ever out of me. Or say yes and marry me and make me the happiest man alive.''

Jenna knew what this was costing a man like Jake. If all this didn't prove his love for her, nothing ever would. ''I don't want to make a fool out of you, Jake.'' Jenna paused as she laid a hand over the strong, steady beat of his heart. "I want you to be a fool over me, the same way I'm a complete and utter fool *over* you. But that's rather a different thing."

Jake grinned back as he drew her all the way into his arms. "Well, that I am, woman."

They kissed again, deeply, passionately, then stayed locked in each other's arms. They drank in the sight and scent and feel of each other. There was so much to say. And yet, finally, nothing else that really needed to be said. They had only to look at each other to see all the affection and wonder in each other's eyes.

"I love you, Jenna Lockhart," Jake said quietly. He kissed the back of her hand tenderly. "And I mean that with all my heart and soul."

"I love you, too," Jenna said, knowing she had never been as happy as she was at that very moment.

Jake regarded her smugly. He leaned forward, kissed her brow, and took her all the way into his arms, sweeping a hand down her spine. "I know."

Jenna drew back, to look into his face. "You do?"

Jake nodded solemnly and laid his hand across her heart. "You can't hide what's in here from me. You can't hide the kind of love we have." The corners of his lips lifted ruefully. "That's always been our problem, Jenna. We tried to hide our love from others instead of bringing it out in the open and letting it flourish." He tucked his hand under chin, lifted her face to his, and looked at her with serious gray eyes. "I'm ready to let our love grow. Are you?"

Jenna nodded, tears of joy sparkling in her eyes. She kissed him again. Warmly. Thoroughly. "Yes, Jake. Yes."

JAKE WAS RIGHT, Jenna realized moments later. The inside of the warehouse had been transformed into the most beautiful wedding chapel Jenna had ever seen. Beneath a white satin ceiling, the floor had been covered with plush carpeting. The ends of the pews were decorated with garlands of pale pink-

and-white roses and plush greenery. Stands of antique silver candelabra lit the altar.

The hundreds of guests turned as they entered, as the hauntingly beautiful strains of a string quintet rose to meet them.

Jake took his place next to the minister and his three groomsmen. And the ceremony Jenna had been waiting her whole life for began.

Jenna's three sisters, wearing matching pastel gowns, led the way down the aisle. Alexandra followed, looking every bit the proper young lady as she tossed rose petals in their wake. Jenna's nephew Jeremy was next, carefully bearing the rings on a velvet pillow. Last but not least was Jenna, escorted down the aisle by her new brother-in-law, Beau Chamberlain.

When they reached the altar, Beau lifted Jenna's veil, kissed her, and gave her away.

Then Jake and Jenna clasped hands and took their place in front of Jenna's childhood minister. "For as much as these two persons have come to become one..."

"...to have and to hold...from this day forward..." Jenna promised.

"...for better, for worse, for richer, for poorer, as long as we both shall live..." Jake agreed.

"I love you," Jake whispered as he bent to kiss his bride.

"I love you, too," Jenna whispered fiercely, kissing him back.

As soon as the embrace had ended, Alexandra rushed over to join them in a family hug-and-kiss session. Watching joyously, the whole congregation erupted in cheers, tears and applause.

To Jake and Jenna's pleasure, the reception was held at the Remingtons' summer ranch, and was every bit as lively and joyous and well-attended as their wedding ceremony had been.

"Thank you for everything," Jenna told Jake's folks sincerely as the evening got underway.

Patricia smiled, with warmth, understanding and acceptance

in her eyes. "We wanted you to know we meant it when we said we welcomed you to the family," she said thickly.

Danforth—a man as physically reserved as Jake was affectionate—nodded. He wrapped his arm around Jenna's shoulders. "We hope you feel like you belong here now."

At long last, to her relief and surprise, Jenna did. Happiness soared through her as she and Jake laughed through the toasts on their behalf, danced their first dance together as man and wife and cut the cake. Later, as Jake took a turn on the dance floor with his daughter, Jenna danced with John McCabe. Lilah caught up with Jenna shortly thereafter. Lilah shot a glance heavenward, murmuring, "I can't help but think your parents are watching over you today, Jenna, and that they approve of the match you've made with all their hearts."

Jenna had that feeling, too. She'd never felt her parents love more fiercely than she did that day. It did her soul good to know she wasn't the only one who'd felt their presence. Glad for Lilah's soothing maternal presence in her life, Jenna smiled and confided, "You were right, at the barbecue Saturday night, when you said Jake and I belonged together."

Lilah wrapped an arm around Jenna's shoulders and squeezed them warmly. "I'm happy you and Dani are both married. Now if only Meg and Kelsey would follow suit and settle down, too. You four Lockhart girls would be all set!"

Jenna knew Lilah had matchmaking in her blood, a trait that had only intensified since the McCabes had recently managed to marry off all four of their sons. Jenna grinned as she and Lilah helped themselves to some more champagne while the party rocked on around them. "Speaking of my sisters, where is Kelsey?" Jenna asked curiously.

Lilah looked around at the crowd. "Last I saw she was dancing with Rafe Marshall, the elementary-school principal."

And one of her fickle baby sister's many ex-boyfriends, Jenna thought.

"Her new business partner Brady Anderson did not look happy about it, either," Lilah continued.

That did not surprise Jenna. Brady had been looking a mite romantically interested in Kelsey, even before they decided, against all sisterly advice, to jointly purchase the old Lockhart Ranch and enter into business together. "And Meg?" Jenna asked curiously.

Lilah continued looking around at the crowd, but to no avail—Meg was nowhere in sight. "Meg's been edgy ever since we all arrived at the reception. The new chief of family medicine has been trying to talk to her."

Jenna smiled as Jake and Alex finished their father-daughter dance, and headed her way. "What about?"

Lilah shrugged, clearly baffled by Meg's behavior. "I don't know. Every time he gets close to her, she heads off the other way."

Jenna felt equally perplexed. "It's not like Meg to avoid someone like that. Especially a colleague she's supposed to work closely with." Meg was always so polite and responsible. Jenna paused, figuring if anyone had a clue what was going on, it would be Lilah. "Well, what do you think?" she asked.

"I don't know." Lilah McCabe frowned, looking worried. "But I'd swear there's another romance in the making there."

Jenna laughed and shook her head. "You really expect all four of us to get married before the summer is over, don't you?"

Lilah smiled. "You bet I do."

Meg and Kelsey still have to make their way down the aisle—Cathy Gillen Thacker and Harlequin American Romance won't leave you hanging! Look for the next two LOCKHARTS OF TEXAS *titles coming in February and April 2001* plus *a very special McCabe-Lockhart single title in March 2001!*

Coming in October 2000

brings you national bestselling author

ANNE STUART

with her dramatic new story...

A man untamed, locked in silence.
A woman finally ready to break free.

Available at your favorite retail outlet.

If you enjoyed what you just read,
then we've got an offer you can't resist!

Take 2 bestselling love stories FREE!

Plus get a FREE surprise gift!

Clip this page and mail it to Harlequin Reader Service®

IN U.S.A.
3010 Walden Ave.
P.O. Box 1867
Buffalo, N.Y. 14240-1867

IN CANADA
P.O. Box 609
Fort Erie, Ontario
L2A 5X3

YES! Please send me 2 free Harlequin American Romance® novels and my free surprise gift. Then send me 4 brand-new novels every month, which I will receive months before they're available in stores. In the U.S.A., bill me at the bargain price of $3.57 plus 25¢ delivery per book and applicable sales tax, if any*. In Canada, bill me at the bargain price of $3.96 plus 25¢ delivery per book and applicable taxes**. That's the complete price and a savings of at least 10% off the cover prices—what a great deal! I understand that accepting the 2 free books and gift places me under no obligation ever to buy any books. I can always return a shipment and cancel at any time. Even if I never buy another book from Harlequin, the 2 free books and gift are mine to keep forever. So why not take us up on our invitation. You'll be glad you did!

154 HEN C22W
354 HEN C22X

Name	(PLEASE PRINT)	
Address	Apt.#	
City	State/Prov.	Zip/Postal Code

* Terms and prices subject to change without notice. Sales tax applicable in N.Y.
** Canadian residents will be charged applicable provincial taxes and GST.
   All orders subject to approval. Offer limited to one per household.
   ® are registered trademarks of Harlequin Enterprises Limited.

AMER00   ©1998 Harlequin Enterprises Limited

HARLEQUIN®

makes any time special—online...

your romantic
life

➤ Talk to Dr. Romance, find a romantic recipe, or send a virtual hint to the love of your life. You'll find great articles and advice on romantic issues that are close to your heart.

your romantic
books

➤ Visit our *Author's Alcove* and try your hand in the Writing Round Robin—contribute a chapter to an online book in the making.

➤ Enter the *Reading Room* for an interactive novel—help determine the fate of a story being created now by one of your favorite authors.

➤ Drop into *Books & More!* for the latest releases—read an excerpt, find this month's Harlequin top sellers.

your romantic
escapes

➤ Escape into romantic movies at *Reel Love,* learn what the stars have in store for you with *Lovescopes,* treat yourself to our *Indulgences Guides* and get away to the latest romantic hot spots in *Romantic Travel.*

All this and more available at
www.eHarlequin.com
on Women.com Networks

HECHAN1

Some secrets are better left buried...

Yesterday's Scandal by

Gina WILKINS

A mysterious stranger has come to town...

Former cop Mac Cordero was going undercover one last time to find and exact revenge on the man who fathered, then abandoned him. All he knew was that the man's name was McBride—a name, that is synonymous with scandal.

...and he wants her!

Responsible, reliable Sharon Henderson was drawn to the sexy-assin stranger. She couldn't help falling for him hard and fast. Then she discovered that their love was based on a lie....

YOU WON'T WANT TO MISS IT!

On sale September 2000 at your favorite retail outlet.

HARLEQUIN®
Makes any time special ™

HARLEQUIN®

A M E R I C A N ◆ R O M A N C E ®

COMING NEXT MONTH

#845 WILD THING by Anne Stuart
He had no identity and no past, but what the silent mystery man did
have was the body of a god. It was Dr. Elizabeth Holden's job to uncover
his secrets, but could she succeed before her primal instincts
got the best of her?

#846 SPECIAL ORDER GROOM by Tina Leonard
Happily Wedded After
Bridal salon owner Crystal Jennings would rather stick a straight pin in
her eye than wear one of her own creations. But when her meddlesome
family dared her to date the first man who walked into her store, she
didn't expect it to be Mitch McStern—the one man who just might get
her to walk down the aisle!

#847 OPEN IN NINE MONTHS by Leanna Wilson
Joy Chase was keeping a secret—a little nine-month secret—from
handsome Sam McCall. And when she ran into the dashing single dad,
could the romance-weary woman find a way to reveal her secret—
without revealing her heart's desire?

#848 A LITTLE OFFICE ROMANCE by Michele Dunaway
Desperate for some quick cash, Julia Grayson agreed to pose as her best
friend's brother's new temporary secretary. Yet working for the
deliciously tempting Alex Ravenwood soon had Julia hoping for a
permanent little office romance!

Visit us at www.eHarlequin.com